GRADING ON CURVES

Tara Mills

Grading on Curves

ISBN-10: 1518726305
ISBN-13: 978-1518726309

This book is a work of fiction and any resemblance to persons, living or dead, or places, events or locales is purely coincidental. The characters are products of the author's imagination and used fictitiously.

Published in the United States of America by Sherman Hills Press

Dedication

For the teachers who touch so many lives
—and for those who love them.

Chapter 1

When Sally interrupted Mia right in the middle of ordering at a local coffee shop, she couldn't possibly imagine she was about to experience one of the more significant moments of her life. She was too annoyed.

"Mia, *look*!" Sally gave the arm of her only—therefore *favorite*—cashmere sweater an urgent tug.

"Would you wait?" Mia hissed in an undertone. She gave the barista a pained smile. "I'm sorry. I'll have a latte, please." *Now* she turned to her friend.

"What is so important that you had to stretch out my sleeve?"

"Nine o'clock," said Sally in an excited hush. "Look, look."

Mia glanced casually over her friend's shoulder. "Ooo, ouch."

"That body's tighter than my daughter's braces," Sally agreed. "Nice face too. Is it too late to trade in Larry for an upgrade?"

Mia snorted in amusement. "You love Larry."

"I think I love this guy more."

"It's lust."

"You can build a lot on lust."

Laughing, Mia shook her head then took another peek at the man while her friend moved forward to place her order.

The dreamy customer glanced up from his laptop

and caught Mia watching him. His left eyebrow arched and drew the corner of his mouth up with it. He gave her an imperceptible nod.

Busted!

Mia blushed and turned abruptly away. Shaken and embarrassed, she retrieved her drink from the counter.

"Let's take a table," Sally proposed, grabbing her chai tea.

"No. I want to get out of here—now."

"What's wrong?"

"Nothing."

"Oh my god. That guy is watching us." Sally peeked again. "No. He's watching *you*."

"Let's just go."

"Come on. Let's go talk to him."

"Sally."

"But he's so cute...and you're *so* available."

"He's so *young*."

"Even better."

"I'm leaving," Mia insisted. "Are you coming?"

"Coward."

To Mia's dismay, their hasty departure did not go unnoticed—or evidently misunderstood by the young man. He smiled at her once more before returning to his screen.

♡

Three days later, the midday sun radiated off the

baking bricks of Wrigley Middle School. The deep blue sky and rampant spring fever drew the kids outside in droves during their lunch hour. One group of boys chose to play a disorganized game of football on the island of grass out front.

"I'm open! I'm open!" Casey yelled, waving his arms wildly for the pass.

The football made a wobbly arc into his hands and he spun and got tackled before he could take a single step. The weight of the other boy drove him into the ground. It wasn't until the bruiser climbed off of him that he felt the sharp, stabbing pain in his wrist. When it started to radiate up his forearm, he rolled away from the ball and onto his back, groaning and stomping his heels as he cradled his arm.

"This was supposed to be *tag* football, you moron!" he snapped at the white-faced boy standing over him.

"I'm sorry. I'm so sorry. I got carried away."

"Holy shit, Casey. Do you think it's broken?" asked another kid, moving in so close his mass of freckles seemed to melt together.

"Feels like it." He grit his teeth and fought back tears. He'd rather die than bawl in front of the guys. But the longer they stared at him from this ever tightening circle, the more touch and go it felt.

"What happened?" A man's voice parted the circle of boys to admit him into the huddle.

"It was an accident, Mr. Walden," the tackler told

him.

“I’m sure it was.” The teacher went to his knee beside Casey. “It’s going to be all right. What’s your name?”

Just answering was a struggle for him. “Casey.”

Mr. Walden put a reassuring hand on his shoulder. “Okay, Casey, let’s get you to the nurse.”

The injured boy fought back the pain and gave the teacher a grateful nod.

The bell sounded just as they entered the building and called the rest of the students back to class.

♡

Some days seemed to drag more than others. Particularly Fridays. Once Mia’s lunch break was behind her, and half the office had bailed for the weekend, it was pretty hard not to wallow in self-pity.

The sound of crickets chirping wouldn’t be out of place in this mausoleum of empty cubicles, she thought as she walked to the break room. She needed a pick-me-up and a minute away from her desk or she was going to chew all her nails off in complete boredom. A Diet Coke and a candy bar were just the things to chase away the doldrums, and yes, she knew how stupid the combination sounded.

She took a meandering route back to her desk, not in any hurry to shackle her ankle again. Why did she have recurring visions of a slave barge and giant oars on Fridays? Feeling a little resentful perhaps? Nah, not her. *Right*!

She wasn't the only one holding down the fort. Every department had one or two employees keeping chairs warm, but it was such a gorgeous day and she was knee deep in spring fever right now. It wasn't easy coming back from lunch when almost everyone else got to hit the road. But since she chose these hours because they worked best with the school's schedule, she couldn't bitch. Well, *shouldn't* bitch anyway.

Zoning out in front of the computer screen earlier, she'd dreamed of seed catalogues and all the eye-catching plants on sale inside and outside every store she passed lately. She was so ready to get down and dirty in the garden.

A phone rang somewhere ahead, intruding on the peace and quiet. Mia knew right away it was coming from her desk. She took off running the last thirty feet then cut a sharp right into her cubicle. Grabbing the phone, she clapped it against her ear so hard it drove the back of her earring into her skin.

"*Ow*." She winced. "Mia Page, can I help you?"

She worked a finger behind her ear and tried to erase the painful mark. Unfortunately, the rattle of her earring against the handset was so loud she didn't catch what the caller said. "I'm sorry. Could you repeat that?"

"Mrs. Page, this is Margaret Nixon at Wrigley Middle School. I'm calling about your son, Casey."

"What's wrong? Is he okay?"

"The school nurse thinks he may have broken his wrist. There's a lot of swelling and he's in a good deal of pain. He needs to see a doctor."

"Damn it."

"Excuse me?"

"Sorry, I wasn't expecting this. I'll leave right now, but it's going to take me some time to get there. I'm forty-five minutes away on a good day. Being that it's Friday afternoon, it's going to take even longer. Is there anything you can do for him in the meantime?"

"The teacher who brought Casey to the nurse is still with him. You have the Sterling Clinic listed as your primary provider on Casey's emergency card. It's so close Mr. Walden offered to run him over there now if that's what you want."

"He'd do that?" Mia pressed her hand to her heart with relief. "Yes, *please*. I'll phone the clinic and let them know they're coming then head straight there myself. Thank you."

As soon as she cut the call, Mia phoned the clinic. She shut down her computer while speaking with the receptionist. Now it was time to bail. Grabbing her purse from the drawer, she shoved in her chair and took off, completely forgetting the unopened can of Diet Coke sweating away on her desk.

The door to her boss's corner office was open but she stopped to take a quick peek before barging in, just in case he was on the phone. He glanced up at her knock, his reading glasses perched precariously on the very tip of his nose.

"Bill, I just got a call from Casey's school. He may have broken his wrist. I have to go."

He set down the form in his hand with a frown of concern. "Of course. Go."

She remembered something as she turned to leave and swung back around. "Don't forget Jane already left for the day so you'll have to listen for the phones out here too."

He slid his glasses back up his nose. "I'll manage. Get going. Hope he's all right."

"Thanks."

They shared a quick, parting smile then Mia fled the building as fast as her high heels could carry her.

One phone call. All it took was one stinking phone call to obliterate Mia's boredom and send her heart into a panicky flutter. Ten minutes ago she was a clock watcher, desperate for an end to this miserable week of inconvenient meetings and training sessions on a new computer system that, come Monday, would send the office into a chaotic transition. Now she was scrambling to find out if her only child was okay.

Burning rubber out of the parking lot, it struck her as funny, though probably inappropriate, that on this occasion there was no way Casey could tease her for driving like an old lady.

Holy hell, it was stifling in the truck. She hit all four power window buttons at once and sighed with relief as cooler air flooded in. It was a stupid move to leave the SUV closed up tight on a day like this. Their parking lot didn't offer much shade and those spaces were claimed early. She really should have cracked a couple of windows this morning.

It wasn't until she blew through the second intersection that the interior temperature dropped into a bearable range. Still, she continued to pluck at the front of her blouse, hoping to get a little breeze down her shirt.

Changing lanes, her thoughts shifted seamlessly back to Casey and what might have happened today. Scenarios played across her mind in old-fashioned Technicolor. Was it the hard concrete steps in the school? Those had always made her nervous. What if he was running to class and lost it on his way down? Or, what if he got nailed by one of those heavy classroom doors? Then her eyes narrowed as an unwelcome thought occurred to her. What if he was screwing around with his friends and got hurt doing something he shouldn't have been doing? Or worse—was he fighting? Mia snorted at the idea. No way. That wasn't Casey's style.

Still, the more she tried to find an explanation, the worse she felt. Plagued by an imagination that was rarely a comfort to her, Mia was good at chilling her own blood. She supposed it was simply the curse of parenthood. Just an inkling of an idea could take on a life of its own. Like a parched cactus, a modest watering would revive it, all thorny and bloated.

It was almost an hour later that she turned into the clinic parking lot and pulled into an open space. She stopped mere inches from the bumper in front of her. Having learned her lesson, this time she left the windows open before she jogged for the entrance.

Her heart sank when she spotted an elderly woman with a cane hobbling to the door at the same time. The distance between them forced Mia to adjust her stride. Barreling in first and dropping the door behind her would be unforgivably rude. It wasn't an option.

Naturally, Mia reached the door first. She pulled it open then stood back like a doorman and allowed the older woman to shuffle in ahead of her.

"Thank you." The woman gave her a sweet smile.

Mia smothered her impatience with a smile of her own. "You're welcome."

A second set of doors was right inside and she hustled around the woman and yanked those open too. Answering the woman's appreciative smile with a polite nod was harder than expected. Mia's anxiety had grown from a tickle at the back of her throat into a full-blown virus.

Without another word, she dashed around the slower woman and reached the front desk well ahead of her only to be thwarted when the receptionist held up her hand for patience while she dealt with a phone call. Mia slumped in frustration.

Completely focused on the receptionist, she didn't see her kid sneaking up behind her until he tapped her on the shoulder.

She spun in surprise. "Where did you come from?" she asked, looking past him.

He nodded toward the far door. "There." Then he broke into a big grin. "What are you doing here?"

"The school called me. Are you okay?" Only now did she see his sling. She actually felt the color drain from her face and had to grab her son's shoulder or sway on her heels. "Oh, Case."

The old woman was watching them. Giving her a pained smile, Mia turned Casey around and walked him out of line.

"We're in the way. Come on."

They stopped in a quiet spot among the chairs in the waiting area.

"Check it out." Casey held up his right arm and modeled his cast for her, beaming with pride. "What do you think?"

Her hand hovered tentatively over it before she ventured to touch it. "So it *is* broken." It was more of a statement than a question.

"Yep." He shoved a sheet of paper at her. "Care and handling instructions. They could have put ice cream on there."

Mia snorted and scanned the form. "Quit kidding around. How are you feeling?"

"A lot better. Wish I'd broken my ankle though."

Mia shook her head in confusion. "Hang on. You actually wanted a broken bone?"

"Well yeah. I was like the only one of my friends who hadn't broken *something* yet. I can't believe my luck. Anyone who shows up at school with crutches is golden. Everyone wants to try 'em. But no, I'm stuck with a cast that doesn't even go over my elbow. Stupid wrist."

No doubt about it—boys were weird creatures. "Stay right here. I'll check at the desk to see if there's anything I need to sign before we leave."

Only a few people remained in the waiting area, and no one else was at the desk when Mia proffered her health insurance card to the receptionist. "Quiet in here today," she remarked.

"It was crazy this morning," said the woman as she typed the numbers into the computer. "Your son lucked out. They took him back right away."

"I know. I didn't expect him to be ready so soon."

A nurse walking through set a file on top of a stack on the desk and glanced at Mia. "Oh, you're Casey's mom?"

"Yes."

"We were just back from lunch when he came in. No waiting for the x-ray. He's probably going to find holding a pencil feels a little awkward at first, but that's common. It shouldn't stop him from doing his schoolwork."

Mia laughed and accepted the return of her card.

"Thanks for telling me. I'll be ready for excuses."

Their business concluded, Mia turned back to Casey and reeled at what she saw. Mr. Coffee Shop Guy was standing with him. A thrilling rush of nervous energy shot through her bloodstream.

He looked equally startled to see her when they made eye contact.

She walked unsteadily over to them and he offered his hand. "Hi. Curt Walden. I'm a teacher at Wrigley Middle."

Her initial surprise was elbowed roughly aside by outright gawking. She was drowning in the most potent bedroom eyes she'd ever seen, a heady blend of perfection and depth. Heaven help her, here she thought he was incredible from a distance. Fool. She was horrified that she was staring, but since she couldn't seem to help it, she decided to keep her expectations more realistic. Closing her mouth was a good start.

They clasped hands and Mia's body temperature spiked from ninety-eight point six to boiling. That one touch plunged her into a mental abyss that jettisoned a good fifty IQ points in the process. His fantastic, kissable mouth was moving, but all she could hear was white noise. Then he stopped talking and looked at her expectantly.

Oh hell. What did he just say? Crap, crap, crap! She had absolutely no idea. How was she supposed to respond now?

With little choice, she ignored his question and blundered on in her own direction. "I'm Casey's mom. Mia Page. Thank you for looking after him for me."

She felt weak with relief when her words came out sounding normal and not as incoherent gibberish.

"My pleasure." He glanced down at their joined hands and a lengthy beat passed before he finally released hers.

She almost dried her sweaty palm on her skirt, but stopped herself in time. No need to make it any more obvious she'd suddenly gone from complete indifference to men after her divorce to a full-body arousal. Who could predict when or where something like that would hit? Never in a million years would she imagine herself this close to a sexual swoon, in a clinic of all places, standing right next to her kid. Yet, there she was. Embarrassed, her cheeks flared with color and her mouth hovered somewhere between a smile and a grimace.

Oddly enough, his smile deepened at her blush and they simply stared at one another for a full minute like two lunatics who'd been transported to a place all their own and time was irrelevant—at least for *them*.

Casey looked back and forth between the two spellbound adults and started to fidget. "Can we get out of here?"

His question snapped Mia back to the present. "Yes. We're all set." She risked a quick glance at the teacher—she knew now it wasn't smart to dwell on him—and said, "I suppose you need to get back to school."

"I do. Oh—" He snapped his fingers. "The doctor said if his arm starts to bother him, ibuprofen should do the trick, but rough play is out for a while."

As they passed through the exit, Casey finally told her how he got hurt. She was surprised to hear it wasn't one of the scenarios she'd pictured.

Out on the sidewalk, Mia faced the teacher. "Thanks again for staying with him until I could get here." She ruffled Casey's hair affectionately and he ducked away, embarrassed, too old for that kind of thing.

"My pleasure."

"I hope it didn't completely foul up the rest of your afternoon," she went on.

Curt Walden shook his head, his easy laugh decidedly forgiving. "Actually, we were finishing a film we started watching with the other science class yesterday so it worked out all right. I should make it back in time to see the kids onto the buses." Then he gave her a smile capable of charming the panties right off of her. "See ya."

Both males peeled away in opposite directions, leaving Mia alone on the sidewalk.

She scrambled to think of anything, anything at all, to prolong the moment. "Hey! Curt? Excuse me? Does Casey need to go back to school for any reason?"

Lame, lame, lame.

He stopped and turned. “No. I’ll square it with the office. Take him home. Have a nice weekend, Mrs. Page.” He flashed another heart-melting smile then kept going.

Casey was almost to the Explorer, but Mia barely noticed. Her entire focus was centered on the sexy teacher instead.

She could feel the beads of perspiration popping out all over her at the way his lightweight shirt caught the breeze and billowed out of the back of his pants. Was that linen? Rayon? Whatever it was, he wasn’t exactly dressed to roam school hallways or stand with his back to a class while he wrote on a chalkboard. She envied and pitied the poor adolescent girls who had to look at that supremely scrumptious derriere every day then suffer each night in a private torture all their own.

No, this guy belonged on a beach, seated at an umbrella shaded table with his long masculine fingers curled around a glass of wine.

Okay, putting Curt on a beach was probably a mistake. In a flash she had him bounding out of the surf in low slung swim trunks as water ran down his sun-kissed body. She moaned softly at the damp line of glittering hair bisecting his chest. It tapered away across his solid abs then picked up again at his navel like an arrow plunging into is shorts. Mia’s fingers twitched as she did a virtual walkthrough, quite willing to follow that trail wherever it led. Exploration was highly underrated these days.

"Mom! Are you coming?"

Casey's shout jolted her back to reality. Well, one thing she could say for certain, this fantasy was galaxies better than the usual gloom and doom.

Hurrying to the SUV, Mia climbed in and drew her seatbelt across her lap.

"Did I hear Mr. Walden say he teaches science?" No response. She looked up to find Casey watching her strangely. "What?"

"Don't even think about asking me to pass him a note at school," he told her flatly.

She gave a startled laugh. "Are you *serious*?"

The boy shook his head slowly. "I know that look, Mom. I've seen it a hundred times this year, and I'm not doing it. Don't even ask."

♡

Curt twisted and threw his arm over the passenger seat as he backed out of the parking space. Agitated, he stomped on the brake harder than intended and jerked to a stop. *Shit. Calm down.*

Easier said than done.

He shifted into drive and headed for the exit wondering, *what are the odds?* He'd actually faltered at the sight of her, suddenly blown away by a gale of emotions: elation, gratitude, longing, and hope. Then he'd noticed her ring and the wind abruptly died and sent him spiraling back to earth with a mighty crash.

It wasn't fair. He didn't even want to calculate how many quiet, distracted hours he'd spent thinking about that woman recently, hoping to see her again. Now his heart sank with disappointment. Clearly the powerful yearning he'd felt at their brief, yet innocent, encounter in the coffee shop a week ago was nothing but a fantasy. He could easily see the resemblance between mother and son now. Maybe his subconscious recognized it too. Is that why he'd insisted on taking the kid to the clinic himself?

Curt groaned at how close he'd come to making a total ass of himself. He'd been one second—make that one *nanosecond*—away from asking her out without giving a rip about her marital status—and in the lobby of a health clinic too! Not to mention her kid was standing right there. He gave himself a mental belt to the head, thoroughly disgusted. Fortunately, Casey inadvertently saved him from himself and for that, he'd be forever grateful.

But damn it. Life had a cruel sense of humor. No matter how strong the temptation, he was *not* a home wrecker.

Chapter 2

Curt knocked on the doorframe before walking into the quiet classroom. Vibrant travel posters for Madrid, Barcelona, Toledo, Granada, and Seville covered every wall. Splashes of color, both jarring and wonderful, stirred the senses.

The pretty dark-haired woman seated at the desk looked up with a smile. “Hola.”

“Buenas tardes. I have your keys. Gracias for the loan.”

She laughed. “Well, it’s not like you could take him on those handlebars of yours.”

Curt smiled, acknowledging the point with a casual shrug.

“So, how is he?” she asked.

“Just a broken wrist, not the arm. He’ll be fine.” Curt set the keys in her outstretched hand and started to turn, but her next question made him reluctantly pause.

“Do you want to catch some dinner? It’s rib night at Rafferty’s.”

“I’m sorry, Holly. I can’t. I have plans.” It was a lie, a white lie, but still a lie. He didn’t want to hurt her. “Another time, okay?”

“Sure,” she said with a feeble smile. “Have a nice weekend, Curt.”

“You too.”

♡

Holly watched Curt go with naked longing in her heart. There were so many things she would change now, if given the chance. But he wasn't going to grant her one. He was slipping away from her, she could feel it. Why did she have to seduce him? By rushing things, she'd damaged their friendship and now there was a chasm between them wider than the Gulf of Mexico.

Maybe it wasn't too late to salvage what they had. She needed to be patient and back off, let him come back to her when he was ready. They could start over as friends again if he would just stop avoiding her. Good things come to those who wait. She knew that now. So she'd wait. It was all she could do. She missed him, so much.

It was even harder to see him at school every day and feel his hesitation whenever they had to interact with each other. It had never been like this between them. Now he avoided the teacher's lounge, and when they monitored the lunchroom together, he no longer stood along the wall and engaged in conversation with her. Rather, he chose to pace between the long stretches of tables and chat with the students instead. It was painful. He was never unkind, just...distant.

She'd lost her best friend that night. She wanted him back.

♡

Mia pulled into the driveway and pressed the garage door opener. “Case, would you roll the empty garbage can into the garage?”

He held up his arm. “*Um,* I have a cast.”

“Um, you have *two* arms. I think you can manage.”

“Jeeze,” he swore and got out to shuffle over to the container.

Mia ignored the teen tantrum and drove out of the sunshine and into the garage. She scooped up Casey’s backpack, along with her purse, and brought them into the house.

Down the hallway, behind the bedroom door at the end, Mia unzipped her skirt, peeled down her pantyhose, and shrugged out of her blouse. She went back to her dirty clothes basket in the corner and shook out a pair of jeans before pulling them on. She did, however, choose a clean, though paint stained t-shirt before going on a hunt for two matching socks.

“Knock, knock!” Sally called from the front door.

Mia went to meet her.

“Don’t you look spiffy?” Sally grinned at her. “You didn’t have to dress up on my account.”

“Funny. Actually, I stopped to pick up a flat of flowers on my way home. I was just about to plant them.”

“Front or back?”

“These are going in the window boxes out front. I’m not sure what I’m doing in the backyard yet.”

"You're still giving me some of your lilies-of-the-valley, right?"

"And a few of the hostas."

"Just checking. I suppose I should figure out where I want them."

"That'd help. Come into the kitchen." Mia led the way. "Something to drink?"

"Sure."

"I've got raspberry iced tea." Mia turned from the refrigerator with a pitcher in her hand.

"Now you're talking."

"So what brings you over?"

"Becky. She told me Casey broke his arm at school today. Is it true?"

"His wrist." Mia poured two tall glasses and put the pitcher back. "He has a cast and he's thrilled."

Sally's eyebrows shot up.

"Don't ask. Let's go sit on the deck, okay?"

They went out through the patio door. Choosing chairs around the glass table, they relaxed under the bright green shade of new leaves, the deck around them dappled with sunshine.

"You sure you don't want to trade houses?" Sally asked her.

"Sorry." Mia kicked back in utter comfort. This was bliss.

"Worth a shot. So how did he get hurt?"

"Casey?"

"Santa."

She resisted the urge to roll her eyes. "Playing football during lunch."

"Ah."

Mia traced her finger around the rim of her glass slowly, thoughtfully. "You'll never guess who took him to the clinic."

Not one to play that game, Sally gave Mia an impatient look. "Just tell me."

"That guy from thc coffee shop."

Sally's eyebrows jumped in surprise. "The hottie with the laptop?"

Mia flipped her wrist. "That's the one."

"Wow. *Why*?"

"He's a teacher at Wrigley."

"I didn't know that!"

"It's true."

"Huh. What does he teach?"

"I think he said science, but just seeing the guy again fried my circuits so don't quote me on that."

Sally gave her a significant look. "Biology?"

"You're so transparent. I don't know. Maybe."

"Just imagine having to sit through *his* sex-ed class."

Mia shivered. "Oh that would be cruel. Sal, you would not believe his eyes. They're incredible."

"But you're not interested," Sally reminded her with a skeptical smirk.

"You know I'm not. I told you before, he's too young."

"So you said. Are you going to tell me his name?"

Mia's mind drifted back to the clinic, back to those eyes, that smile of his. "I'm sorry. What was the question?"

Sally laughed. "His name?"

"Oh. It's Curt, Curt Walden. Perfect for a science teacher, don't you think? Conjures up Walden Pond in my mind."

"I think the word perfect can apply to all kinds of things on that guy."

Mia sighed. Sometimes Sally nailed it.

Chapter 3

Curt couldn't see Casey Page in the hallways without acknowledging him with a smile or a nod. Even without the hopeless torch he carried for the kid's mom, the two of them had a link, of sorts, because of the accident. Admittedly, it was a pretty weak link. Still, he felt a compelling need to preserve it.

"How's the arm, Casey?" he asked the following Friday as they passed each other in the cafeteria.

"It's good." Casey eyed the teacher meditatively before walking out with his friends.

"Of course it is," Curt muttered under his breath, feeling obvious and pathetic for craving any kind of connection with a woman he could never have.

He didn't know himself anymore.

♡

Just after three in the afternoon and Mia sat waiting for Casey on the circle drive in front of the school, one idling vehicle among many lined up bumper to bumper.

Watching the side door closest to his locker, she eventually saw his head bobbing above all the others when he walked out into the sunshine. He'd sprouted like a weed recently and it didn't look like he was even close to done yet. He said something to his friends then, with a wave, broke off and headed her way.

"How was school?" she asked when he climbed in then jerked back when his book bag flew right past her face and into the back seat. "Casey! That almost hit me."

"It did?" His eyes bugged out. "I'm sorry."

"Just watch it next time."

"Okay."

Dropping it, she scanned the sea of faces beyond the windshield. "Are you buckled?" She knew who she was looking for, she just wasn't comfortable admitting it—even to herself.

"Yes," he grumbled at the predictable question. "Hey, Mom, since its Friday, can I rent a game tonight?"

"What's wrong with the games you have?"

"I've beat 'em all, except Quest for Excalibur. I'm afraid if I play it with this thing on—" He held out his graffiti covered cast. "I'm gonna mess up my levels." He gave her a long, pleading look, the one he'd perfected by the age of five.

She knew she'd give in, she was such a pushover, but the script had to be followed.

"There are so many other things to do in this great, wide, wonderful world of ours. Honestly, I don't understand why you aren't bored with video games by now. I know *I* would be if that's all I ever did."

"Mom, you can't compare the games we have

today with what you used to play. If I was stuck with Pac Man and Frogger, I'd get bored too."

Mia frowned at him. "How old do you think I am? Forget it. The point I'm trying to make is that my friends and I did all kinds of things. With summer just around the corner, you should be outside more."

Casey snorted and held up his arm. "That's how I did this."

Mia laughed. "Fair point. Just don't expect me to let you sit around inside playing games all the time."

He pressed his advantage. "You know, if you let me get a skateboard, you'd make both of us happy."

The sneaky little bugger.

"You really *do* want to break your leg next, don't you?"

He huffed in exasperation. "I'm not going to break anything else."

"Right." She glanced at him through narrowed eyes. "We'll talk about it later."

He gave a doubtful snort. "Sure."

The kid was on to her.

With the discussion at another standoff, Casey tuned her out and switched the radio to his favorite station. For once, Mia didn't care. She had a lot on her mind too.

For starters, she didn't understand how an innocent meeting with Curt Walden could send her on a covert mission to Casey's bedroom to raid his stash of batteries. Her face still burned with shame, her prurient intentions extremely embarrassing, yet oh-so-satisfying. She knew she'd do it again. She was going to do it again.

For four years she'd had no—repeat, *no*—interest in men or sex. The main focus of her life was her son. But that doting and obsessive mom was gone, and she was looking for reasons to get Casey out of the house so she could live out her erotic, mechanical fantasies of the hot, young teacher. Oh god, she was sick. What would Curt Walden think of her if he found out he was the carrot for her stick, so to speak? Ugh. She needed therapy.

And she couldn't stop mentally undressing him. She might as well add depravity to this growing list of heretofore undiscovered attributes of hers. Of course Sally was no help at all. How was she supposed to expunge the guy from her head when Sally kept bringing him up, asking if she'd heard from him or seen him again? Simple answer, she couldn't.

It had been seven days now since she'd actually met him, ten since she first saw him, and it wasn't getting any easier. Monday and Tuesday were particularly hellish because she couldn't keep her mind from drifting off to where it shouldn't go. Three times, *three extremely embarrassing times*, they'd had to call the IT guys to fix her computer. She'd always felt comfortable with their system, even with programming changes and quirky updates, but now she looked like an imbecile. How could she even begin to explain that kind of distraction?

This obsession wasn't healthy. In fact, it felt on the low side of nasty. Well, it was his fault—had to be. That's the only thing that could explain it. Yes, simple. He disturbed her. Something about him disturbed her. She'd been struck by a bout of Curt Walden and only isolation and bed rest—without entertaining shenanigans—would see her on the road to recovery.

But shifting the responsibility for her unusual response solely onto Curt's shoulders wasn't entirely fair. It didn't begin to explain or soften the realization that it really was four years since she'd been intimate with a man and even longer since she'd wanted to be.

The last time had been a Friday too. That night Casey was staying at a friend's house so Mia threw together a simple pasta dish for dinner and Greg uncorked the wine. Once their silent meal was over, they lingered at the table and opened a second bottle, both preoccupied with their independent thoughts.

The discussion, when it finally came, was calm. The decision to divorce, welcome. They found themselves in bed after that. Considering what they were about to do, it should have been momentous. It wasn't. It was routine and predictable, merely emphasizing what was missing between them. They loved as friends, but felt no passion, no desire for one another. At least it was mutual. It was time to end their pretense of a marriage.

Mia couldn't even say when her sexual appetite waned. The fade was so gradual she didn't notice it was missing. Only now did she brood on questions she'd never broached before as she ran in and out of the drycleaners.

Greg started dating within a month of separating and encouraged her to do the same, yet she'd declined every invitation until they eventually dried up. To be honest, she couldn't find a spark of attraction for any of the men who asked her out. Since that was her biggest problem with Greg, maybe a part of her simply didn't want to revert back into the same pattern with a different partner. Oh, they were all nice, of course, normal and decent, but none of them had that extra something to tempt her into a new relationship.

Until now. Unfortunately, the man who somehow managed to rekindle her sexual interest wasn't an option.

Mia stopped off at the strip mall last because it was closest to home. Taking the time of day into account, they were lucky to find a parking space right in front of the video store. She dug into her purse for their membership card and some cash, but just as Casey reached for it, Mia pulled back.

"Wait. You know the rules. No excessive violence, no random acts of mayhem, no explicit images, and no games with mature ratings."

"Mom, you know I'm not old enough to rent those—yet."

She looked at Casey, imagining his boyish face transforming before her eyes. The day was coming, soon, and then he'd be able to stroll in there without worrying they were going to card him. "Just choose something I don't have to take away from you," she said with a weary sigh.

"You know I can play mature games just about everywhere else, right?"

Mia dropped her head against her headrest and grumbled. "Yes. But that doesn't mean I have to make it easier for you."

With a parting laugh, Casey jumped out of the truck and disappeared into the video store. In case he beat her back, Mia left the SUV unlocked and headed for Zack's Deli.

♡

Curt turned from the menu board, already tasting the turkey club in his mind, when he saw Mia right outside the door. He left the line and moved to the end just so he could talk with her again.

The bell above the door tinkled when she walked in. Her head was tipped back as she read the menu and shuffled in a distracted way to the end of the queue. He played it casual, spying on her over his shoulder. However, rather than notice him after she finished reading, her gaze drifted off to a far corner of the deli instead, her expression a complete blank.

Okay. Curt watched her quizzically, both amused

and intrigued.

She really was cute, in a rather vacant way. He'd seen more than a few students over the years with that exact expression on their faces. It had never struck him as adorable—until now.

He stole a glance out the window to see if Casey was around too. He was nowhere in sight.

Things were looking up.

Mia turned slowly, her roaming gaze brushing over the two employees behind the counter then skimming over the line of people ahead of them. It eventually flickered up at Curt then trailed off again.

Wait for it.

Ever so slowly, Mia's head swiveled back and her perfect little brows arched, tugging her lashes and lids along with them. He nearly burst out laughing when her jaw succumbed to the pull of gravity.

Holding it together, *barely*, Curt grinned. "Hello, Mrs. Page."

Chapter 4

"I can't believe I did that!" Mia clapped a hand over her mouth.

"What? Overlooked me?"

"Yes." She cringed. "I'm so sorry."

Curt smiled. "I wouldn't worry about it. You seemed preoccupied when you came in. A lot on your mind?"

Her face flared hot as her beach fantasy returned full throttle. This time, her hands were smoothing over Curt's bare chest and sliding down that arrow of damp hair. She could almost feel her index finger slipping between his warm stomach and his swim trunks, feel the resistance of the elastic band as she pulled it out to take a long, appraising look at him

A lot on her mind? You could say that. But *she* wasn't going to. This was so incredibly inconvenient. She shuddered, absolutely appalled at herself.

"I'm not normally this scatterbrained." *Or perverted.* "I'm having a rough week."

His eyes softened with understanding. "I didn't think you were."

"I appreciate that." She dared a quick peek into those mesmerizing eyes of his and felt a clutch in her belly. Whoa, she needed to relax. "And it's *Mia* Page, by the way—not Mrs. I mean, I'm not a Mrs. anymore."

God. She winced on the inside. Why was she babbling this at him? How obvious could she be? He was too young, for crying out loud. Like he'd be interested in her personal history. Get real. She was an idiot. A total boob.

Yet, Curt cocked his head at the news and his smile grew. Odd.

"I just assumed when I saw the ring."

"Oh." She laughed and twisted the ring on her finger. "This was my grandmother's. I wear it on my left hand because it's more comfortable. I don't clank it on everything that way."

His smile warmed. "Okay, *Mia*. And in case you forgot, Curt Walden—science teacher extraordinaire."

She laughed and asked, "Do you come here often, Mr. Walden?"

That wasn't a pick-up line. Honest.

"No." He grinned roguishly. "And it's Curt."

His beautiful eyes unsettled her. There was something intimate in how he looked at her and she wasn't prepared for it. He gave her the impression, foolish perhaps, that he could probe her private thoughts; use her pupils like a peephole in a door. It was an alarming idea. Paranoid of betraying herself and the fantasies playing in her mind like a movie, Mia only risked brief peeks at him.

Using the menu board as a focal point, Mia said idly, "Science, huh? I should probably confess it wasn't my best subject." She snorted at the understatement. "No. I was pretty lousy, actually."

His laugh was warm, rich, and intensely seductive. It seduced her eyes away from the menu, but she couldn't quite bring herself to look up at him again, not when her shoes were so fascinating. God, *please* make them fascinating. Damn it.

"Maybe you just needed a good tutor. A little one-on-one attention?" he suggested, humor in his voice. "I'm free most evenings. I'd be happy to bring you up to speed."

That brought her eyes up. *Holy shit! Is he flirting with me?* As if she didn't have enough to contend with just trying to keep things light. Man, it was getting warm in here. How about turning on those ceiling fans?

Mia was depressingly out of practice with flirting and now it was doing strange and uncomfortable things to her. She forgot herself and looked up at him—and knew right away it was a mistake. She melted like a caramel on a hot dashboard when their eyes connected. Panicked, she broke away, despising her weakness.

Another set of customers walked out and the line shuffled forward. Curt turned toward the counter for a second and a tiny gold post in his ear flashed in the light.

How did she miss something like that? Nine-one-one emergency! Please, someone help her, she was about to spontaneously combust. The mere sight of that earring kicked Mia's bodily fluids into overdrive. Her eyes began to tear, her mouth watered—and that was just *above* the waist. What the hell was happening?

"Are you okay?" He'd noticed her hot flash and now he was concerned about her. Lovely. "Do you need a glass of water or maybe a chair?"

"I'm fine," she assured him, anxious to downplay her system overload before he figured out what was really going on. That would be bad. "I've just...I've been running around so I think I'm still a little keyed up."

"You sure?"

"Yes. I'm fine."

"Okay." He looked her up and down slowly, clearly weighing something. Then he asked, "No Casey tonight?"

"What?" *Wake up you idiot, he's talking again.* It was time to shut down the arousing thoughts of flicking that earring with her tongue. *Just concentrate on his mouth and listen to what he's saying. How hard is that?*

"It's Friday night. I was wondering what you and Casey were up to."

"Oh." Mia shrugged. "Not much. Casey's renting a video game next door and I'm picking up dinner. That's it. I'll probably kick off my shoes and curl up on the couch with the remote. The usual."

"Sounds nice."

"Yeah." Actually, for once it sounded depressing.

"You know what sounds even better?"

Mia's eyes rose to his of their own volition and, though she hesitated to ask, she did anyway. "What?"

"A bottle of wine and good conversation."

"I have a deck."

"Cards?"

She burst out laughing. "No, a deck, as in a nice place to sit outside."

Now *he* laughed. "Perfect. Tell you what. After I get my sandwich, I'll run next door and buy a bottle of wine then meet you at your house. Do you like red or white?"

"Both. I'll leave it up to you."

"Great."

Curt stepped up to the counter and ordered a turkey club. While they made it, he turned back to her. "So where do you live?"

"Two blocks away. Fifteen twenty-seven Jasper. It's a white stucco house, gray trim and shutters. Ours has flagstone climbing up around the front door, and I just planted purple and blue flowers in the window boxes out front. Left side of the street."

"Fifteen twenty-seven Jasper. I'll see you soon, Mia." He collected his change and saluted her with his sandwich before pushing out the door.

Did he just finagle an invite out of her? Why? What did it mean? And how old *is* he? Obviously younger than her, but by how much? Did she honestly care? Was *he* going to care when she told him *her* age? Wait a second. She was making some pretty big assumptions here. Who said he was interested in her romantically? Wow. Talk about letting a fantasy get the better of you. Still, he was more than just a good looking guy. The way he'd focused on her left her disturbed, unsettled, and excited beyond explanation.

"Ma'am?" the clerk called. The others in line began to mutter and snicker.

Mia's head snapped up and she quickly placed her order, handing the cashier the exact change so she could slip out fast. The hostile impatience radiating off the man behind her made her uncomfortable. If that weren't enough, she was getting really tired of looking like a flighty idiot today. What was wrong with her?

Sandwiches in hand, she fled from the deli and found Casey waiting in the truck. Even from a distance, she could see him turning a game over in his hands. Based on the expression on his face, she'd be lucky to hear ten words from him the entire weekend.

"What did you find?" she asked when she climbed into the driver's seat.

He flashed the game at her. "It's Search for the Lost City."

"Sounds exciting."

"I've played it at Tony's. It's really fun, but I never have time to get past the tower ruins. There's so much you have to find before you can start looking for the hidden entrances. I always get sidetracked going down false paths, and end up dying. Tony's made it into the hidden city. There's a ton of treasure in there. But getting it out is even harder because now there's dragons and gargoyles after you. I have to learn where all the traps are if I'm gonna make it inside. The last time I played, I got pecked to death by huge birds. They ate my eyeballs."

"Ew. Gross." Shaking off the revolting thought, she said, "Well, that should keep you busy, anyway."

She checked her mirrors and windows, scanning all the other cars for Curt. What was he driving? Was that him behind her? Could he be waiting at her house already? Impossible.

"Case?"

In a world of his own, he didn't hear her. Yep, he was her son all right.

"Casey!"

He looked over. "What?"

"What can you tell me about Mr. Walden? Is he a good guy? Do the kids like him?"

"Mom…why are you asking me all this?"

"Just curious. I ran into him in Zack's and invited him over. I wouldn't mind the company. You'll be playing your game anyway." Her attempt to sound casual was totally ruined by her rushed, breathless delivery.

Casey gave her a long, calculating look.

"What?" she asked. "It was a spur of the moment thing." The compulsion to explain was unbelievable.

Based on the way Casey was looking at her, she wasn't fooling anyone.

"Mr. Walden is one of the seventh grade science teachers," he told her. "Kids seem to like him. More than Mr. Strong. *He* smells like dirty socks. Just going by Mr. Strong's classroom is enough to make you gag sometimes. It's even worse now because it's getting warmer. He must be sweating more."

"That's not very nice, you know."

"But it's true. We don't hold our noses when we see him, but kids don't hang around his classroom any longer than they have to either. I wish I'd had Mr. Walden last year."

"A ringing endorsement," she said dryly.

Damn! He didn't tell her *anything*. How was she supposed to entertain a person she knew nothing about?

'So, I hear you don't have bad BO like your colleague.'

She didn't think so. Would she be able to control her inner monologue if conversation stalled? What if she discovered they feel very differently about all kinds of things and it became impossible to keep civil as conversation went on? She hoped that wouldn't happen. If she had to ask him to leave, could she do it? Yes. *But why, Mia, why would you need to ask yourself such a question?*

"Stop it!" she blurted out.

Casey looked at her in confusion. "What?"

"Nothing, I was just thinking, that's all."

They pulled into the garage and Mia raced into the house, dropping the sandwiches on the dining room table. Casey went straight to his room. She heard his book bag hit the floor with a heavy *whump*.

Now it was time to panic.

She dashed into the kitchen and saw to her relief that it looked okay. Casey had actually put his cereal bowl in the dishwasher that morning. She popped her coffee mug in with it then ran to look over the living room. All she had to do there was tidy the couch cushions and straighten magazines. There were stray shoes by the front door and she scooped those up and dumped them in the closet. Kicking the ones she was wearing onto the pile, she shut the door. Next she raced to the bathroom to give the toilet a quick once-over and rinse the sink. She hid their toothbrushes in a drawer and yanked the questionable hand towel off the rack and replaced it with a fresh one.

Her chest was heaving when she slapped her hands together. "Done."

Scrambling to her bedroom, she was just stepping out of her skirt when the doorbell rang.

"Case, that's Mr. Walden. Would you let him in, please?" she yelled through her closed door.

She tugged dresser drawers open, one after another, trying to figure out what she should wear. The last thing she wanted to do was give him the wrong impression.

The wrong impression? Just what was that exactly? That she might welcome more flirty suggestions? That she might enjoy locking every detail of his face and body into her head for salacious purposes later? Heavens no. Was there any way she could sit across from him without giving her steamy, sexy thoughts away? Probably not, but she had to try.

She pulled on her favorite pair of jeans, the ones she'd laundered so many times they were faded to white in spots and incredibly soft to the touch. She finished it off with a simple pullover then checked herself in the mirror on the back of her door.

Yes, this was exactly the look she wanted—casual but attractive. She fluffed her hair, loosening it a little, and liked it even better. There was nothing about her appearance that said eager or easy. Of course not, she was at home, at ease, definitely not contemplating a fling with a younger man.

Liar.

Chapter 5

Mia just about had a heart attack when she rounded the corner and caught Curt bent over in the entryway. Had a shockingly loud tearing sound not yanked her eyes off his muscular ass and to his pant leg instead, who knows what could have happened. Evidently, his cuffs came with Velcro straps. He must have sensed her behind him because he straightened up and turned with a killer smile.

"You know, I was wondering about your pants earlier," she admitted then dropped the subject before she blurted out how incredible they looked on him, particularly after seeing them pulled so nice and snug.

"No kidding? They're actually camping/hiking pants, but I discovered they're perfect for biking too. I love all the pockets, and the breathable fabric is light and comfortable. Doesn't hurt that they dry fast if I get caught in the rain."

"Well, they look great." Mia laughed when she realized how that sounded.

Curt gave her a flirty wink.

"So you biked over?" she asked.

"I did."

"Cool. Come into the kitchen with me."

Curt slid his hand through the strap of his pack and followed her. "I brought two bottles, a Beaujolais I discovered recently and a Sauvignon Blanc.

Unfortunately, the white isn't chilled so consider it a hostess gift."

"You didn't have to do that. Thank you." She leaned against the counter and watched him pull the bottles from his backpack. It took her a second to remember she had something to do too. "Oh, glasses."

Amused at how fast he'd distracted her, she took two stemmed glasses and three tumblers out of the cabinet then went rummaging in a drawer for the corkscrew.

"Case, do you want juice?" she called to him in the next room as she slid the drawer closed.

"Yes, please."

Curt held out his hand for the corkscrew. "Here, let me open the wine while you pour the juice, okay?"

"Great." Mia passed it to him and turned to the refrigerator for the pitcher. Just as she reached in to grab it, Curt slipped up from behind and bent right over her, his body so close she felt him lightly nudge her in the ass with his hip as he reached around to slide the bottle of white onto the lower shelf. She froze, suspended by surprise, and far too aware of their posture and the contact of their bodies. Then he moved back, unintentionally brushing her across the ribs with the inside of his arm. The explosion of goose bumps was instantaneous and spread along her side and down to her hand. Her nipples went diamond hard.

She was shocked. Was that all it took to get her flushed and aroused?

Mia concentrated on calming herself while she filled their water glasses and carried them to the table. Curt followed with the Beaujolais, the stemware hanging from the fingers of his other hand. He returned to the kitchen for his sandwich. Mia was just pouring the wine when he got back. He paused to look at the four chairs, obviously wondering where he should sit. Mia drew out one chair. Casey claimed the opposite. That decided, Curt chose the chair on Mia's left and she set his wine in front of him.

"No mayo, right?" Casey asked her, peeling his bun back suspiciously.

"Have I ever ordered you mayo?"

His face fell. "Hey, you know I don't like lettuce."

"Eat it. It's good for you," Mia said firmly. "If I really wanted to torture you, I would have told them to put tomatoes and onions on it too. Consider yourself lucky."

Sulking, Casey began to eat without further complaint.

Curt smiled at the two of them, evidently amused by their minor skirmish.

Then she looked around the table and back to Curt. "What was I thinking? The least I could have done is grab paper plates. You shouldn't have to eat on the wrapper. Obviously we don't entertain much."

Curt put his hand on her arm and stopped her before she jumped up. "Don't bother. I'm fine with this. It's how I do it at home. Save a tree."

Relieved, she settled back in her chair. "Okay."

"Do we have any chips?" Casey asked.

"Maybe. You know where to look."

He hopped up from the table and they could hear a cupboard open in the kitchen. He came back with tortilla chips.

"Mr. Walden?" He offered the bag.

"No, thank you. I'm good."

"Mom?"

Mia shook her head. "No, but thanks."

Casey poured a pile of chips onto his wrapper and crunched away. The kid was completely unaware he was the center of attention for the two adults. His utter absorption in his meal provided a brief delay before the pressure of small talk began. But the distraction he provided was over as soon as he crumpled his wrapper, downed the last of his juice, and looked at his mom with a hopeful request.

"Can I be excused?"

"Yes. Put the chips away before you turn on your game, okay?"

"Okay."

Casey pushed away from the table and left them alone without a backwards glance. Curt and Mia glanced at one another with awkward hesitation. Now what?

"You have a nice kid there," Curt said, breaking the ice all over again.

She could have kissed him for taking the initiative, and for the compliment. "Thank you. I know I'm biased, but I have to agree. I'm lucky."

"You are. I'm glad you realize it. You wouldn't believe how many little monsters there are. I've had my share in the classroom. Sometimes I wonder if I should even bother calling their parents in for a conference. So many would rather turn their kid's bullying, bad grades, and disruptive behavior back on the teacher rather than let their kid assume any of the responsibility. Those parents aren't generally open to hearing anything but false flattery."

"That's gotta be frustrating." Not exactly sure what to say next, she made an offer instead. "I have cookies in the cupboard. Would you like one? Or I could cut up some fruit."

"No. I've had enough." Curt rolled the remainder of his sandwich back up.

Mia did the same. Then she lifted her glass of wine and studied it thoughtfully. "You were right. This is good."

"It's a crowd pleaser."

She looked over and found him watching her with a faint smile, his left cheek raised slightly higher than the right. But it was his eyes that unraveled her. Shaken, she felt an unreasonable need to distract him.

"Why don't we go out on the deck?" She tipped her head towards the patio door.

"Sure." Curt stood and went to take a look. "You

have a beautiful back yard."

Catching the double entendre, he glanced back with an easy laugh and winked at her.

Mia hid her smile and shook her head, choosing to play it straight for now. "Thanks. I spend a lot of time out there—weather permitting. Are you up for a mini-tour?"

"I'd love one."

He went back to the table for the bottle. She slid the door open and turned to see if he was coming when he was suddenly there. His warm hand closed around hers, two hands to support one glass of wine. Their eyes met and held for a beat before he topped off her glass then released her to add to his own.

The guy didn't even have to try to rattle her. It wasn't fair. This was her turf. She should have the home field advantage and yet, she was losing ground. Practically bolting outside, she took a deep calming breath of fresh air, hoping it would clear her head. It was a short-term solution.

The deck was shaded and cool. A slight breeze set the leaves fluttering above, creating a camouflage pattern on the floor. There was an enormous amount of bird activity at the various feeders around the yard and somewhere in the distance, the sound of a lawn mower cutting grass. Curt set the open bottle on the table and followed her down two steps and onto the grass.

They started on the left, at the gate attached to the

corner of the garage, and followed the wooden privacy fence enclosing the rear of the property. All along the fencing was an undulating border of spring beds filled with perennials and shrubs. The scent of hyacinths was strong, intermingled with tulips and daffodils. The older neighborhood was graced by a lot of mature trees and Mia's yard was no exception. She had some beauties.

Curt paused to admire her flowers. "You know, I can't look at a daffodil without thinking about Gene Wilder in the movie *Willy Wonka and the Chocolate Factory*."

Mia laughed. "I can see that."

"You remember it?"

"Of course."

She cut over to a large metal trash can by the garage and scooped out a pitcher of birdseed. As they walked, she'd stop occasionally to spill a little into her feeders.

"I suppose with all this shade, you probably struggle with your lawn." He'd noticed.

"I've given up fighting it and come to terms with my bald patches."

He chuckled. "I'd give it up too and enjoy what you've created. It's downright tranquil."

Her eyes swept closed for a moment and she smiled. "Mmm, I love that word. But there is one thing this yard needs—a bird bath. Right over there." She pointed with the pitcher to the largest tree in the middle of the yard. "The one I had was a cheap plastic thing. I hated it. But it worked so I couldn't justify buying a new one."

"Where is it?"

"Look up. See that break? A big branch broke off last month and smashed it. My lucky day. Now I have a good excuse to shop for a better one."

♡

The little victory smile she turned on him was enchanting.

Curt had the strongest urge to dip his head and plant a kiss right on that happy smile. Maybe he could share it. Perhaps it would leave a taste that would linger on his lips for hours afterwards like the wild strawberry or watermelon flavored lip glosses the girls used to wear when he was a teen. A lovestruck kid might be forgiven for an impetuous move like that. It was different for an adult.

Mia led him back to the deck, never suspecting how strong the impulse to kiss her was or how close he came to giving in to it.

He followed her up, his eyes on her sexy sway as she took the steps. His voice was a little gruff when he said, "So you like flowers."

She turned, her face serene, and looked out over the yard. "Only if they can look after themselves. I love gardens, but I'm not all that interested in taking care of one. When we bought this house, there were a lot more flowers, but over the years I've planted the beds with flowering shrubs instead, filling in here and there with a few annuals. Basically I'm letting the perennials and bulbs sink or swim. Mine is a lazy man's garden."

They each claimed a chair at the table, but Mia warned him before he sat down, "You might want to wipe that cushion first. They can get a little dirty out here."

After brushing off the thick, waterproof cushion, he made himself comfortable. The spring steel frame allowed for gentle rocking. "This is nice."

"Yeah, I love sitting out here."

Another awkward silence invaded the space between them. This time Mia broke it, broaching a new subject.

"I was wondering what made you decide to teach science."

Smiling faintly at an old memory, Curt traced the stem of his glass. "I had an excellent teacher. His enthusiasm was contagious and it made the class fun for me."

Mia smiled. "Hmm."

"And I wanted my summers off," he added with a laugh.

Her eyebrows drew together. "Do you get your summers off? I thought most teachers worked?"

"It all depends. Believe it or not, I'm still living in the same apartment I rented when I was a student so my finances aren't as strained as a lot of the teachers I know. It was cheap and quiet—still is. I wanted to get through school in four years or less, and renting a room in one of the large, old houses near the university wasn't exactly conducive to studying."

"I can imagine."

Curt emptied the last of the wine into each glass before he leaned back in his chair and took a sip. "Yeah, it was a good move because I was living in party central at the time. I got a little tired of strange people coming and going at all hours."

"That would drive me nuts."

He chuckled. "The apartment I found wasn't exactly close to the university, but that was its only drawback, which turned out to be a blessing in disguise. It's strictly studios and one bedroom apartments, and there's a no kid and no pet rule." He shrugged. "Well, I could have a fish if I could make space for a tank."

"Is yours a studio or one bedroom?"

"I have a studio. I can't complain about the rent either. Keeping my expenses low allows me to travel every summer. There's no reason to blow money on a larger place. I went to Spain with another teacher last summer."

"You did?" Mia's hand went to her heart. "Oh…I envy you. I've always wanted to travel. Years ago, Greg and I planned a trip to the Virgin Islands, but that fell through at the last minute because of a conflict he had with work. We ended up divorcing instead of rescheduling. Money well spent, I suppose." She broke into a fatalistic laugh. "A second honeymoon would have only delayed the inevitable."

"When did you divorce?"

"Four years ago."

Thoughtful, Curt drummed his fingers on the arm of his chair. "You really shouldn't give up on travel. So what if your circumstances have changed? That just means your options have changed too. Who knows, you might even have more possibilities this way."

"At this point, it's either family vacations with Casey or nothing."

His expression softened on her and he smiled. "Don't give up on it, Mia."

They both fell quiet and he simply gazed at her, enjoying the view. Her pretty, natural look pulled at him. He loved that she'd left her hair hanging loose and easy. It moved when she did and looked incredibly soft. Even her makeup was light, subtle, complimenting her delicate features without overwhelming them. He was looking at a woman who was meant to be touched, held, and enjoyed, even if her professional image insisted she was a serious and sensible woman. Perhaps she was both? He wondered if she even knew the truth about herself yet.

Shifting uneasily in her chair, Mia said, "You know, I'm not used to people looking at me the way you are."

Caught off guard, he asked, "How's that? Am I making you uncomfortable? What can I do to fix it?"

She threw up her hands helplessly and laughed. "I wish I knew. You could turn around and face the fence, but that's not going to change anything. This is my issue, not yours. You're not doing anything wrong. I'm just not used to this kind of undivided attention."

"Am I staring?"

"God no, that would be creepy." Her laughter faded. "It's hard to explain. And now I wish I'd never said anything."

"I'm glad you did."

The corner of her mouth twitched. "Right now I feel pretty stupid."

He chuckled, but then a thought struck him. "Is this why you didn't notice me right away at the deli?"

Mia frowned. "I'm not following."

"It is!" He was so excited, he pitched forward. "You avoid eye contact."

Unsettled, she ran her hand up and down on her armrest. "So?"

"I think you're afraid to catch people looking at you. That's why you avoid looking at *them*."

"People don't look at me," she argued softly.

"Yes, they do. You just don't want to notice it."

She scoffed, "Why would they bother?"

"I think that's fairly obvious. You're pretty." He calmly sat back and waited for her to refute it.

Her eyes flickered to him then away again. “I wasn’t digging for a compliment.”

“I’m just stating a fact.”

They sat quietly for a moment.

How could she be so unsure of herself, so uneasy in her own skin? Could it be? It was worth asking.

“You haven’t dated much since your divorce, have you?”

“How can you tell?”

“Call it a hunch,” he said with a sad smile.

She looked at him and slowly shook her head. “I haven’t been out at all.”

Her admission wasn’t just shocking, it was incomprehensible. “Not once? You must have had offers.”

“Sure.” She shrugged a shoulder.

“Why didn’t you accept any of them? What are you hiding from?”

She drew her right knee up against her chest in a defensive posture and started to pluck at the inside seam with her thumbnail. He watched her, patiently waiting for an explanation.

“It wasn’t that,” she said eventually.

“Then why?”

Mia hesitated before going on. “I just…I wasn’t interested, okay? I’m a single mom. That gives me plenty to worry about. Men weren’t a priority.”

Something had changed.

“And now?” he asked and held his breath.

She looked away, avoiding eye contact. Her words, when they came, were barely a whisper. "I don't know anymore."

He smiled with relief, encouraged by the inroads he was making. "Seriously, what do you do for fun?"

Her laugh was hollow. "Oh, I live it up. I go home after work. I read a lot. Watch television. If I'm not hanging with my neighbor, Sally, I'm suffocating Casey. I manage to keep busy."

Curt tipped his head in a thoughtful way. "Is it safe to assume you don't have plans tomorrow?"

Her eyebrows shot up. "Why?"

"I want to hit the art fair. Have you ever gone?"

"Never," Mia admitted.

"How about it? Feel like meeting me there?"

"Okay."

Yes!

"Good. It's a date."

Chapter 6

Even though it was just shy of ten in the morning, it was already quite warm. Mia waved from the driveway as Greg backed out with Casey buckled beside him. As soon as they were off, she turned with an energetic step, excited about the day ahead. Her rendezvous with Curt was less than an hour away. There was no time to dilly dally.

"Morning!" Sally called and crossed the grass with a coffee mug in her hand. "I see Casey left."

Mia silently groaned at the unfortunate timing. "Yep. Guy stuff. I don't even ask anymore. It's probably better that way."

Sally laughed. "Yeah, I still get chills remembering how loud you got when he told you about the climbing wall—after the fact."

"Don't remind me. I apologized to the neighbors."

"The cookies were a nice touch. So what's up? Feel like digging some hostas?"

"Actually, I already did. I left four pots for you along the back of the garage. Help yourself."

"Oh. Going somewhere?"

"I am. I'm meeting a friend at the art fair."

"Art fair?" She made a face. "I was going to ask if I could tag along, but forget it. Tell Jane I said hello." Sally returned home with a backhanded wave.

"Will do."

Mia darted inside, her secret safe—for now.

Staring into her closet, she slid hanger after hanger down the rod hoping to find the perfect something. Too bad she didn't know what that was exactly. Then her hand brushed against a long forgotten top at the very back. She drew it into the light. This was it! *On second thought*. Her smile wavered and she leaned in to take a cautious sniff. Finding the top smelled as fresh as the day it was laundered, she turned the hanger to admire it from every angle.

She used to call this her princess top. The style was decidedly feminine and meant to hug a woman's hourglass shape. Flared at the bottom and cut provocatively low in front, it accentuated the bust and offered a tantalizing hint of cleavage from above. It was a bit risqué, but what the hell? The retro look was perfect for today.

Paired with slimming jeans, she kept the rest simple; comfortable tennis shoes for walking, a light brush of mascara, and a neutral lip gloss. It wasn't until she was brushing out her hair she realized this look called for something other than her usual nine-to-five jewelry. It took a minute, but she found her old sterling dangle earrings and passed them through her lobes.

Now it was time to fly.

Of course, knowing she was running late, it was

inevitable she'd get caught behind a slow moving line of cars outside of town. Parking was going to be a nightmare. She turned on the radio and discovered the police had closed off three downtown blocks and they were diverting traffic around the art fair.

She followed the line of vehicles up a side street, but when they turned down the first road looking for open parking spaces, she kept going to the next block and turned onto a residential side street instead. She lucked out and found a spot under a beautiful old elm.

Locking the doors, she slid her purse strap to her shoulder and checked the time. She had seven minutes to get there.

♡

When she saw him, Curt was leaning back on an oversized planter in front of the Stylus Pub enjoying whatever shade the spindly young tree offered. He slowly panned over the crowd and she realized, with a thrilling little jolt, he was watching for her as he took a sip from the bottle in his hand. Then his head swung back around and he broke into a smile when he spotted her. Mia's heart started to pound when he pushed off from the planter and strolled over.

He stopped in front of her and raised his sun-glasses to take a warm, appreciative look at her.

"You look beautiful."

She blinked up at him and stammered, "You...so do you."

Oh god. Did she really say that? Fortunately, she'd made him laugh. Whew.

"Thanks." Then he added confidentially, "I love it when you blush."

She slapped her cheeks and cringed. "I wish I could stop doing that."

"Don't you dare."

She didn't know how to respond to that so she changed the subject instead. "Looks like this is the place to be."

"One of many. Would you like something to drink before we get started?" He folded his glasses and slid them into his breast pocket and turned those sinful eyes on her.

With his dark shades out of the way, this was going to be tougher than she thought. Mia felt fluttery just looking at him.

"No thanks. I finished a bottle of water in the car."

"Let me know if you change your mind. It's pretty warm today."

"You'll be the first to know."

They stood rocking back and forth on their heels for a minute, looking at each other, that unwelcome awkwardness slipping between them again.

Finally, Mia gave him a helpless shrug. "Since you've done this before, why don't you show me around?"

A gorgeous dimple in his left cheek made a brief,

inspirational appearance. "Sure. Let me drop this off inside first. I'll be right back." He wagged the bottle then popped into the pub. When he returned, he explained, "I know the guys in there. They'll hang onto it for me until I get back. If I'm lucky, they'll fill it."

"Handy."

"Ready?" he asked.

"Yep. Lead on."

They set off down the sidewalk. There were canvas stalls everywhere, running down the center of the street back to back and single rows backed up against the curbs and facing the middle rows. Occasional wide breaks between stalls allowed easy access to both sidewalks and the stores beyond. Most of the shops had tables or racks right on the sidewalk to take advantage of all the extra foot traffic. Then there were the food vendors set up in the intersections, creating a mobile food court.

Curt and Mia stopped by several stalls to look at pictures—both paintings and photographs. Once he knew what she liked, he was able to steer them to more appropriate vendors and artists.

She was filing slowly through a box of prints, admiring the haunting black and white photos, when he sidled over and said, "If you like those, you should see the ones hanging in my apartment."

She turned with a laugh. "I'll think about it." She wasn't about to commit to anything yet. Still, that didn't mean he should stop trying.

At another booth farther along, she was struggling to comprehend the strange configurations of welded pipes in bold color combinations when he chuckled at the bemused expression on her face.

Walking over, his hand landed lightly on the small of her back and he leaned in with a soft, "Come with me."

That did it. He just fried her brain. She could actually hear the sizzling. She stared blankly up at him, so rattled by his touch she couldn't think straight.

"Huh?" she asked stupidly.

"Come on," he repeated, easing her away. "I want you to see the next booth. You're going to love this guy's stuff."

Mia was in no condition to argue, especially when his hand remained where it was, floating lightly on her lower back. Evidently, he wasn't in any hurry to break the contact either. Could she get a hallelujah? *Oh yeah.*

It was hard to fault Curt's taste. The next artist was a metal smith who'd fashioned his wonderful pieces from glowing brass, copper, and highly polished steel. Mia found a birdbath she absolutely loved. Had it been anywhere close to her price range, she would have bought it. There were other items as well that she could picture in her yard, from the whimsical fountains that gurgled merrily to ornate sundials. She took a business card.

Farther along was a mask maker with a wide variety, from the largest Mardi Gras parade masks down to the most beautiful miniatures. A lot of the masks were meant to be worn, and people were trying on the comical, frightening, and exotic for their friends and families to laugh over. The best selling size however were the finely detailed miniatures.

As they continued to wander, Curt suddenly pulled her close to allow a couple with a stroller to slip around them.

"Hey. Are you hungry?" he asked her afterwards. "Because I could eat."

"Sure. What do you have in mind?"

He gave a nod to the right. "There's usually a gyro stand over there. Those are good."

She crinkled her nose. "Would I have to eat lamb?"

He chuckled. "No."

"Okay."

Once she got a look at the menu board, Mia moved out of the way while Curt joined the crowded line. He eventually brought back a steak pita for her and a classic lamb for himself. She relieved him of her lunch before he dropped the bottle of Coke dangling from between two fingers underneath it.

"Thanks." He readjusted his hold. "I thought I was gonna lose it."

Since there wasn't any seating available, they tried walking while they ate. In the end, they decided to sit on the curb while they finished their lunch.

"It's not the best you'll ever have," Curt admitted, "But it's not the worst. Trust me."

Mia blotted her mouth with a napkin. "I don't know. I'm enjoying it."

He eyed her skeptically. "Can I have a taste?"

She held it up to him and he took a bite. Chewing thoughtfully, he finally conceded, "Not bad."

"*You* suggested the place," she reminded him.

"Out of all the other garbage on sale here today, you bet your sweet bottom I did. But now you need a proper comparison. I'll have to give it some thought. If I can't come up with something better locally, I'll cook for you myself."

"You cook?"

"I'm single. If I don't cook, I don't eat."

"Oh. Right. That makes sense." Her gaze landed on the side of his hand and the creamy sauce slowly trickling out his palm. "Look out. You've got a drip."

Curt turned his hand and licked it clean, but there was more where that came from. "I think I've sprung a leak."

Mia laughed and dabbed his hand with her napkin, hoping to stop the flow. It was useless. "Keep it." She stuffed her napkin into his sticky palm.

"What a mess." He did what he could to contain it, but when that proved futile, he admitted defeat. "I think I'm done." He rolled everything, including her soaking napkin, up in the wrapper.

Feeling bad for the guy, Mia nudged him with her elbow. "If you're still hungry, you can finish mine." She held it out to him.

"Don't *you* want it?" He didn't wait for her answer. "No. Forget it. I'll find something else."

"I'm never going to finish this. It's huge. I'm willing to share if you are. We're already sharing the Coke."

"Hey. I offered to get you your own pop."

"Don't get defensive. I didn't want my own, remember?"

"You're such a woman."

"Thank you."

He smiled. "You sure about sharing?"

"I suggested it, didn't I?"

"Let me throw this out first." He got up and took his messy wad to the nearest trash can.

Watching him, Mia noticed how he walked, the way he moved. The word *balance* floated through her head. Yes, the word fit him perfectly; his temperament, his carriage, the perfect symmetry of his body itself. Being an avid bike rider, it probably came in handy. She had a hunch it would be pretty hard to throw off the guy's equilibrium.

When Curt came back, he sat closer to her, hip to hip, thigh to thigh, and they passed the pita and the Coke back and forth. The quiet intimacy of their meal did not escape either of them.

Satisfied, she urged him to finish the last bite.

"I'm done. Go ahead."

He crumpled up the paper afterwards. Then with a smile and a gentle bump of his shoulder, he asked, "Shall we continue?"

"Let's do it." She slapped the tops of her thighs and stood before he could offer a sticky helping hand.

A perceptive man, he took it in stride. "Just point me to the first water you see, okay?"

It turned out to be a fountain. He dried his hands on his pants.

"I have an idea. Why don't *you* take *me* where you want to go now?" he said with a courtly gesture.

It was on their return circuit that Mia discovered her favorite artist, a glassmaker. His pieces were exquisite, wonderful and fluid, often just hinting at what the figure was supposed to be. The graceful nudes were particularly lovely. She helped herself to another business card.

"Curt!"

They both turned at hearing his name.

An attractive young woman with dark swinging hair and an enviable complexion was walking right for him.

Mia tactfully stepped away to give them a minute, but Curt caught her hand and tugged her back. He gave it a reassuring squeeze.

"Hi, Holly. I wondered if I'd see you here. Notice anything new this year?"

"A few things," she said slowly, eyeing Mia

before her gaze dropped to their hands.

Mia felt Curt's tension in his grip.

"Holly Patton, Mia Page. Holly is a teacher at Wrigley Middle too," he told her.

"Oh." Mia smiled, not exactly sure how to interpret all this, yet oddly relieved to hear they were merely colleagues. "Nice to meet you."

"It was Mia's son I helped last week—the wrist," he went on, as if anxious to smooth something over. Then he told Mia, "Holly let me use her car to take him to the clinic."

"I'm grateful. Truly. Thank you, so much." When her words appeared to fall on deaf ears, Mia tried again. "What do *you* teach, Holly?"

Mia's warm smile suddenly crackled at the edges from the unexpected blast of frigid air.

Lovely.

Chapter 7

"Spanish," was Holly's cool reply. "What's your son's name?"

Mia wasn't sure she wanted to tell her now. However, good manners won out over, *'Piss off, bitch.'*

"Casey, but he takes French so you probably don't know him."

"Mrs. Thompson is a terrific teacher. I hope he sticks with it. Universities like to see a foreign language on a student's resume." She leaned in and gave Mia a confidential poke. "I know it's a little soon to plant this seed, but when he graduates, he could really benefit from a trip to Europe. There's nothing like it to get you thinking more globally. Our trip to Spain last summer was fantastic, wasn't it, Curt?" She flashed him a brilliant smile. He nodded slowly, almost painfully.

Nice bomb. Mia returned Holly's superficial smile in kind. "I hope he will. I hope *I* will."

"You really should. Don't wait. Book a trip now. You should ask Curt to show you the pictures he took while we were there sometime. He's talented."

"I'm already planning on it."

Mia's announcement seemed to surprise Curt almost as much as it surprised her. Evidently, it was time to mark her territory.

Just how serious were they? Mia glanced at Curt

to see if she could read anything on his face, but he was annoyingly impassive.

"Do you want to meet up later?" Holly asked him.

"Sorry. We're probably leaving soon," he begged off gracefully.

"Well, in that case…Oh hey, I see my sister. We got separated once already. I'd better catch her before I lose her again. It was nice meeting you, Mia. Curt, I'll see you Monday." Holly scurried off, cutting through the crowd.

Adios, bitch.

Mia was glad to see her go. She didn't appreciate the catty baiting. Obviously there were some questions she needed to clear up if she was going to pal around with Curt in the future. Judging by how the day was going so far, it was pretty clear he was herding her in that direction. Not that she minded. God no. But just how many antagonistic female *friends* did he have waiting in the wings ready to take her down? Was he going to have to keep his two sides separate—his love life away from his social life? She wasn't interested in being a marginalized mistress.

Broaching the subject wasn't going to be easy though. Her head wanted to stop her, playing on her fears that she was misinterpreting his signals, but it was hard to pretend she didn't know where they were heading. As the day wore on, he'd found more excuses to touch her and fewer reasons to withdraw. She loved it.

One thing she had to make clear, however, was *if* she was going to make herself sexually available to him, it had to be on an exclusive basis. It didn't matter whether the affair lasted weeks or months—it had to be monogamous. She wasn't immune to jealousy. A closet Don Juan could easily turn her into an insecure mess right out of the box. The last thing she wanted to be was another Holly when faced with a romantic rival.

They closed their full circuit back at the Stylus Pub.

"Feel like going inside for something to drink?" He clearly favored the idea. "It's air conditioned."

Still a bit prickly, Mia declined.

"Would you wait while I run in for my cup? I want to walk you to your car."

"Sure."

When he returned, he went over to the bike rack nearby and unlocked one of the bikes. Freeing the tire, he slid his cup into a holder on the frame.

"All set," he announced with a smile.

"Riding a bike here today was pretty smart. No parking hassles."

"It's all I have. I don't own a car."

"No way."

He laughed. "Way."

"I just thought you were *choosing* to bike instead of drive. You know, going green? You must save a ton of money."

"Not having a car *is* a choice. And you're right, I can't complain about the money I save."

"What do you do in the winter?"

"Carpool. Buses, when I can't ride."

As they walked away from the crowded town, Mia turned that information over in her mind, adding it to what she'd already observed about him. Before she could stop herself, she'd blurted out, "Well, that explains it."

"Explains what?" He looked at her with curiosity.

Crap. Talk about stepping in it. "Nothing. Just something I noticed," she said evasively.

"Tell me." He goaded her with a cocky grin.

"Forget it. It's way too embarrassing."

"Now I *have* to know. Come on." He tugged her to a standstill.

She nipped her lower lip before breaking into a pained smile. "It explains your phenomenal butt." Heat bloomed across her face and she cringed inside. "I can't stop staring at it," she admitted. The damage was done anyway.

Curt's head dropped back and he burst out laughing. "Do you have any idea how happy you just made me?" He shook his head in amazement. "Here I thought you were immune. I mean, let's face it; you didn't exactly give me much encouragement. There was a point yesterday where I wondered if you were just being nice when you agreed to meet me here."

Mia chuckled at his error. "No. Trust me, I

noticed you. I started fantasizing right away. It made me feel like a freakish pervert."

"Now you've really got me going here." He winked. "Feel free to ogle me anytime."

She cuffed him playfully on the arm. "Don't tease. I'm already embarrassed."

"No," he said, completely serious now. "I *want* you to see me, in every sense of the word."

Her footsteps faltered and he reached out to steady her.

"In fact," he went on. "I wouldn't mind getting into some fantasy discussions too, if you feel like sharing. We can compare notes."

She looked away with a bashful laugh. "I'll think about it."

It wasn't until Mia saw the sign for the street where she'd parked that she finally got up the nerve to ask him about his relationship with Holly.

The *click, click, click* of his rolling bicycle counted off their steps for a minute before he answered her.

"Holly and I have been good friends for almost five years now. We discovered we travel well together because we have a lot of the same tastes and interests. I enjoy her company."

"No," she persisted. "I mean, did you two *date*?" There, she'd asked it.

"We never dated. I should probably apologize to you for Holly. She's a nice person. We're just sorting out some issues right now. It has nothing to do with you."

"Are you sure?"

"I am. I'm just not sure she understands that yet."

"The more you say, the more confusing this is getting for me. How is that possible?"

He laughed. "Crazy, I know. I guess I should explain. Is this your street?"

"Yes. We go left here."

"As you know, we went to Spain last summer. It was beautiful. Amazing. On our last night, we partied hard with some of the locals. We drank too much. It was pretty late—or really early, I'm still fuzzy on the details—but I do remember we had one of those moments, the kind where you're suddenly looking at each other, wondering things you probably shouldn't. Do you know what I mean?"

"Yes."

"We ended up spending the night together before flying home the next morning. I knew it was a mistake right away, but I could tell Holly and I weren't on the same page. She was building dreams, a relationship off that one stupid night. There I was, regretting what we'd done, and she was having feelings for me I couldn't reciprocate."

"This is my car."

"You drive an SUV?"

"Don't start."

He held up his hand in peace. "Now what?"

"I'm not ready to say goodbye yet," she admitted.

He looked relieved. "Me neither. What time is your ex bringing Casey home?"

"Three."

He glanced at his watch and his face fell. "Damn. Doesn't give us much time." Looking at her, he had an idea. "Wait right there."

He rolled his bike behind the truck and propped it against the bumper. When he came back, he held out his hand for her keys. Curious, she gave them up and he popped the locks and opened the back door for her.

"Get in." He closed her in and walked around to the other side.

She was glad she'd left the windows down. The interior was quite comfortable. Or at least it was until the other door opened and Curt slid into the back with her.

"Where were we?" he asked softly.

Chapter 8

"Holly wants you," Mia prompted him.

"Oh yeah," Curt said with a sad smile. "So we talked. I reminded her why I wasn't the right guy for her and we were better as friends. She agreed. But over time, I noticed she wasn't dating anymore. Willing or not, I was in the way, so I backed off. Now we only see each other in school."

"If you were such a good fit otherwise, how do you know you couldn't be more?"

"You can't force an attraction." He sighed. "Don't get me wrong, she's pretty. But if there's no spark, there's no spark."

Mia found herself on familiar ground, though Holly was obviously hoping Curt's feelings for her would change. She was circling the airport waiting for the runway to clear. No wonder she was hostile.

"It must be a strain to see each other at school every day."

"No more than for anyone else in this situation. I don't think it's all that unique."

"I suppose not." She almost felt sorry for Holly. Almost. "At least you didn't marry her." Mia gave him a rueful smile and pointed a finger at herself.

"You?"

"Oh yeah. Greg and I always got along better as friends. We should have split up before the wedding because our feelings had already faded to a warm affection by then. Our marriage was flat lining by the time Casey came along. Even he couldn't rescue it. I can't tell you what a relief it was to finally sit down and have the *'I love you, I'm just not* in *love with you,'* talk."

"So you were both okay with it?"

"Better than okay. Greg's pretty serious about the woman he's seeing now. She makes him happier than I ever did. I'm glad too, because he's a great guy."

"And your friendship?"

"Better than ever."

"So there's hope for Holly and me eventually?"

"Anything's possible."

"And how about *us*?" He slid his hand along the back of the seat behind her and that's what triggered their sudden move into the middle.

He reached out to caress her cheek, his palm cupping her jaw, his thumb tracing her cheekbone. If she'd thought his eyes were potent before, she was mistaken. She knew this smoldering look. This hungry, almost wild yearning had frightened her when she was younger and unprepared to unleash the desire coiled like a spring inside a man. *How things changed.* Now, as a woman, it thrilled her.

He moved in slowly, tentatively, perhaps expecting her to pull back. When she didn't, his lips pressed over hers ever so softly.

Their restraint didn't last.

Mia caught hold of his collar and Curt drove his fingers up from her neck straight into her hair. A simultaneous groan of longing escaped them both and they laughed at themselves before going back on the attack, the intensity of their next kiss almost painful. The need to touch and move as one was agony. She opened her mouth to him and he thrust inside. Frantic, even manic, they gripped. They gasped. They devoured. They made the truck rock on its axels. This was the kind of kiss she'd been missing—the kind she forgot even existed.

Their hands flowed over each other, impatiently exploring. Mia's spread over his chest and plucked his hard nipples through the soft fabric of his shirt. He broke away from her lips to kiss and nuzzle the tops of her breasts, scooping them up to enjoy more of her cleavage.

She twined her fingers in his hair and held on for dear life. She could feel the moist heat of his mouth, his breath, penetrate her shirt and lacy bra and dampen her sensitive nipples underneath. He bit gently and sucked until her hips involuntarily thrust up from the edge of the seat.

His chuckle was low and sexy as he slid his hand between her legs and rubbed along the inside seam of her jeans. She whimpered and pushed back against his magical fingers, damp, aching, and needlessly ready.

When their eyes connected, she saw her naked lust reflected back at her. Their mouths collided again and, desperately hungry, they fed from each other until they were panting for air, yet still reluctant to stop. Only when they were both lightheaded did they break off to draw long, ragged gasps.

"My head is spinning." She needed both hands to steady it.

He nodded, more than a little dazed himself.

There was nothing she wanted more than to ask him back to the house. She wanted him so bad it took real effort to remember Casey would be home soon. As if sensing the intrusion of time, their kisses gentled, their touches tamed.

"I have to go," she reminded him sadly, her head reeling at how fast she'd lost control with him.

"I know."

Rather than move, they sat forehead to forehead, chests rising and falling, each lost in their own private thoughts.

Mia wasn't ready to part. She was so disappointed, so unacceptably unsatisfied she could have wept. The ferocity of her rekindled sexuality left her shaken. She couldn't recall ever feeling this stirred up.

Curt released her and got out of the truck. He walked around and opened her door then took her hand as she slid off the seat and pulled her against him. They held each other close, wonderfully close, full contact, and she realized that parting here and now was probably a very good idea. Had they continued in such a public place, they would have been caught like two horny teenagers in the back of a parent's car.

Curt was clearly up for action. Pressed against her like this, it wasn't as if he could hide it from her. For once, the anatomical inconveniences between the sexes seemed weighted in a woman's favor. At least her sexual arousal wasn't so obvious.

Without letting her go, he reached around and opened the driver's side door. Mia gave him one final squeeze then climbed in. As soon as she started the engine, she rolled down the window the rest of the way. He reached in and took her hand off the wheel. His thumb stroked back and forth over her knuckles.

"Can I see you tomorrow?" he asked.

"I'd like that."

"When?"

Her eyes dropped to her hand cradled in his and she smiled. "Anytime. Plan on staying a while."

"Maybe I'll take you and Casey biking. What do you think?"

"Sounds nice."

He stretched in through the window to kiss her goodbye then moved back so she could pull away from the curb.

It was impossible not to watch him through the rearview mirror as he walked his bike in the opposite direction. Poor guy wouldn't be riding for a minute or two. She hated to admit it, but the thought lifted her spirits considerably.

Chapter 9

Mia expected Greg and Casey back at any time so she was surprised when her ex called instead. She'd just changed into a fresh tank top and yoga pants when the telephone rang.

"Hey, Mia. I was wondering if Casey could stay overnight. We can swing by for a change of clothes and his toothbrush. I want to talk to you about something anyway. Will that work for you?"

"Is something wrong?"

"No. But I'd rather tell you in person. Can I come over?"

"Sure. I'll get an overnight bag ready for him."

"Good. See you soon."

She hung up and wandered to the window. What was this about? Without any point of reference, she couldn't answer that question, though, it didn't stop her from worrying.

Rather than torture herself with dire possibilities, she went into the kitchen to see what she had in the fridge to offer him. Not much. She grabbed the last of the cans of Coke from the pantry and slid them onto the shelf alongside the bottle of white wine. Curt's bottle.

Seeing it made her sorry she didn't know about Casey's sleepover sooner. She could have stayed out longer. Mia glanced at the drawer with the telephone book and contemplated looking up Curt's number. She could ask him over. Why not? No harm in extending a simple, friendly invitation.

Right. Like she could sit there and pretend she didn't know exactly where it would lead. *'My son's gone. Come on over and we can crack open that bottle you brought.'*

How obvious did she want to look? Why not answer the door in a negligee and scrap the pretense of respectability altogether?

No, it was better this way. If he wanted her, he was going to have to work for her a little. She'd never been easy and she wasn't about to change that no matter how tempted. A fling was one thing. A one night stand was out of the question.

Tonight she'd put Curt out of her mind, draw a relaxing bath, light some candles, and sink into scented water with a good book.

Good plan.

Packing for Casey wasn't easy. The deeper she dug through his clothes, the more she pitched into the laundry basket. Finding crusty, smelly, wadded up socks in his dresser was the last straw. *Why* did he put them in there? Revolted, she took the cleanest pair she could find and tucked them inside his bag then upended the entire drawer over the basket and hauled it down to the washing machine.

She was on her way back up, the machine agitating away behind her, when Greg pulled into the driveway. They reached the front door at the same time and Mia threw open the screen for him.

"Come on in." She stepped back.

He dipped to kiss her on the cheek. "How are you?"

"Since this morning?" she asked. "Transformed."

Though she was kidding, once it was out, she realized it was true. Stunned, she waved him into the kitchen.

"How about a Coke?"

"Sure."

"Where's Casey?" She grabbed one for him and took a Diet for herself then shut the fridge.

"Watching Anime. Should be over by the time I get back."

"Let's go sit at the table," she suggested.

They settled in their old, familiar chairs and popped their cans, releasing a harmonic hiss of fizz along with it. Mia took a sip and watched her ex-husband as she set down the can.

He was radiating stress like asphalt radiated heat. It was disturbing and contagious. Then he started to fiddle with the tab on his can. Suddenly realizing she was watching him, waiting, he gave her a pained smile. The fine hairs on the back of her neck stood straight up.

"Greg, you're freaking me out. What's going on?"

"I'm getting married," he blurted out, clearly afraid of how she'd react. He shouldn't have worried.

"But that's great news!"

"Are you just saying that?" he asked softly.

"Don't be an idiot. My god, I'm so happy for you. For both of you!"

She could actually see his tension evaporate and his body relax. His bright, open smile was back.

"I asked Liz on Thursday night," he told her. "We've been talking about moving in together for a while. Hell, we're practically living together now. But then I realized, I don't just want to live with her, I want to marry her. I love her." He took a moment, clearly weighing something. Then he added, "We'd like to have a baby. *I'd* like to have another baby. I'm not getting any younger."

Casey would have a little brother or sister? Mia tried to picture it. She remembered how nervous he was during her pregnancy, so unsure about parenthood. His doubts melted away once he held their son the first time. Just picturing Greg's face, so full of wonder when he looked at the newborn in his arms made Mia smile all over again.

"I think you *should* have another baby. Have two, if that's what you want. You're a great dad." She reached over and squeezed his arm.

He covered her hand and squeezed back. "I'm an idiot. I don't know why I was so worried about telling you."

Mia laughed. "Worrying is what we do. You had me going there for a minute."

"Sorry." Greg smiled sheepishly. "Oh, and I'm going to ask Casey to be my best man."

"Really?" The idea pleased her. "I think it would mean a lot to him."

"I thought I'd take him shopping for matching suits tomorrow. Just us guys."

Mia's smile wavered. "Greg, Casey's growing pretty fast right now—I swear I can hear his bones creaking. Just how soon is the wedding? Have you set a date?"

"We're pushing for the end of the month, maybe early June. We want it small, close family and friends at the arboretum. Liz's uncle is a judge and he's agreed to officiate."

"That's fast."

"We know what we want."

Mia smiled. "I never realized you could be so romantic."

He shuddered. "Call it decisive—*please*."

"Whatever." She laughed at his denial.

"Well, I'd better get back." Greg stood and looked around. "Is Casey's bag ready?"

"I put it in the hall. Make sure he changes his underwear. He's good about changing his socks, but if you don't remind him…well, you can imagine."

They walked to the door and shared a warm hug.

"I'm really happy for you." Mia drew back. "Tell Liz congratulations from me, okay?"

"Of course. You'll be there, right?"

"I wouldn't miss it."

"Good." He went out the door and looked back. "I'll have Casey home before dinner tomorrow."

They each gave a final wave then Mia closed the door. Her thoughts were light and happy when she went down to transfer the clothes to the dryer. Imagine—Greg was getting married again. The idea pleased her.

On the way back upstairs, she thought about how much she treasured their friendship. She supposed it might be normal to feel a little jealousy when your ex remarries, but she didn't. Greg and Liz were great together, and seeing it only emphasized how premature *they'd* been to settle so soon. How could they be so young and idealistic, yet at the same time, so cynical about the most important thing in life—love? The reasons escaped her. They should have held out for the fairy tale. When did they decide that the love in great novels and movies was only fantasy? She didn't remember any conversations and yet they'd nearly sabotaged each other, interfering with the possibility of finding and experiencing something wondrous—a love with true and lasting substance. She was glad to see it working out for him now.

Suddenly inspired, Mia decided tonight was hers. She had love and possibilities dancing in her mind—happy endings and fairy tales. Why waste it at home?

Returning to her bedroom to change for the third time that day, she was humming when she backed out of the garage and left the dark house behind.

♡

The mall lot was packed. Well, it was Saturday. What did she expect? She eventually found a parking space in the twilight zone and followed a group of squirrelly teens and a middle-aged couple to the line of doors in the distance.

Evidently, this crowd was going to the movies. She veered around the long ticket line and continued on to the bookstore.

The tables just inside were filled with popular picks and new releases. She took her time browsing. Sometimes she'd turn one over to read a dust jacket, but mostly she left them alone.

By the third table, she'd grown discouraged. Sometimes, the sheer volume of books overwhelmed her. That's when the enormity of the challenge of finding the right book to satisfy a mood would hit. More often than not lately, she'd lose her enthusiasm and leave empty handed. She didn't want to do that tonight, but how do you nurture and sustain a positive outlook when faced with a mass of options like this?

Taking a deep breath, she pressed on, scrutinizing the end-of-shelf displays. Nothing was hitting her. She wandered over to the fiction section, confident that what she wanted was a story, an escape. She shouldn't rush this.

Since the shelves were in alphabetical order, she

began at the beginning, scanning titles and eliminating any she knew at a glance weren't what she wanted. She was in the mood for happiness, not murder. Attraction, not angst. She pulled several off the shelf to read their jackets before putting them back. A couple of times she was curious enough to crack the spine to sample the writing. By the third bookcase, she had one potential in her hand and she wasn't exactly wild about it. She was settling. Her enthusiasm was seriously waning when she crouched down to skim the titles along the bottom. It was another disappointing nothing.

That's it. Might as well give up and grab a magazine instead. Disheartened, Mia rose stiffly to her feet and stumbled backwards into the person behind her.

"I'm so sorry!" Her mortification turned to shock when she saw who'd caught her. "Curt?"

Chapter 10

Mia couldn't believe it. There he was, right there, his gorgeous smile locked on her as he supported her by the elbow.

"Well hello." Pleasantly surprised, Curt set her upright. "I was looking forward to seeing you tomorrow, but this is even better. Are you okay?"

Embarrassed, Mia looked at her feet. "Blame my footwear."

"Nice boots. Heels make a woman's legs look great, but they're not good for you."

"Is anything these days?"

"Good point. Is Casey with you?" He looked around.

"Not tonight. I'm alone." Mia pointed to the shelves behind him. "Looking for anything in particular?"

"Not really. Just something fresh. You?"

"Actually, I'm about to give up," she admitted.

He tipped his head to see what she was holding. Mia turned it toward him. He shrugged after reading the cover.

"My sentiments exactly," she agreed.

"I've been reading a lot more non-fiction lately," he told her. "It's easier to find books I know will interest me—less hit or miss. I have a lot of political, environmental, and philosophical books at home." He leaned close and lowered his voice confidentially. "I'm a little ashamed to admit this, but I just don't know many current fiction writers anymore. I find I'm re-reading the same old books when I'm in the mood for a story because there's so many. Where to begin?"

She understood. "I do that too."

"Tell you what. Why don't we look together? We should be able to find something. Neither of us should give up already."

"Why not? Where should we start?"

"Here?"

"I'm game."

"What type of book are you in the mood for tonight?" he asked.

She thought about it. "Nothing dark. I'm not into murders and gore. And I really don't want to join someone on a sad and depressing journey back from dependency or share in a quest for salvation. I want something light, fun, and entertaining." She smiled in apology. "I know how tough I'm making this, but if I have to read one more book about dysfunctional families trying to heal and understand one another, I swear I'll tear my hair out."

Curt laughed. "So, you're a happy ending kind of person."

"I guess I am. Life is tough enough without wallowing in the low points."

"Okay. We're looking for happy endings and escapism. Maybe some laughs. I think we can fill that order. Let me see that book again." Mia passed it to him. He flipped it open and scanned the description before closing the cover and handing it back. "I don't think this book is what you're looking for. Just an opinion," he added.

"I know. But I hated rejecting everything. What kinds of books do you like?"

"Me? I like intrigue with smart, exciting plots. Political thrillers with a good pace." He paused, obviously weighing something, then shrugged and threw it out there. "I've always been a fan of sci-fi, but a friend turned me on to fantasy recently."

"And that makes you uncomfortable?"

"People don't exactly see it as *literature*." His air quotes were so unexpectedly cute, she smiled.

"But you *like* it."

"I do," he said.

She glanced around, making sure there was no one close enough to overhear her then whispered, "I read romance."

"Your secret's safe with me." Curt grinned. "Then why are we wasting our time over here? I'll help you find a romance if you'll help me find an interesting fantasy."

"I don't know anything about fantasy."

"Well, I've never read a romance."

"Two babes in a bookstore," she said with a laugh. "Okay, let's hit it."

They went to the romance section first since it

was closest. Curt started pulling books out right away. He even read the beginnings of a few. Mia was amused at first, but grew more serious as they went on.

Eventually, Curt looked up from the open book in his hand and asked, "How steamy do you like these?"

This was embarrassing, but might as well fess up. It was better than boredom. "The hotter the better."

That earned a big smile. "Good answer. Look at this one."

Accepting it from him, she took a peek. It had everything—tension, a plausible story, emotion, and steamy sex.

"Ding, ding, ding. We have a winner." She tucked it under her arm. "Your turn."

There were two teens and one adult, all male, looking at books in the fantasy section. Mia found that interesting.

She turned to Curt. "Do you have a favorite author?"

"Not yet."

"Okay." Mia jumped ahead of him, so they wouldn't knock into each other, and began to look over the colorful spines. The more she saw, the more the genre intrigued her.

"Hey. What do you think of this one?" Curt showed her a book.

"I like the cover." She took the book from him and flipped it over to read the back. It had everything he described, but within a realm of magic. It even had romance. Mia smiled. “Could I read this when you’re done with it?”

He gave her a playful nudge and took the book back. “Of course. Maybe we can swap.”

He’d surprised her.

“You’d read a romance?”

“Sure.” He shrugged. “How can I have an opinion about them one way or another if I’ve never read one? I try to avoid making unqualified judgments about anything, if I can help it.”

Their choices in hand, they paused to put the rejected book back where she’d found it on their way to the registers. Curt’s transaction went faster than Mia’s so he waited for her near the entrance.

Her purchase made, she came to a happy stop in front of him. He smiled back and gestured to the mall beyond.

“How about a drink from the food court?”

“Sure.”

They made idle chitchat as they strolled, the lazy swing of their matching bags perfectly synchronized. The broad corridor opened up before them into a spacious atrium that echoed with sound. They stopped at the edge of a sea of tables and considered their options.

“I’d rather not have coffee this late,” Curt said.

“Agreed.”

“Fresh fruit juice?”

Mia followed his nod to the left and considered the quiet stand. A girl in a visor was slouched against the counter people watching with a bored look on her face.

"I'm game. Let's give her something to do."

The girl straightened up when they walked over. There was no mistaking the instant she recognized Curt because she broke into a big, metallic smile.

"Mr. Walden!" She must have gone up on her toes because she seemed to grow three inches.

"Hi, Jenni. How are you?" he asked with a kind smile.

"I'm great!" Her eyes cut to Mia then back to him. "What can I get 'cha?"

Mia?" Curt raised his eyebrows at her.

She crept forward, eyes scanning the menu. "The Berry Blend sounds good," she said slowly.

"It's a-*mazing,*" the girl told her. "Mr. Walden?"

"I'll have a Pineapple Citrus Breeze."

"It'll just be a minute."

While they waited, the girl threw all kinds of fresh fruit into the idle blenders. When the loud blades engaged, they glanced at each other and laughed, rocking back and forth on their heels, uncomfortably aware of all the people looking their way because of the unexpected racket. Fortunately, the noise was short-lived. Jenni poured the contents of both into two tall, disposable cups, capped them, and then set them in front of the waiting couple.

"That'll be seven dollars," she said and stepped behind the register.

Mia started to reach into her purse for money. Curt stopped her.

"My treat. *I* asked *you.*"

"Thanks."

He paid and they took their beverages to a table that was partially screened by large planters.

"I take it you're a feminist," he surmised with a smile.

Swiveling back and forth in her seat, she laughed. "Of course I am. Why do you bring it up?"

"I just didn't expect you to go Dutch on me. Thanks for not jumping down my throat for wanting to pay."

"I wouldn't do that. My mother would disown me for not appreciating a simple courtesy. However, since you brought it up, the reason I was ready to pay for my own is because I don't like to make assumptions."

"Fair enough." He leaned in. "Next time I invite you out, I'll expect to pay. Just so we're clear."

"And if I ask you, I'll treat."

"Fine." He sat back in his chair and took a tug from his straw. "I'm trying to figure out how this very feminine woman, who reads romance novels, can be a feminist."

"You see a contradiction?"

"I don't know. Maybe. You don't seem like the bra burner type."

"Not when I love expensive lingerie." She laughed at his instant and predictable reaction. "Seriously, don't you think that's a pretty tired stereotype? Women are making headway in the equal pay and opportunity fight, but we're still behind. If you don't believe me, look at the numbers."

"I'm not questioning you on that."

"Good. It wouldn't hurt to see more businesses adopt family-friendly policies either."

He raised his eyebrows. "Such as?"

"You know, flex time, off-site options, that kind of thing. It isn't like there's a happy homemaker taking care of the kids and the households anymore. Is it any wonder modern families are under so much strain?"

"Since I haven't been in your situation—a woman, single, with a child—I guess I never thought about it, but you make sense."

"Thank you. Now if we could only get everyone working for our cause, we might make real progress."

His smile warmed. "I think you and Holly would get along great. She feels the same way."

Maybe if he weren't already between them. Mia took a sip of her juice and chose a new subject. "You said you read philosophy?"

"Some."

"Then tell me, what's the meaning of life? And don't say forty-two." She teased, now that she knew he liked science fiction.

"Reproduction," he said without hesitation. "But that's the scientist talking."

His certainty surprised her.

"Are you saying there *is* no other point?"

"Pretty much. Everything else is just a means to that end. Fortunately, we humans don't have to be slaves to the biological imperative anymore. That's not to say we don't still struggle with our sex drives. It just means we have choices past generations didn't."

"Do you teach sex-ed?"

He laughed. "It's part of the seventh grade curriculum, so yes, I'm qualified to teach it."

"I'll bet you are."

He smiled modestly. "Any other questions?"

"Oh goody. Let me see. Condoms in school?"

He thrust his cup into the air and declared, "All for it. Beats the hell out of pregnant teens in school."

"I agree. Genetically modified produce, yea or nay?"

His right eyebrow twitched. "Do you honestly think what you're eating now is in its original form? Humans have been modifying crops, grafting trees, playing with plant and animal genetics for as long as we've been cultivating our own food sources. Ever eat a grapefruit?"

"Sure."

"Notice anything different about it, like how much sweeter they are now compared to the tart varieties we grew up with?"

"Huh. You're right. They're a lot sweeter. I don't even sugar it anymore."

Curt drew the beads of condensation down his clear cup and asked, "How about apples? Look at all the varieties we have. It's virtually impossible to be a purist these days. Who'd want to be? Think of all the things we'd have to do without. How could we feed the world, move away from pesticides and herbicides, protect groundwater, or preserve topsoil without scientific breakthroughs?"

"I guess I never thought about that."

"Don't worry. There's no test."

Grinning now, Mia chewed the end of her straw flat. "Do you believe in UFOs?"

He laughed. "No. At least not the ones you're talking about. I'm not saying there isn't the potential for life to exist in some form or another somewhere else in the universe. Statistically, that's a very real possibility, but I haven't seen any compelling evidence to suggest aliens are dropping by Earth on a regular basis either." He smiled at her. "Any other questions?"

"How about cellphones in school?"

His expression soured. "That's a big no. My classroom is a no-phone zone. I confiscate any phones I see."

Mia laughed. "So you do have limits."

"I expect my students to pay attention when they're in my class. Girls are the worst. I take a lot more phones away from them than boys."

"I notice you don't use your phone much."

His eyebrow rose flirtatiously. "Neither do you."

"Hey, I'm with you right now. Why would I want to talk to someone else?"

"You just won yourself a lot of points for saying that."

Suddenly bashful, she poked her straw up and down and glanced away, her eyes landing on the bored girl who'd served them. "This juice is pretty tasty."

"I'm enjoying mine."

"I take it our little Jenni over there is one of your students?"

"She was…a couple of years ago."

"I think she had a crush on you."

Curt grimaced. "I don't even want to go there."

"Aw. Didn't you ever have a crush on a teacher?"

"One or two," he admitted with a little smile. "You?"

"Not until now."

His eyes twinkled. "You're racking up the points there, honey."

With those thoughts lingering in the air between them, they finished their drinks and tossed their trash into the first waste basket they passed as they left the echoes of the food court behind.

"Where are you parked?" he asked her.

"By the theater. Not the smartest decision I've made."

He chuckled. “Mind if I walk you out?”

“I’d like that.”

“Here, let me carry your book.”

Mia passed him the bag. He slid it against his then offered his free hand to her. She smiled and took it, meshing her fingers with his as they strolled to the exit.

It was dark and overcast when they stepped outside. Ominous rumbles and flashes of intermittent lightning sliced through the rolling gray clouds overhead.

Eyeing the thunderheads, Curt expelled a sigh. “Here comes the rain.”

“We could use it. Where’s your bike?”

“I walked. I don’t live far from here.”

“Come on.” She waved him along. “I’ll drive you home.”

“You don’t have to.”

“I know,” she said lightly.

He smiled. “Okay.”

Somehow, quite naturally, they found themselves drawn together. Curt’s arm went around her shoulders. Mia’s arm slipped around his waist and she hooked her thumb through one of his belt loops and held on. It slowly dawned on her he’d matched his stride to hers so their tandem stroll down the line of cars felt right somehow, surprisingly comfortable.

He interrupted her thoughts to tease, “You sure you parked far enough away?”

"Cheap shot. I already admitted it was a mistake to park by the theater entrance on a Saturday night."

She hit her truck remote and the locks clicked and the interior lights flashed on inside the SUV.

He came to a dead stop and shook his head. "I can't believe I'm considering riding in one of these."

"Get over it. I feel safer in this."

"Three words, Mia. Global. Climate. Change."

"No one said you have to *take* this ride. I'd hate to see you sacrifice your principles."

He glanced up at the threatening clouds, the first sprinkles already falling, and sighed. "I'll take the ride."

"You sure?" she asked, needling him for the fun of it.

"I'll get over it. I'm fundamentally unaltered."

"So where are we going?"

"Forty-Seventh and McGowan. You know where that is?"

"The general area. Just let me know when we get close."

"Got it."

They left the mall behind, but traffic wasn't any better until they turned off the commercial street. Mia had to pay attention to the road, but she could feel it whenever his eyes strayed her way.

"It's just up ahead." He pointed. "On the right."

Mia pulled along the curb and put the truck into park.

"Do you want to come in?" His eyes picked up the greenish glow of the dashboard lights and flickered seductively back at her.

The guy didn't make things easy. Her heart wanted to answer yes, but that's not what her mouth was saying. "I would, Curt, I really would, but I can't. It's too soon." The look she gave him begged for patience. "I'm sorry. I need more time."

"I understand." He grew serious. "I don't think it'll come as a shock that I want to take you to bed, but I'm willing to wait, within reason, for you."

"Within reason?"

His smile was back. "Well, you can't expect me not to try to persuade you." He stretched to kiss her. "I'm going to do everything in my power to change your mind. Ultimately, it's up to you. Let me know when you're ready, okay?"

There was a battle going on inside her. She wanted to take him up on his offer *now,* but this was a big step for her. All told, Curt would only be the fourth man to see her naked, counting her old obstetrician. Intimacy with a new man was suddenly a pretty terrifying thought.

Still, her heart raced like a hummingbird's at the expectation in his eyes, the confidence that he was going to be her lover. If she were capable of lying to herself, she might have felt offended by his presumptions, but who was she kidding? She knew the minute she mentally undressed him she'd be an idiot not to jump at the chance to get close to the real deal. Other women would have tripped her down the stairs for the opportunity he was offering. She'd already met one.

"I'll keep you posted," she said softly.

His smile warmed. Squeezing her thigh, he gave her an intoxicating kiss that lingered on her lips after he eased back.

Her eyes slowly opened and locked with his. The corner of his mouth twitched and she answered; her smile a reflection of his. Curt made a deep, little sound. It could have been a breath of contented air escaping or a happy hum. He stretched toward her, intending to kiss her again. She grabbed him by the head with both hands and kissed him first. His fingers bunched in her hair as they sank into the moment one last time. She was sorry when he let go and turned to open his door.

"We're still on for tomorrow, right?" he asked, looking back as he climbed out.

"Absolutely."

"Good night, Mia."

"Good night," she told him wistfully.

His glowing smile could have drawn moths if he stood still long enough, but he shut the door and strode across the grass. She put the truck into gear and pulled away, certain she was right to hold off, but miserable just the same.

She had no idea how she was going to make it

through tomorrow.

Chapter 11

It was good to stay in control, Mia reminded herself. The last thing she wanted to do was complicate things, forfeit her self-respect, and gamble with Curt's good opinion by going to bed with him too fast. They were just getting to know each other, for crying out loud. It shouldn't be all that tough to ignore this overpowering attraction between them, right? *Right?*

Even after her cool shower, and with a quiet house, she still had trouble relaxing. The storm didn't help. She couldn't settle down. Wrestling with her covers and battering her pillows into submission after hurling one of them against the wall, she was eventually able to nod off. But getting a good night's rest was impossible. That's when her dreams took over, tormenting her with erotic images and very real sensations one after another until she moaned herself awake and kicked off the remaining sheet. It was useless.

Grumbling in frustration, she dragged herself into the kitchen and brewed a pot of coffee. By the time the newspaper came, she was beginning to revive. She traipsed out to the curb in her robe and slippers to get it, beyond caring whether anyone saw her or not. Any sane person would still be in bed at this hour.

She made herself comfortable at the table with her newspaper, an English muffin, and her large, warm mug nestled in her hands.

When Curt arrived just before ten in the morning, she'd already changed into a pair of Capri's and a loose, collarless t-shirt over her favorite rose colored bra. She'd worried for hours he wasn't going to show up only to turn around and start worrying he would. In the end, her mixed emotions vanished when he came to the door wearing tight black racer shorts and a coordinated shirt. The fabric hugged his body close and left little to the imagination.

Mercy.

He gave her a warm smile through the screen and they embraced as soon as he crossed the threshold.

"Are you okay?" He pulled back with concern. "You're shaking like a frightened puppy."

She laughed at herself. "Too much caffeine. I'm a little wired."

Relieved, he dipped to kiss her. "Good morning."

"Mmm. It's definitely looking up." This was going to be embarrassing, unavoidable, but embarrassing. Still, she might as well own it. "I need your help."

He brushed his finger under her chin. "Name it."

"I can't get my bike down from the ceiling hook in the garage myself." She shrugged apologetically. "I was going to ask Greg to do it when he dropped by last night. I forgot."

"No sweat. I'll do it."

"Thanks." She led him through the kitchen and out to the garage, opening the big door for more light.

When he saw her bike, Curt stared up at it, speechless. His eyes were dancing, his grin wide when he turned and asked, "How long has it been since you rode that thing?"

"A while," she said vaguely.

He snorted, amused. "Obviously. Well, the baby seat has to come off, and I'm willing to bet those tires are completely flat. You'll be lucky if they hold air at this point."

"No jokes, okay?" she pleaded. "Just give me a minute to find the pump."

Mia went digging behind an old croquet set while he lifted the bike down and went to work.

The no-frills tire pump was dusty but in good condition when she located it. She brought it over and caught the handlebars for him, stabilizing the bike while he removed the infant seat.

"You probably shouldn't expect much from me right away," she told him.

He snickered at that. "Don't worry. I won't."

Mia hauled her long neglected pout out of storage and dusted it off. It worked like a charm.

He held out his hand to her. "Come here. I'm sorry." He mimicked her pout perfectly and she smothered her giggle.

"I don't know." She drew back with a wary smile. "I'm seeing a wicked side of you here."

He winked and tugged her over. The teasing at an end, she bent to accept his apologetic kiss and stayed when it turned passionate. When she finally staggered back, she was tempted to fan herself. Another kiss like that one and she'd forgive him anything.

"All done," he told her.

Ready to go, she ran inside to lock the front door. Rather than take the house keys, she grabbed the garage door opener out of the truck and clipped it to her pocket. Curt relinquished her handlebars and they walked into the bright morning sunshine as the garage door closed behind them.

He grinned at the bike helmet she strapped on her head. "I love it."

"It's Casey's. I've never owned one. Does it look stupid?"

"You look cute."

"I knew it. It *is* stupid."

"It's smart." Curt strapped on his own helmet then threw a long leg over his bike seat and straddled the bar. Kicking his pedal around, he suddenly frowned at her. "Hang on. Where *is* Casey? Isn't he coming with us?"

"Oh, I forgot to tell you, he stayed at his dad's last night so they could go suit shopping today. More news—Greg is getting married again and he wants Casey to be his best man."

"That's great. I guess that means it's just us."

"Yep."

The implications hung between them like a pulsing wave of energy.

They stood there, looking at one another, each a little hesitant.

Finally, Curt waved her forward. "You should lead."

"No. Uh uh. I'm not riding in front of you."

"Why not?"

"For starters? I don't want you staring at my butt."

"Too late." He laughed. "Come on, Mia. You haven't ridden in a long time. With you in front, not only can you set the speed, but I'll be able to react if anything happens to that old bike of yours. My point is, I have to *see* you if I'm going to help."

"I know that all makes sense, but I'm just not comfortable."

"Don't be stubborn. I don't care if you look at mine."

"Why would you? Yours is fantastic. Mine, on the other hand, needs some toning."

"Vanity." He sighed. "Would it help if I said I really like your ass?"

"Flattery won't win this one. Now go."

Without another word, Curt kicked off down the driveway and out onto the road. He led her to the paved network of trails running throughout the community. She was a little wobbly starting out, but once she found her balance, her confidence returned. It took longer to figure out the gears. She accidentally shifted into the wrong one and felt the strain in her legs immediately. It took a minute to get it sorted out and find a more comfortable tension.

Curt glanced back. “How’s it coming?”

“I’m getting there.”

The trail dropped into the woods and followed the creek. Mia was happy enough coasting along beside it, but once they crossed the little bridge, they were faced with a steep climb up the opposite bank. Suddenly panicked, she fussed with her shifter, hoping to find the right gear, and ended up standing on the pedals instead just to keep up her momentum.

Curt watched from the top of the hill. “You’re in the wrong gear.”

“No kidding,” she muttered under her breath and tried another, and lost total pedal power. Freaking out, she jammed the shifter into yet another gear and stood up, fighting hard to recover her speed. Her legs were ready to give up.

“Almost there, Mia,” he called, encouraging her.

She was beginning to hate him. He chuckled when she shot him an irritated glare.

Just when she pulled abreast of him, he cut back onto the trail and forced her to keep going. That really pissed her off. What? He couldn’t give her a minute to catch her breath? That was totally unfair. *He* got to rest! Her resentment grew as she labored and gasped along behind him.

“You’re doing great, Mia,” he called back to her without turning.

She scowled at that fantastic tapered torso of his and the flexing, muscular grace of his buttocks and felt a strong urge to run her front tire straight up his back and leave a nice imprint of her tread on his shirt. It might just be worth the wipe out.

By the time Curt pulled onto the grassy shoulder, Mia's muscles were in outright rebellion and it was impossible to miss her wheezing and panting. His dismount was smooth—poetry in motion. Hers wasn't. Not even close. She dropped her bike to the ground and collapsed beside it like a limp rag. Her head was spinning from shortness of breath as she stared up at the perfect blue sky and wished she'd just die already. Her careening heart rate was beyond scary.

Curt sat next to her and smiled down on her. "How are you holding up?"

"Guess," she snapped sourly. "Hey, you're not even winded!"

"I ride every day," he reminded her simply.

Mia groaned. "I'm never going to make it home."

"Sure you will. We're not as far as you think. We took the short loop this time. The more we ride, the longer the loops are going to get."

She stared at him in horror. "You expect me to do this again?"

"You'll be glad you did."

"A lot you know."

He grinned and squeezed her thigh. "Feel your legs?"

"Those aren't legs, they're spaghetti."

"Your legs are going to get stronger and more toned. You're going to love them so much you're going to forget the pain you feel right now and start looking forward to the exercise. I promise."

"That's what everyone said about childbirth too. Notice how many children I have?"

Curt's laughter turned sympathetic. "Are you ready to get going?"

"Can I have another minute?"

"It won't make it any easier."

She eyed him critically. "You're evil. Do you know that?"

He smiled.

"Fine." She threw out her floppy arms and gave up. "Let's go."

He yanked her to her feet and she eyed her bike with trepidation. Maybe she could throw it under a bus.

Mia didn't realize how saddle sore she was until she got back on the damn thing. Her butt felt like one big bruise. It was worse than the shaking legs. Harder to handle than the burning lungs. More annoying than the stupid sniffles. She hurt and wanted to stop.

At least the path leveled off so she didn't have to deal with more hills. They rejoined the street from an entirely different direction than they went in. When she saw her driveway coming up, her relief was so acute she could have cried.

She hit the garage door opener and they walked their bikes into the garage and stood them against the shelves. Mia closed the door behind them.

"I'm beat." She could barely force herself to take another step.

"Not surprising. Be glad you don't smoke." He gave her a second look. "You don't, do you?"

"No." She panted her answer and stumbled into the kitchen where she dropped forward at the waist and grabbed her knees to keep from falling on her face.

Curt went into the upper cabinet for two glasses and filled them with cold water. He held one out to her. "Here. You need this."

She brought herself back up slowly and accepted it with a grateful, "Thanks." Leaning back against the cabinets, she emptied it in one go.

Smiling, he explained, "The water will help keep your muscles from cramping."

"I know." She studied him in amazement. "I can't believe it. Did you even break a sweat?"

"I'm warm."

"Yeah, but *I* need a shower." She peeled her shirt away from her body and shuddered at how clammy she felt.

"Go and take one."

"Do you need the bathroom first?"

"Give me a second."

He left his empty glass on the counter and Mia set

hers next to it.

While he used the bathroom, she went to find a change of clothes. She heard the toilet seat drop and the inevitable flush through the wall. The faucet came on as she shoved her dresser drawer closed.

The bathroom door opened and he came to a stop just outside her bedroom, silently watching her. He didn't invade her space, and she appreciated that, but he was reminding her he was there.

Suddenly very conscious of that fact herself, she realized she was about to strip naked with Curt in her house—and they were alone.

It wasn't easy brushing past him on her way to the bathroom. Maybe that was the reason she did something completely unexpected and out of character for her. Mia left the bathroom partially open behind her. Curt paused on his way by, perhaps afraid to misinterpret her meaning, but when they made eye contact in the mirror, she gave him a hesitant smile. It was a subtle invitation. He slowly pushed the door open and walked in.

Chapter 12

Mia stepped out of her Capri's and stood nervously in front of him in her panties and loose tee.

"Are you sure about this?" Curt asked, his deep, rich whisper sending shivers down her spine. All she could do was nod.

He let out the breath he was holding and brushed back the wispy hairs that had escaped her ponytail and now framed her face.

"I've wanted you," he said, his seductive eyes unraveling her.

"Wait. I need to tell you something."

"Okay."

"I might be older, but I haven't had much experience outside my marriage. This is a big step for me. I'm going to be rusty and out of practice at this."

He smiled. "*This* as in sex?"

"This as in everything," she said softly.

He ran his finger lightly along the sensitive whorls of her ear. The tickle was exquisite. "Are you having second thoughts? If you are, and want me to go, just say so. I don't want to push you."

Her eyes fell closed for a second as he slowly skimmed the backs of his fingers down the side of her neck. She stepped back, crossed her arms over her stomach, and grabbed the bottom of her shirt and pulled it off. The look in his eyes when she dropped it to the floor made her hot enough to scald on contact and completely obliterated any lingering doubts she may have had.

"Hold that thought." Curt turned to the tub and ran the shower, testing the water with his hand while he visually caressed her body, blindly adjusting the temperature by feel alone. "I can't take my eyes off you." He broke into a wonderful smile.

Mia's chest rose and fell, her heart beating wildly. She wondered if his was doing the same. Were his muscles loading up on adrenaline too? Was he as nervous as she was? Breathing through the sudden flutter of anxiety, she reached back to unhook her bra. Curt stopped her.

"Let me."

His left hand was wet when he placed it over her breast, his right was warm. Her lashes felt weighted, heavy when he cupped her, squeezed her gently, but she fought to keep her eyes open. She didn't want to miss anything. His right hand moved behind her and she felt a quick tug of the elastic a second before the bra sprang away from her ribs. One little shimmy and the straps slid down her arms and the bra landed on her pants.

"Mia," was all he said before he sank to his knees in front of her. Taking a breast in each hand, he drew them out, kissing and nuzzling between them. She gasped with pleasure when he latched onto a sensitive nipple. "You taste salty," he murmured, drawing his teeth lightly over the tight peak.

She swayed, clutching his head as he shifted to the other breast, kissing, licking, and sucking on her until she trembled and groaned. It had been so long, too long since she'd enjoyed this kind of attention.

Curt's hands moved off her breasts to glide down her sides and curve over her hips. He hooked the narrow elastic of her underwear with his thumbs and slowly stroked her legs all the way down, drawing her panties with him. She was so shaken she needed to put a hand on his shoulder before she could step free of them.

Facing her tidy pubis, he moved in to pay her an intimate olfactory visit.

She flushed in alarm. "What are you doing? I'm sweaty." Despite her embarrassment, she couldn't keep from laughing because he didn't seem to care. He inhaled with a rumble of approval.

Strangely flattered, she was trembling when he rose and pulled her to him, his kiss a carnal promise. Yes. She was ready. Mia wanted to flow over his body like water, but he kept her locked where she was with one arm while he reached up to gently tug her ponytail holder out of her hair. He tossed it onto the vanity then combed his fingers through her damp hair.

Mia could see his tension building. The hunger that both unnerved and excited her yesterday was back. She welcomed it with open arms.

She remembered the first time she saw Curt, how

she thought he had the most powerful bedroom eyes she'd ever seen. But she knew nothing—*nothing*. Only now, faced with the raw need swirling inside them, did she understand. She was mesmerized, a captive to his will, like a cobra swaying for the seductive charmer.

"Hey," he touched her under the chin. "You're shaking. Get in the shower and warm up. I'll join you in a minute."

She wasn't cold, but she stepped under the water anyway, her emotions in a whirl, and slid the door closed between them. Her eyes were glued to the rippled glass while Curt stripped. As edgy as it made her, she couldn't look away.

His shirt went up and over his head and flew in an arc onto the counter. She nearly groaned at how amazing he looked. Then he worked his tight shorts down his hips and she saw the energetic spring of his erection when it escaped his clothing. She stopped breathing.

Oh god, she was about to get up close and personal with that part of him, a part that, up until now, she'd only imagined. She had to stare at her polished toes just to calm down. Her fantasy was suddenly very real and it was getting a little overwhelming.

The door slid open and he looked Mia up and down slowly before stepping in with her. He must have seen the wild panic in her eyes because he gave her a reassuring smile and opened his arms. "I'm not going to hurt you."

Relieved to hear it, she moved into him and they held each other until she gradually relaxed. Now, alive to their contrasts, she found she loved how he felt against her; his rough hair brushing her smooth skin, his solid body hard against her soft curves.

Curt tipped her chin up and kissed her gently. Then he turned her into the water and stroked his hands through her hair, carefully wetting it as she ran her hands up and over his chest and his shoulders.

Mia's breath caught in surprise when he slid his arm around her waist and turned her smoothly out of the spray to switch places with her.

Okaaay—strong guy lifting her as if she weighed nothing? That was a definite turn on.

He began to shampoo her hair. The way his fingertips massaged her scalp transformed her into a sopping mess of lust.

"I'm going to faint here," she warned with eyes half closed.

He chuckled and turned her back under the spray.

She sighed. "You must be an incredible dancer. Even *I* feel graceful when you do that."

"Time to rinse," he said with a laugh.

While she worked on her hair, Curt got the washcloth nice and soapy. He started at her neck, but she was purring before he swirled it over and around her breasts, giving them a little extra attention.

"I aim to please," he explained when she raised an

eyebrow.

"Mission accomplished."

Moving on, he found her ticklish spots. She wriggled away with a laugh.

They traded places again so Mia could apply conditioner while Curt washed her back. He shifted to one side so the spray could rinse her down then kissed her on the shoulder.

Working her fingers through her hair, she expelled a dreamy sigh. "Mmm, I like that."

"Good."

He took hold of her left hip and held her flush against him as he reached around with the right to work the suds slowly, methodically, into her pubic curls. He was incredibly gentle as he slid the cloth between her legs, using it to open her and feel his way over and into her sex. Mia sank against him, weak in the knees.

It was impossible not to fixate on his erection pressing into her from behind as he parted her sex and swirled suggestively over her clit. Then his bare hand slid around to replace the cloth covered hand, and she gasped at the skin contact.

He kissed her shoulder again then moved back just enough to allow him to get at her bottom with the washcloth. He proceeded to torture her with both hands simultaneously as the word *yes* thrummed in her head over and over like a drumbeat and her knees quaked. To her relief, he continued down her legs before she actually collapsed at his feet.

Finally, he whispered, "You need to rinse," and spun her back under the spray.

It was embarrassing to admit she needed his help to do it at all. While she rinsed the conditioner out of her hair, he used his hands like a squeegee to remove the last of the soap from her body.

Sensually inspired, an unfamiliar boldness took over in her. She rose up on her tiptoes and kissed him, hard, then dragged her tongue slowly along his lower lip before easing back.

She saw the flash of heat in his eyes right before he grabbed for her.

"Uh, uh, uh," she admonished gently. "It's my turn to wash *you*." Unable to resist, she wrapped her hand around his cock. His eyes rolled back as she ran her thumb along the sensitive underside.

"Is that what you call this?" His low chuckle was sexy and arousing.

"Just wait," she said with a wicked smile and yanked the sudsy washcloth off the soap rack. "I think you'd better hold onto something, Mr. Walden."

She followed the same course he'd used on her, mapping him carefully, unabashedly admiring him the way he'd admired her. She couldn't resist giving his nipples an oral cleansing first, not letting up until they were both a deep, rosy hue. Ah, screw it. She couldn't help herself. She dropped the washcloth so her fingers could take a nice little run through his wonderful chest hair. Curt's eyes fell closed and he smiled. His groan said it all.

Mia retrieved the washcloth and lathered his muscled arms and shoulders, then the small of his back. Her body practically cried out to his as she ran her fingers down the narrow trail of hair bisecting his tight stomach. Her fingertips dipped into his dark navel before returning to his rather compelling erection. Languidly, she soaped the thatch of hair at his groin, rhythmically scratching it before taking hold of his cock and drawing it out in long, easy strokes with the soapy cloth while playing his sack with her other hand. He moaned and threw his arms out, hands planted on the tiled walls while she smiled in delight. *She* was all-powerful now.

As fun as this was, it was time to move on or they were going to run out of hot water. She moved swiftly down his muscular legs and gave his feet a quick scrub while he rinsed the rest of his body.

Only, she couldn't quite leave him like that. There was no way she could ignore the solid, straining length of him winking right at her. Unable to resist, she took hold of him at the root and leaned forward, flicking her tongue out to—

"Mom? Mom, we're back!"

"Oh shit," she gasped.

Curt pulled her to her feet, his eyes wide with horror.

Chapter 13

"I'm in the shower! I'll be right out," Mia yelled through the door. "Are you ready?" she whispered to Curt.

"I was," he whispered back in frustrated defeat.

She felt for the guy. Talk about getting robbed.

"Mom!" Casey called again. "We got our suits! Come see."

"Be right there." She looked at Curt sadly. "I didn't know they'd be back this early."

"Clearly." He chuckled softly at their lousy timing and pulled Mia against him, his hand at the back of her head as she sighed into his shoulder. They both needed to settle down now.

"They can't know you're here." She reached to turn off the faucet.

"Yeah, I figured that."

"I'll distract them so you can sneak into the garage for your bike. Use the side door to get out." She looked at him, sick with disappointment. "I'm so sorry."

"It's okay. I'll survive."

She stepped onto the mat and pulled two bath towels out of the cabinet. She handed him one and they dried off as quickly as they could.

"Hey," he said as she went to open the door. She turned and he caught her hand and pulled her back for a long kiss. “This isn’t finished.”

Mia sighed and eased away, caressing his rough cheek. “I certainly hope not.”

With that, she bolted for her bedroom and left him alone to dress.

She tugged on her terry bathrobe and slippers then went to find her son and his father. Greg held up the garment bag as soon as she walked into the living room.

“Okay, let’s see it.” She carefully maneuvered them around so they faced away from the hallway.

Mia saw Curt dart across the entry and straight through the kitchen. A second later she saw his hand close over the doorknob to the back door. She held her breath and hoped he didn’t make any noise when he opened it, but to her relief, Greg unzipped the bag at exactly the right moment.

“That’s nice.” She touched the lapel, her voice masking the soft closure of the back door.

“We decided to go with dark blue. It looked the best on him.” Greg turned the hanger for her.

“We’re going to match,” Casey added.

“Show her the rest,” Greg prompted him.

“Oh yeah.” Casey went into the bag sitting on the coffee table for a boxed shirt and tie combination.

Mia held it against the suit. “That’s going to look nice together.”

“He still needs socks,” Greg told her.

“And shoes,” Casey added. “Dad says I can’t

wear my Nikes."

"I'll take care of it," she said with a happy smile. "This is so exciting."

Greg looked at their teen as if finally seeing what she'd noticed recently. Their kid was growing up.

"How about taking your stuff to your room now?" he suggested and held out the hanger. Casey came forward for the handoff and disappeared.

Turning to Mia, Greg said, "I'll call you by Wednesday so we can talk about next weekend."

"Fine." She walked him to the front door.

He bent to give her an affectionate peck on the cheek then examined her more closely as he pulled back. "You look really pretty today. You got some color."

"Did I? Must be from my bike ride this morning."

"A little fresh air and exercise, eh?"

"Something like that."

He smiled. "Well, you look good. Keep it up."

"Way ahead of you."

♡

Greg's car had just backed onto the road when Mia's phone rang.

"Hello?"

"Can you talk?"

"Sally?"

"Yes. Can I come over?"

"Not tonight."

"But I know a secret."

Mia's hands went cold. "Oh yeah?"

"A juicy one."

She squeezed her eyes closed and groaned. "I'm not even dressed."

Sally snorted. "Like I care."

"Forget it. I'll take the phone to my room."

"Acceptable."

Swinging her door closed, Mia flopped backwards onto her bed and stared up at the ceiling. "Okay. I'm in my room."

"Me too. I swapped out Larry's beer and he's got ESPN on so I've got time."

"Goody for me," said Mia without enthusiasm.

"Sooo?"

"Oh. You want *me* to start? You're the one with the secret."

"Nice try. You, my dear, were entertaining."

"You caught me."

"Not only did I see you two disappear into your house, but I saw your sexy teacher sneaking out the side door after Greg brought Casey home. Did they catch him there?"

"No."

"How could you keep all this from me?" Sally whined. "I'm your best friend. I *wanted* you to get some of that."

Mia pinched the bridge of her nose and sighed. "I'm sorry. I was going to tell you, but I didn't know how and I didn't even know what to say exactly."

"Huh?"

"Even I'm not sure what's going on yet."

"How long have you been leading this double life?"

"Since Friday."

"FRIDAY?"

"Your door better be closed, Sally, because you just burst my eardrum."

"Sorry. It's closed. *Friday*?" she repeated, more softly this time.

"It was no big deal. We ran into each other and I invited him back here. That's all."

"Uh-huh. And the art fair? You went with *him*, didn't you?"

"Yes." There was no point denying it.

"I knew it." There was a long pause. "Did you..." Sally's question trailed off.

"*No!*" Mia said in a hushed voice.

"Because it looked like you might have..."

"We didn't." *Have time*, Mia finished silently with a cringe.

"You'd tell me, wouldn't you?"

"Of course," *not* she added in her head.

"I don't keep secrets from you," Sally said, laying on the guilt.

"I know." God, did she know. "Tell you what, I'll hang out a dish towel when I finally get lucky and you can throw me a party, okay?"

"Consider it done."

Mia laughed. "Are we better now?"

"I suppose. You know, I think he likes you. I saw how hard he was checking you out at the coffee shop and now this weekend? I...I envy you."

Mia felt her insides warm at the thought. "Sal, don't get ahead of yourself. I'm not sure my little heart can handle what he could throw at it."

"I'll be there to sweep up the pieces with my dustpan."

"Thanks. I'll talk to you tomorrow."

Chapter 14

When Curt spotted Casey in the science wing on Monday, he beckoned to him.

"I'll catch up," Casey told his friends.

The kid ambled over and Curt forced a casual smile. "How's the arm?"

"Fine, I guess." Casey gave him a curious look.

"That's good."

"What's up?"

"Um, can we step in here for a second?" Curt tipped his head toward his empty classroom.

Casey glanced at the clock in the hall and hesitated. "I don't know."

"I'll give you a pass to your next class, if you need one," he offered, understanding perfectly.

"Okay."

They walked in and Curt dropped his voice discreetly. "How's your mom?"

Casey's eyebrows shifted north by a quarter inch. "My *mom*?"

"Yeah."

"Fine," he answered slowly. "You could call her."

"I'd like to, only—" Feeling even more awkward all of a sudden, Curt rubbed the back of his head and admitted, "I don't have her number and you guys aren't listed in the phone book."

Casey snorted, flipped open his notebook, and

gave the end of his mechanical pencil a click. He scribbled away then tore off the sheet and handed it to him. “I put her work number on there too, just in case.”

They both laughed at how weird this was.

“Thanks. Do you need that pass?” Curt asked him.

Casey looked at the clock. “I think I’ll make it.”

“If you have any problems, tell your teacher to talk to me.”

“Don’t worry, you’ll get the blame.”

Curt grinned and waved the paper in his hand. “Thanks again.”

“No problem.” Casey chuckled and took off running.

♡

“Jane? I think I did it again,” Mia said ominously over the divider between their cubicles.

Her coworker came to investigate. They looked at the computer screen and Jane slowly shook her head.

“*No*. This is something different.”

“Worse?”

“How should I know?” She shrugged. “I’m not a computer geek. Call Galen.”

Mia balked at the suggestion. “I think he hates me now.”

Jane snorted, amused. “He doesn’t hate you. He just doesn’t find you all that bright anymore. But I think if you flirted with him a little, you could easily bring him down to your level like *that.*" She snapped her fingers. "It's worth a shot."

"Ha ha. Go away. I've gotta call him."

Ten minutes later, their tech guy was leaning over Mia's shoulder, his hideous burnt orange tie brushing her bare arm. He scratched his nose and frowned at her screen. "Hmm."

"What's hmm?" she asked.

"I'm not sure yet. What were you doing when this popped up?"

"Mail merge."

"And it was working fine?"

"Seemed to be."

"Hmm."

"Galen." Jane came into the cubicle. "Now mine's doing it too."

Someone else from across the way yelled, "What's going on with the computers?"

Their programmer stood up with a curious gleam in his eye. If Mia wasn't mistaken, he was actually excited about this new glitch.

"Don't touch *anything*. I have to dig into this downstairs on the mainframe," he told her then called out over the multitude of desks, "Computers are down, everyone. Finish what you're doing, if you can, before you're locked out!" He sprinted for the back stairs and was gone.

"That was weird."

"*He's* weird," Jane agreed and wandered back to

her desk right as Mia's phone rang.

"Mia Page, can I help you?"

"Hi. It's Curt."

"Curt?" The sound of his voice sent a jolt of electricity through her body that threw her back in her chair. Could the right guy actually fry a woman's hard drive? Was she sizzling and smoking? Could she go up to Jane and zap her with a single poke? Might be fun to find out.

"Am I calling at a bad time?"

She grabbed her nutty head and laughed. "Actually, it's the perfect time. We're locked out of the system for a few minutes, at least. How did you get my number?"

Jane peeked over the top of the divider with prying eyes. Mia waved her impatiently away.

"I got it from Casey."

"Oh." Okay, that felt a little weird. "What's up?"

"I want to see you again."

"Really?" She cringed at how girly that came out.

He chuckled. "Yes. Are you free tonight?"

"No, I have plans with Sally."

"Tomorrow?"

"That's open. What did you have in mind?"

"Dinner, pleasant conversation, hopefully a little skin contact."

"I still have that bottle of wine chilling in my fridge."

"I think we should do something about that."

Mia laughed. "I'll cook. I have to feed Casey anyway. Afterwards, I'm all yours."

"Don't toy with me."

"Within reason."

"I'll take what I can get. How are you?" he asked softly.

"I can hardly sit today, my butt is so sore. Otherwise I'm great."

"*Ah.* Don't worry, we'll toughen you up. What time should I come over?"

"Come as soon as you can. We're just going straight home after I pick up Casey."

"Okay. I'll see you tomorrow."

"Can't wait."

Mia hung up with a smile and turned to find Jane standing right behind her.

"Did I hear you make a *date*?"

"Possibly."

"And he's why you can't handle sitting longer than an hour without getting up to walk around like a colonoscopy patient?"

"We went for a long bike ride. That's it. I swear."

"Mmm-hmm," murmured Jane skeptically.

Mia rolled her eyes. "Don't be disgusting."

♡

Mia made turkey burgers for dinner then sent Casey to his room to do his homework while she went to move the coffee table and set up the living room.

Sally walked in a short time later waving her latest yoga video. “Ta-da!”

Mia held out her hand for it and popped it into the DVD player while Sally unrolled her mat.

“The Bahamas?” Mia asked her.

“Yep. Next best thing to being there.”

They closed their eyes and breathed in slowly, centering themselves into the mountain pose. The soothing music began without blocking out the sounds of the surf behind it.

For thirty minutes they went through the various poses in silence until Mia adapted the routine and chose to do a bent-leg twist rather than the seated forward bend.

Sally noticed. “What are you doing?”

“Something more comfortable. I need a new bike seat if I’m going to keep riding.”

“We need to talk.”

“Later.”

Later came when Casey walked through, snorted at them, and said, “I’m going over to Tony’s now.”

Mia looked up through her feet at him. “Is your homework done?”

“Yes.”

“No later than nine. It’s a school night.”

“Okay.”

Sally rolled onto her back and went into the relaxation pose. Mia joined her.

They were rolling up their mats when Sally asked,

"Any new developments with your hottie?"

"He called me at work today."

"Interesting."

Mia blushed. "He wanted to get together tonight."

"And you said no?"

"I had plans with you."

"I would have understood."

"I'm seeing Curt tomorrow."

Sally brightened. "Even better. So what does this mean?"

Mia shrugged. "I think I might be dating him."

Sally laughed. "Maybe you'd better find out."

Chapter 15

Mia and Casey beat Curt to their house by twenty minutes on Tuesday. It allowed her just enough time to change out of her work clothes before she let him in herself.

He hovered around the kitchen while she scavenged through the cupboards for dinner ideas. Just having him there was distracting, especially when he moved up behind her and trapped her against the counter. Successfully corralled, he proceeded to kiss his way from her ear to her shoulder. She melted against him then slowly turned in his arms.

"There she is," he said with a smile and bent her back to claim her mouth next.

Her mind went blank of everything but his arms around her, his body pressed against hers. On the verge of a total, lightheaded surrender, Mia grappled her way back to sanity. She planted her hand on the center of his chest and walked him backwards to the opposite counter and held him there, all too aware of how close he brought her to combustion.

"Stay," she ordered. "You're not making this easy on me."

He squeezed her hand. "Then give me something to do. Tell me how I can help."

"Go sit down."

"Mia, I'd really like to help."

"Honestly?"

"I wouldn't ask otherwise."

"You could open the wine."

"It's a start."

"I was thinking of chicken," she said and pulled a package of boneless breasts out of the fridge. "Is that all right?"

"Fine."

"I could grill them, but they always dry out." She wasn't optimistic.

"Really?" he asked in surprise and twisted the screw into the cork. "Let me throw a marinade together for it."

"You can do that?"

"Sure." The cork came free with a pleasant pop and he poured two glasses before setting the bottle aside. He picked up the glasses and handed one to her.

She smiled. "Thanks."

"Are you okay with me looking through your cabinets?"

"Go for it."

"Great. I'll take care of the meat and you can do the vegetable, okay?"

"I like that idea."

Pointed in the right direction, Curt opened her spice cabinet and spun the Lazy Susan to see what she had. "You don't have any fresh herbs in the garden by any chance, do you?"

"Not yet."

"I figured. I'll make do." He pulled two bottles out, but was careful not to let her see what he had. "Olive oil?"

"In the lower cabinet right in front of you."

"Ah." He put the bottle on the counter and went searching through the upper cabinets again.

She paused over the carrot she was peeling to ask, "What are you looking for now?"

"A large bowl."

She went to the end cabinet and took a heavy glass bowl from underneath. "Will this work?"

"Perfect." He poured a bit of the olive oil into the bowl then shook the herbs on top of it. "Hey, you wouldn't happen to have fresh garlic, would you?"

"I would." Mia retrieved it from the onion drawer and set it on the counter.

Curt pulled a clove free and smashed it on the cutting board with the flat of his knife. He minced it fine and added it to the oil then poured a bit of wine over the top.

"You actually look like you know what you're doing," she said in amazement.

"I'm a man of many talents." He winked at her and shook salt and pepper into the mix.

"You don't have to convince me." Mia laughed and went back to her carrots.

Once the chicken was added to the marinade, Curt went outside to light the grill and Mia finished de-veining the pea pods. Prep done, they sat at the table and played a game of gin rummy while the coals burned down.

That's where they were, deep in their game and enjoying the wine, when Greg dropped by.

"What are you doing here?" she asked, catching her ex coming through the kitchen.

"Casey left his Civics book at my place on Sunday. He didn't mention it?"

"No."

"Huh." Greg was clearly bewildered. "He called me about it last night. Here." He handed the text book to her. "Where is he, anyway?"

"Tony's. He'll be back in time for dinner. Drink?" Mia asked as they walked back to the dining area.

Seeing them, Curt pushed out of his chair to offer his hand. "Hi. Curt Walden. I'm a friend of Mia's."

Greg's surprise was comical, and though his eyebrows were still a tad higher than normal when he shook Curt's hand, his voice was steady. "Greg Page."

Curt gave him an easy smile. "I understand congratulations are in order."

"Yeah, well, I thought it was about time I got off my…well, you know. Thanks." He grinned at Curt, obviously wondering where he'd come from. "*How* do you know Mia?"

"I teach science at Wrigley Middle. You've got a great kid there, by the way."

"Thanks."

Mia broke in. "Greg, can you stay and have a

drink with us?"

"Love to, but no. Liz has dinner going already. I have to get back." He looked at Curt. "It was nice meeting you. Maybe we'll run into each other again."

"I hope so."

"*Mia,*" Greg said with an insinuating smirk.

She rolled her eyes and waved her ex-husband away.

"He seems nice," Curt said as soon as the front door closed. "It's my turn, right?" He arched a brow as he laid down a card.

She studied him thoughtfully. "Are you referring to our game or taking a crack at me?"

He smiled. "A little of both."

She laughed. "You have a way about you, Mr. Walden."

"So what was that look he gave you, if you don't mind my asking?"

"Greg's a great guy, but I can just imagine what he's thinking right now, finding us alone in the house like this. I know him. He's going to give me so much shit."

"He wouldn't do that, would he?"

"Oh yes he would."

♡

After dinner, Sally turned up dressed in her workout gear, her yoga mat under her arm.

"Hi," she said with a perky grin and craned her

neck to see around Mia as soon as she opened the door.

Mia groaned. “What are you doing?”

“What does it look like I’m doing? I’m here to work out.”

Liar. “Sally, you know we didn’t—”

She leaned in and whispered, “Is he here?”

“Yes.”

“Can I come in?”

“No!” Mia hissed.

“Aw, come on.”

“*Sal*...this is *so* embarrassing.”

Curt, obviously overhearing their exchange, poked his head around the corner as he dried his hands on the dish towel.

“Hi.” He gave Sally a friendly smile. “I remember you.”

“You look familiar,” she said, playing dumb.

“Coffee shop,” he reminded her.

“That’s it!”

Mia rolled her eyes. “Curt Walden, meet my good friend and pesky neighbor, Sally Larson.”

Sally threw her hand out and slapped it into Curt’s palm.

He laughed. “Good grip.”

“You too.” She gave his hand one more pump for the road. “Well, I guess three’s a crowd.”

Mia nodded, biting her tongue. “See you tomorrow, Sally.”

"Okay. Nice meeting you, Curt."

"You too."

Mia closed the door. "I'm so sorry about that."

He chuckled. "I have a two-handshake-a-day limit. That should be the last one, right? Nobody else?"

"It better be. I can't believe she did that. On second thought, yes, I can."

"So now what?" he asked. "Wanna get out of here?"

"And go where?"

"We could walk the trails."

"All right."

Mia changed her shoes and grabbed a light jacket out of the closet. Curt helped her into it.

"Thanks." She poked her head around the corner and called down the hallway to Casey. "We're going for a walk, Case. Back in a bit."

"Okay."

Once outside, Curt reached for her hand. He brought it to his lips and kissed the knuckles before letting their linked hands swing lazily between them as they strolled. Smooth. The guy knew exactly how to brighten a woman's mood.

"You know what I like about you?" she asked.

He smiled at her. "What's that?"

"You actually *like* to hold hands. Greg never offered and Casey outgrew it years ago."

He gave her fingers a little squeeze. "Call me old-fashioned."

"You?" she teased.

He laughed. "As a matter of fact."

"On your left," called a masculine voice behind them.

They shifted to the right and the bicyclist rode safely by. The coast clear, Mia was about to return to the path when Curt tugged her back and tipped her chin up. Their eyes locked and she felt the earth tilt beneath her because his were beautiful, compelling, sexual, and absolutely confident. She wished she had half his self-assurance.

"You want to kiss me."

His cheek tightened and stretched the corner of his mouth. "I do."

"Why?" The question was out before she knew it was coming.

He cocked his head in confusion. "*Why?*"

"I'm curious."

"Because you're pretty, funny, sweet, luscious, and I can't get you out of my mind."

With that, he cupped her cheek and gave her a tender kiss, lingering close afterwards to nuzzle her nose. Their breath mingled between them. It was intoxicating.

"But what's happening with us?" she asked even as she pressed into his hand.

She felt drugged whenever he was around and obsessed whenever he wasn't. It was so odd, so unsettling. No, downright scary, like venturing onto thin ice, knowing you were going to drop through, take a misstep, you just didn't know which step that would be. When was she going to take her icy plunge, and why couldn't she stop herself from risking it?

"You don't know?"

"I don't *understand*," she clarified.

"What's not to understand? We have chemistry."

"Something, as a science teacher, you know all about."

"As a matter of fact." He pressed two fingers to her neck. "Elevated heart rate, pupils are dilated, and your skin is flushed. It's not the walk that's got you breathing faster, Mia, and you know it."

She pulled back, embarrassed. "Don't."

"It's nothing to be ashamed of. We all go through it." He placed her hand over his thudding heart and looked into her eyes. "See."

"I don't know what I'm doing," she told him helplessly. "What am I *doing*?"

"What comes naturally."

"This," she said, wagging her hand between them, "is not natural. I feel out of control, like I'm some kind of pervert or something."

"What? Why would you think that?"

"How old are you?" she asked softly.

"Twenty-eight—not that it's relevant."

"How can't it be?"

"I'm well past the age of consent, for starters."

"But I'm thirty-six."

"Okay."

"I'm *thirty-six.*"

"You said that."

"And it doesn't bother you?"

A young couple rode by, the little boy towed behind his dad on a tag along as the mom followed protectively after them.

"Come on. Over here. We're not having this conversation right next to the path." Curt strode across the grass to a tree in the distance where they could have a private word.

She shook her head and followed. He took a seat on the grass and Mia sank to the ground facing him.

"No. It doesn't bother me," he said, picking up where they left off. "Why the hell would it?"

"But you're so young. You should be dating women your own age, or *younger*. What are you doing wasting time with me?"

He took her hand, gently squeezed it, and wouldn't let go when she tried to pull it away.

"Look at me. *Mia,* look at me." His eyes softened on her and he smiled. "I'm sitting with the woman I want. Why is that so hard to understand?"

"But what if I grow emotionally attached to you and you go and ditch me for someone younger?"

"Ah." Curt expelled a deep breath. "Your issue is really about *men* chasing younger women. Do you honestly think you'd be safer or feel more secure if I was forty-something? Would you rather be involved with a guy about to hit his midlife crisis? Come on."

"Fair point. It just makes more sense that you'd find a younger woman more attractive."

"Why is that?"

"Don't make me list the reasons," she murmured.

"Then listen to mine." He thought carefully about his words before he spoke them. "Age is the last thing I'm thinking about when I look at you. I'm so attracted, it doesn't even register. But now that you've brought it up, let me explain something. I've been in a couple of serious relationships with women my age. Both times we started out in sync, but that changed. A friend would have a baby and suddenly, I'm the sum of my parts, a potential father. She's dissecting me with her eyes and wondering how our features will blend in our offspring. It's biological—I get that. But now they *want* the white wedding and the baby stroller."

"What's wrong with that?"

"*I* don't."

Mia's face fell.

Curt gripped her hand. "Don't misunderstand me. I want to get married someday. Very much. I'm not the lifelong bachelor type. I'm just not interested in having kids of my own."

"*I* have a son. Why get involved with me when he's in the picture?"

"You have a terrific kid, and you're a great mom.

I credit Casey for bringing us together. But he's a teen. He's growing up and you're both moving in your own individual directions now. You can't stop that. I don't think you'd want to. Would you?"

"Of course not."

He studied her thoughtfully. "*Did* you want another child?"

Mia slowly shook her head. "Honestly? I never really thought about it. I suppose because after the divorce, I was so focused on Casey. In my head I was Super Mother. Probably more like *Smother* in his." She crinkled her nose and gave a little laugh. 'I was a tad obsessive sometimes."

Curt smiled. "Clearly, it worked out."

Only now did she realize she'd been so tense about this talk, she'd actually ripped up a tuft of grass next to her. She pressed it back into place and gave it a guilty pat.

"My bad." Wiping her dirty hand on her pant leg, she slowly raised her eyes to his. "So then we're—"

"Exploring a potential relationship?" Curt finished, his head cocked as he waited for her reaction.

Mia smiled. "Good answer."

Chapter 16

Mia took the stairs back up from the lunch room. It was exercise, and quicker than waiting around for the elevators.

"Your beverage, madam," she said and set the cold can on Jane's desk.

"Thanks."

"Welcome. I was looking for an excuse to take a break from the computer anyway."

Jane looked up with a disconcerting twinkle in her eye, obviously on the scent of something. "Greg's holding for you."

And now she knew what it was. Mia sighed. "Yeah, I was expecting him."

She went back to her desk, flopped down on her chair, and reached for her phone.

"It's always the quiet ones," she heard Jane say breezily from the other side of their partition.

Mia froze, her finger hovering over the blinking light on her phone. "What's that supposed to mean?"

"No wonder you're distracted and exhausted. A younger man?"

She blew out a heavy breath. "It's not like that."

"That's not what I hear. Way to go. I can't wait for the juicy details."

Irritated with her ex now, Mia pecked the button harder than necessary and snapped, "What!" He didn't deserve a courteous greeting.

Greg chuckled. "Mrs. Robinson, I presume?"

"Very funny. *Why* did you have to tell Jane about Curt?"

He didn't bother to deny it. "I was looking for a little Intel. Casey didn't prepare me."

"Casey didn't know I'd be seeing him again."

"Ah. Well anyway, I assumed you'd already dished to the girls. Why the secrecy?"

"Because I didn't want to be the hot topic around here. Now everyone is going to be gossiping and asking impertinent questions. Just like you."

"It'll blow over in no time," he said, casually dismissing her concerns.

Mia was not appeased. "And what possessed you to mention Curt's age? He's an adult, you know. I'm not robbing the cradle."

"I never said you were. I was just fishing for a little more info."

"Then ask *me* next time."

"O*kay*." he said with an expectant pause.

"You can be so irritating sometimes. He's twenty-eight. Are you satisfied?"

"Only if you are," Greg said with a wicked laugh.

Mia groaned. "Puleeze."

Finally acknowledging her mood, he said, "Easy. Why are you so sensitive about this?"

"*Why*? Because now Jane thinks Curt is screwing my brains out," she hissed in an undertone.

"Isn't he?"

"Of course not! You know me better than that. We're taking it slow."

"You're right. I'm sorry. I couldn't resist messing with you. But honey, you've been squeaky clean for too long. I was starting to worry that maybe I'd messed things up for you and the right guy."

"You were?"

"Yeah. I thought about it—wondered sometimes."

Her mood softened. "You had nothing to do with it. Don't blame yourself. I wasn't ready."

"And now you are."

She spun in her chair, broadcasting her radiant smile to the world. "And now I am."

"Mia." Greg paused a moment, obviously weighing his words first. "Don't let anyone give you a hard time about the age difference, okay? If you and Curt are hitting each other right, that's all that matters. Everything else is incidental. Are you happy?"

"Incredibly."

"I'm glad. Really glad. How about meeting up with Liz and me for dinner sometime this week? Bring Curt."

"It's too soon to subject him to an interrogation from the ex."

"You wound me. Do you honestly think I'd do that?"

"No," she conceded with a sigh. "I take it back."

"Let me know if you need a little one-on-one time

with him. I'll hang out with Casey."

His offer touched her. "Thanks. We haven't made any more plans yet."

"Just ask, okay? Love you, Mia."

"Love you too."

They clicked off. As far as exes went, she'd lucked out in that department.

♡

Mia sat outside the school at three-fifteen, waiting for Casey. A slow trickle of students started coming out of the building at five after. Now it was a steady stream of kids walking, rolling, running, and horsing their way out the doors. It wouldn't be long.

The sun hit her across the chest and neck and made her warm and drowsy. Her arm draped lazily out the open window and her head lolled on the headrest. She gave in to the pull of her heavy lashes and rested her eyes. Maybe having Casey as a second driver in a couple of years wouldn't be so bad after all. She could nod off in the passenger seat when she felt like this.

Something brushed across her bare arm and she jerked in surprise.

"Curt!"

"Hey, beautiful. When I saw you out here, I had to come say hello."

His eyes sparkled in the sunlight. His chin and upper lip were shadowed by a hint of whisker. It was incredibly sexy. She wanted to stroke his face, feel the light rasp of his cheek along her neck and shoulder. They held hands instead.

"What are you doing tonight?" she asked, trying not to sound too hopeful.

"Paperwork." He gave her a disappointed smile. "I still have to grade Friday's quiz. For some strange reason, I lost total interest in getting it done over the weekend. Now I have make-up work."

"Bummer."

"Say, maybe you could meet me at the Stylus tomorrow night." he suggested, his unexpected change of mood bringing hers up too. "Anytime between eight and ten."

"I'll see if I can arrange it." She knew she could. Her heart beat wildly just thinking about it.

"Good. I'd like to see you."

He leaned in for a kiss, but Mia spotted Sally's daughter Becky walking over with Casey and pulled back. Curt turned to look over his shoulder.

"You snooze, you lose," he said ruefully. Giving her hand a light squeeze before he let go, he moved back. "I'll check in with you tomorrow."

"Okay." *Damn.*

Casey assessed the scene with a comical smirk. "Hi, Mr. Walden."

"Hi, Casey. Hello," he added to the girl.

"Sir." Becky blushed.

"I'll talk to you later," he told Mia, then with a parting wave to all three, walked back to the building.

Casey stepped up to his mom's open window. "Cheer was cancelled so I told Becky we could give her a ride home today."

"Of course. Any time."

Mia's eyes swung back to follow Curt up the sidewalk as the kids climbed in. He disappeared inside the school, taking the warmth of the sun with him.

♡

After dropping Becky off, Mia wheedled Casey into taking a bike ride with her. Still unfamiliar with the extensive trail system, she voted that they stick to the same route she took with Curt rather than risk getting lost.

"I know these trails, Mom," Casey told her.

"I'm sure you do. But what if we get separated?"

He laughed. "You're not going to get lost."

"I could."

He snorted. "Yeah, *you* probably could. I have a better sense of direction and I don't even drive yet. I promise I won't ditch you."

"Thanks, smart-aleck."

God, it hurt getting back on that seat. Her muscles protested right from the start and her butt was incredibly tender as they rolled down the street, but she was getting the hang of it again—sort of. She also noticed she was wobbling less.

"Not so fast," she called to Casey.

He checked his speed and she caught up.

“We’re going to tip over if we go any slower,” he grumbled.

“Just peddle.” She fussed with her gears until she found one that satisfied them both.

Fifteen minutes later, Mia recognized the stream and the crossing with the steep bank on the opposite side coming up. She stood on her pedals and gave it her all—and lost her oomph about six feet shy of the crest. She dropped off the seat and trudged the rest of the way on foot, and without complaint. At least that hurdle was behind her now.

Her lungs working overtime and her legs shaking with fatigue, Mia gave Casey a weak wave to keep going. She got back on her bike and pushed off, slowly bringing her speed back up again.

“Your left!” a woman shouted from behind.

Mia steered right and hugged the edge of the path, but to her shock and alarm, the other cyclist nearly clipped her anyway, forcing her into the dense brush growing along that part of the trail.

She shot a quick glare at the woman even as she crashed through the thicket. The other cyclist rounded the next curve and kept going, but not fast enough. Mia recognized the profile and glossy black ponytail.

Holly.

Her front tire lurched to a violent stop and launched Mia over the handlebars. Branches whipped her across the face and body right before her hands hit the hard ground and her elbows buckled. She was screaming when she did an ungainly face plant into the underbrush.

"Mom! Are you okay?" Casey was suddenly next to her, pulling her back by the arm.

"Case!" she cried out in pain. "My arm doesn't bend that way."

"Sorry." He let go.

She worked herself up to her knees and turned, dismayed to see him pale with worry. "Do I look that bad?"

"Is anything broken?"

"Only my pride."

"You have leaves in your hair. And sticks." He plucked one out and showed it to her.

She snorted. "There's a shocker."

He helped her to her feet and she brushed her battered palms on her dirty knees.

"That's going to sting tomorrow," he said, looking at her hands when she examined them.

"They hurt now."

"Can you ride home?"

"I don't know. Let's see."

They tugged her bike free, looked it over for damage, and pulled stray weeds and branches out of the spokes and pedals.

"Thanks for your help, honey." She threw her stiff leg over the bar and winced.

"No problem. How'd that happen anyway?"

"A little help from my friends," she said dryly.

"What?"

"Don't sweat it, kid. Let's go home. I need a good soak after this."

Once their bikes were put away in the garage, Casey went to finish his homework and Mia ran herself a warm bath. While the tub filled, she phoned Greg to tell him about her date.

"Taking me up on my offer already?" he asked with a chuckle.

"I guess so. I hate to leave Casey alone on a school night."

"I'm happy to help."

"Thank you."

"So what are you two going to do?"

"Not a clue." She wasn't even sure if she was going to mention the sneak attack by Holly.

"Talk to you tomorrow."

"Sounds good."

♡

Greg called the following afternoon and caught Mia just before she left to pick up Casey after school.

"Here's a thought," he said. "Since you're going out anyway, why don't Liz and I hang out at your place? That way Casey can turn in at his normal time."

"Good idea."

"Liz is going to bring a movie."

"Which one?"

"Not sure. Something she heard about at work.

Supposed to be good."

"Okay. I'll see you later."

Mia headed over to Wrigley Middle. When she didn't see Curt this time, she felt seriously let down. She watched for him so intently, she didn't notice Casey until he opened the passenger door. Shaking off her disappointment, she reminded herself she was going to meet him tonight.

The telephone was ringing when they walked into the house. This time it was Liz on the line.

"So I was thinking, since we're coming anyway, Greg and I can stop for food on our way over."

"Perfect. I'm not really in the mood to cook anyway."

"Great. Anything hitting you? There's a Chinese restaurant we like by our place or we can pick up burgers, Mexican?"

"Honestly, I could eat anything, I'm really hungry. Are you leaning one way or another?"

"Not really."

"Let me check with Casey." Mia came back with the predictable answer.

"Let me guess," Liz said. "Pizza?"

"Bingo."

"Well, that makes it easy for us.

"I'll call it in and have it delivered. Okay?

"Sounds good. We'll see you around five-thirty or six."

Mia hung up and went to her room to pick out an

outfit for the evening. She settled on black jeans, a lacy tank top, and her midnight blue blazer. She swapped her more conservative earrings for silver hoops now so she wouldn't forget to do it later then returned to the kitchen and ordered the pizza.

She was reading the newspaper when Greg pulled into the driveway. She folded it up and went to greet them. Liz was first through the door and Mia threw her arms around her.

"Congratulations!" She stepped back and pulled out Liz's left hand. "Let's see the ring."

Laughing, Liz turned it in the light so the diamond flashed and sparkled. "What do you think?"

"It's beautiful."

"I picked it out myself." She glanced back at Greg coming through the door. He saw what they were doing and streaked right on through with his six pack of beer. "You can't trust a man for something like this."

"Oh, I don't know. My ring was pretty," Mia said then called after him, "but a hell of a lot smaller."

He cringed and put the beer, minus one bottle, in the fridge and twisted off the cap. "Hey, I was broke back then and you know it."

"You know I'm only teasing. I owed you one."

"Now we're even." He smiled and raised his bottle to her before tipping it back.

Mia went into the fridge herself and looked back at Liz. "What are you drinking?"

"Is that iced tea?"

"Yep. Raspberry."

"Ooo, I'll have that."

"I'll join you."

Interestingly enough, Liz and Mia got along famously. Liz was attractive, thirty-five, and self-assured. Her quick wit and sense of humor made her terrific company. She was the kind of friend Mia would have chosen for herself if she'd met her first. Mia loved how the couple played off one another, almost as if they were scripted. It was a good pairing and she approved. Naturally, everyone was relieved they all got along so well together. It made it easier on Casey too.

Greg picked up the sports page and scanned the headlines. Liz took advantage of his distraction to give Mia a sly look.

"So, tell me about Curt," she whispered.

Mia pointed down the hallway. "Let's go to my room." She glanced at her ex. "Grab a chair. Get comfortable. We'll be right back."

She closed the door and Liz sat down on the corner of the bed and smiled up at her. "Well? I'm dying of curiosity."

Mia laughed and fiddled with a belt lying on her dresser. "I'm trying to downplay this because I really haven't talked to Casey about dating anyone yet. It makes me uncomfortable."

Liz frowned. "Why is that? Do you think he'll

have a problem with it? Greg dated right after your separation and Casey handled that just fine."

"But I'm his mom. It's different, isn't it?"

"I don't see how." Her brow creased in thought, Liz asked, "Is that why you didn't date?"

Mia sank down beside her. "No. I wasn't interested in anyone, never tempted…until Curt."

"Ooo, now I'm really intrigued. I can't wait to meet the guy who finally lured you out of your cloistered existence."

"Funny." Mia snorted.

Liz's smile faded. "Casey's not a little kid anymore, Mia. He's smart enough to figure things out on his own, whether you talk to him or not, so be open with him."

Mia felt foolish. Liz was right. She just needed to find the right opportunity. Even if this attraction was doomed to fizzle after tonight, she still had to admit she was out there now. Whether the next date would be with Curt Walden was yet to be determined. A lot could change in a matter of hours.

That was a painful thought. She didn't want to hope her way into a big disappointment.

"Is this what you're wearing tonight?" Liz asked, picking up the top.

"Yes. What do you think?"

"You're going to knock his socks off."

Chapter 17

Since Mia didn't want to arrive at the Stylus too early, she killed a little time driving around town first. Oddly enough, the more she delayed, the more nervous she felt. This was stupid. What was she afraid of? Doubling back, she parked down the street from the pub, engaged the locks, and headed over there, fiddling with her keys as her low heels clopped softly on the sidewalk.

She saw the planter in front of the pub and remembered how her heart raced when she saw Curt leaning casually against it, his dark sunglasses hiding his wonderful eyes as he watched for her. Was he watching for her right now through those tinted windows? It was impossible to tell. She took a deep breath and walked in to find out.

The interior was dim but not enough to prevent her from looking with interest at all the old album covers and records affixed to the walls. She did a quick scan for Curt but didn't see him yet. Evidently, she'd beaten him here. Nearly all the tables on this side of the central bar were vacant, but there was a boisterous bunch on the other side where a band was playing live music on the small stage.

She chose a table near the front so they'd easily see each other when Curt walked in. A book of appetizers stood in the center of the table. She looked it over. She felt exposed sitting alone in this island of misfit chairs. Fortunately, it didn't take long for a server to come over. She ordered a glass of red wine.

Left alone to consider her surroundings, Mia decided the Stylus Pub was actually nicer than she'd initially presumed. If she had to choose a corner bar, this one wouldn't be bad. She could tell by the conversations floating her way that most of the patrons seemed to know each other because there were good-natured insults and comments flying back and forth between the tables and the band on stage. She laughed softly when she heard a barrage of choice zingers hit their mark.

The server came back with her wine and set it down.

"Thank you."

Mia drew it close and self-consciously traced the base of the glass with her finger while keeping one ear trained on the music while she watched the door.

The server returned unexpectedly a minute later with a cautious question. "Excuse me, but are you Mia?"

"Yes," she said, startled.

The server smiled. "Great. Curt asked me to bring you back to him. I can carry your wine if you want."

"Thanks, I've got it."

Curious, Mia rose, grabbed her purse, and followed the young woman. She led her around the bar and toward the stage. Mia did a double-take. Now she understood. Curt was playing guitar and harmonizing with another singer up there. He smiled down at her and she grinned like an idiot right back.

He had a warm and wonderful baritone. Mia's heart rate took off without her and left her trembling like a love-struck teen. What was he doing up there? The band sounded incredibly good.

The server showed her to a table at the front and Mia set down her purse and wine then groped for the back of a chair without breaking eye contact with the man on stage. She sank onto it and simply soaked everything in—the atmosphere, the music, but most of all, the intimate gaze locked on her.

Curt's fingers danced across the strings and she was mesmerized. She tried to keep her reaction casual, but every time their eyes reconnected she got the distinct impression he was performing for her alone. How did he always manage to bring her out in a blush?

The group played two more songs before leaving the stage. They dropped down from the raised platform, stowed away their instruments first, and then joined her at their table.

Curt cut between the chairs straight for her. Excited now, she smiled up at him and he bent to kiss her and lingered to caress her cheek.

"You made it. I'm glad." His voice was as warm and soothing as rich cocoa. He kept his hand on her shoulder when he sat in the chair next to hers.

"This was unexpected." Mia gestured at the stage.

"Yeah, I thought it might be." His smile was killer. "This is my Thursday night crowd. Guys," he called out and looked around the table at the faces watching them, "say hello to Mia."

"Hey, Mia," the other guitarist greeted her. The others smiled and nodded.

Curt turned and signaled the server. "Crystal, can we get another pitcher?"

"Sure thing, Curt."

He squeezed Mia's shoulder and beamed again, clearly pleased she was there. "Let me introduce you to my friends. That ugly bastard across from you is Brad."

Brad wasn't remotely ugly. Not even close, but he was more the boy-next-door variety.

"That goon over there is Rollie."

Rollie rolled his eyes at Curt and gave Mia a friendly salute.

"And that's Eric."

Or Thor in a mortal body, she thought.

Mia scrolled back one face. "Did he say Rollie?" she asked the man directly.

The other guys found her question intensely amusing and started ribbing him.

Curt smiled and explained, "His last name is Rollins, but he prefers that to his first name."

"I'm sorry," she apologized to the man in question, "but now I have to ask."

"Of course you do." He threw out his hand in defeat.

Curt was struggling not to laugh. The other guys didn't even bother trying. They let it out.

"Mia, meet Herbert," Curt said with a suppressed chuckle. "He's a junior."

Rollie nodded sadly, playing the tragic, wounded party to the hilt. "It's true. My parents didn't love me enough to spare me the name."

Her sympathy was at war with her amusement. Laughter won out. She blamed his hammy performance. When she could trust herself enough to speak without giggling, she said, "You guys are good. Do you get paid to play here?"

Curt smiled and shook his head. "No. Thursdays are open mike. We meet here and jam a bit. Brad's the only one of us professionally trained. He took up the sax to meet women and, surprise, surprise—met one. Would you believe he turned down a traveling job with the Bloomberg Symphony Orchestra to stay close to her? Now he's reduced to teaching band at the school with me like a commoner. Maybe you'll meet his wife Desiree here next week. It all depends on whether or not they can line up a sitter for the baby."

"I think it's sweet that he chose love over adventure," Mia defended him then turned to Eric. "And what do you do?"

She could tell just by looking at him she'd asked the wrong question and she regretted it.

"Sales," he said in a sullen voice. "What sucks is I'm good at it, but I hate it with a passion. Really hate it. I'm trying hard to hit on something that suits me better. I keep reminding myself it's just a job and a job doesn't define a person. At least it shouldn't."

"There's always bodyguard or offensive tackle," Brad threw out there with a grin.

Mia ignored the interruption and focused on Eric. "No, I totally get what you're saying. I'd hate to be judged solely by my job."

"What do you do?" he asked her.

"I'm an office drone."

Curt looked as if he were about to say something when Crystal stopped back with the fresh pitcher of beer and put an end to the subject. Brad caught the handle first and topped off his glass then passed the pitcher down the table.

By this time the next band started to play, conversation at their table was so animated they never paused to listen to the performance. Evidently, this wasn't unusual, and no one on stage seemed to mind. The musicians obviously played more for themselves than for the people in the pub.

Mia was sorry when the party broke up. She couldn't remember the last time she'd had such a fun evening out with friends. It had been years. Truthfully, she didn't know exactly what to expect when she left the house tonight. She never imagined this, so it was a pleasant surprise.

Out on the sidewalk, the friends called goodnight to one another and went their separate ways. Curt had his arm around Mia when Brad walked outside after settling his tab.

"Curt, you need a ride home?" he asked him.

Curt looked at Mia. "Do I?"

Her smile was slow, but certain. "No."

He grinned and turned back to Brad. "Thanks anyway. I'll see you tomorrow."

"Later." Brad walked off, waving his hand over his head at them. "Nice meeting you, Mia."

She gave the hand spilling over her shoulder a playful tug. "Didn't you bike?"

"Not with this." Curt raised his guitar case and she realized she'd asked a pretty stupid question.

"Then how did you get here?"

"Brad picked me up."

"Ah. I suppose you'd better get in."

She popped the SUV's locks. Curt put his guitar on the back seat then got into the front with her.

He snickered as they buckled in. "I have to tell you, that's one of the cleaner back seats I've seen."

"No one ever sits back there."

"Then why drive a big monster? The carbon emissions are—"

Mia groaned. "Not this again."

"Knee-jerk reaction. Sorry, I can't help it if I want to save the planet."

"Try harder. So are we going to your place or are

you going to sit there struggling with the ethics of riding with me again?"

He laughed. "You know, I'm torn."

"Ass," she said, chuckling herself now.

They drove in silence, lost in thought as an old R&B station played on the stereo. She nearly jumped in surprise when he reached over and lightly stroked her thigh.

The ride was too short. Mia saw his bike locked up in front of the building and her heart sank.

"Pull into the parking lot," he directed her. "You can use my spot."

He pointed out the space marked sixteen and she turned into it, though she was afraid to shift into park. That P glowing back at her carried all sorts of connotations. Was she ready for them?

Curt gave her leg a squeeze. "Would you come in?"

His face was so earnest, so hopeful. It was like looking inside herself.

The clock on the dashboard read nine-forty three. She had time, but not much. Still, it was pointless to pretend she didn't know he was about to put the moves on her and she wanted him to.

She put the truck in park and shut off the engine. "Okay."

They walked across the lot with Mia tucked under his arm. Curt let them in the locked door and held it for her. She paused inside, waiting for him to point the way.

"We go up," he said softly and, taking her hand, led her up the carpeted steps.

They took a right at the top and went to the last door on the left. The hallway was dim; the decorative sconces more form than function. He used the glow of the streetlights coming through the window at the end of the corridor to find his apartment key.

She stood aside while he dealt with the lock then pushed the door open and reached inside to flip the switch. A single lamp went on.

Curt's apartment reminded her of a one-room hotel suite, only there was a mini kitchen tacked on the far end. The only door, other than the bi-fold closets, led to the bathroom. His queen bed took up a good portion of the space, though he'd set up a sitting area separate from the sleeping area. His flat screen television was tucked inside a shelf system and could swivel toward the bed or the chairs along the adjoining wall. Two more bookcases, loaded with books, stood against the interior hallway wall, a compact desk with a notebook computer between them.

He'd used every inch of available space and it worked. It was just the right size for one person. His decorating was tasteful, yet minimal, white walls and various shades of gray on the bedspread and the upholstery of the chairs. There were splashes of deep cherry red to add interest to a pillow here or a frame there. The wall behind the chairs was covered in photographs, all black-and-white, in sleek, pewter frames. Mia wandered over to look at them.

"Are these yours?" He nodded. "They're good," she said, admiring the intriguing narrow lanes, the quaint details of old buildings, and marble plazas.

"Thanks." Curt came up behind her and wound his arms around her waist, drawing her against him. He dipped his head and kissed her shoulder.

Mia's knees gave a little when he moved up her neck but she pushed on, her heart racing at where she was and what it meant. "Nice place. I've wondered about it."

He chuckled. "It's improved over the years. Gone are the milk crate tables, the sheets over the windows, and the uncomfortable futon. I had the shag carpet pulled up years ago."

"Shag carpet?" She shuddered and turned in his arms so she could hold him back.

He kissed the tip of her nose and smiled. "Harvest gold."

"Ew. This is better. So tell me, are you always this neat or did you clean the place hoping I might drop by tonight?"

"I'm normally neat. The apartment is so small it looks like shit if I get sloppy. Drives me nuts. I did give the bathroom a good cleaning for you though."

"Aww. That's sweet." She used the teasing tone to mask her nervousness. Like it or not, taking a new man out for a test drive wasn't something she did every day.

The wordplay was over, the reason she was here in his arms was obvious to them both. Still, she couldn't make herself move.

Curt seemed to understand how much she needed him to guide her, needed him to initiate what was about to come. He brought his lips down to hers and backed her against the wall.

"I need to see you again, Mia. Feel you naked against me again," he whispered and slid his hand under her top to cover her breast. He gave it a gentle squeeze. "Not enough, not nearly enough." He popped the hooks on her bra and shoved her shirt up so he could scoop her up with both hands, his smile victorious.

Her eyes glazed over and she sank back, needing the wall for support. "Oh god," she groaned.

Curt's lips were on hers again, this kiss deeper, harder. She gripped his head as he brought her nipples to hard points. She felt drugged when he played with them, drawing them out again and again while his tongue explored her mouth.

Then he moved back and said, "This has to go." He tugged her blazer down her arms.

They both took a moment to contemplate her rolled shirt, tangled up with her bra. Without a word, Mia whipped it off and tossed it onto the nearest chair.

Curt smiled in gratitude. "That would have taken me longer."

"We don't want that."

"No, we don't." He caught her by the waistband and tugged her close and popped the snap. "These look great on you," he said with a naughty smile. "But they have to go."

Together, they worked both pants and panties down her hips. She kicked out of her shoes and stepped free of everything.

"I'm keeping these." He snatched her panties off the floor.

"I can't go home without underwear."

"Do you want to bet?"

"Nice," she said dryly.

He moved in on her, close, and whispered in her ear, his tone, and his breath, warm and seductive. "I want to be nice to you. Let me show you how nice I can be when I'm properly motivated."

"How do I know if you're properly motivated?" she taunted wickedly.

He took her hand and placed it over his bulging fly. "Does this answer your question?"

Mia inhaled sharply at what she felt under her palm. "I should say so. Uncomfortable?"

"A bit."

"We can't have that."

"No." He shook his head then stepped back and whipped his shirt off and sent it flying.

She stared at his bare chest, unable to resist the urge to run her hands over his warm skin again. Her tactile tour left her breathless with excitement. Curt was luscious, firm, intensely beautiful, and she was about to sample the goods. She leaned in to tease his left nipple with her tongue and her mouth started to water.

"Um, Mia," he said tentatively. "I love that, I do, but it's not helping in the restricted pants department."

She laughed at herself. "Sorry. Sidetracked." Her hands started to shake as she fumbled with his fly.

He noticed and caught her wrist to stop her. "Would you rather I do it?"

"No. *I* want to."

"What the—" Arrested by a flash of deep pink, he turned her hand for a closer look. "How did this happen?"

"I wiped out on my bike. I'm fine."

"Be careful." With that, he kissed her wounded palm and let it go.

"I will."

She opened his pants, turned her wrist, and slid her hand down his stomach and under the waistband. Her fingertips brushed warm, springy hair. She looked up and found him watching her. Their eyes locked as she ventured farther and found the solid bend she was seeking. Mia followed it down and gently grabbed hold, turning his erection carefully in the right direction.

Curt exhaled in relief. "Better."

Mia withdrew her hand and gave his boxers a tug.

"Of course you know these have to go?"

Chapter 18

Five minutes later, Mia stared down at the top of Curt's head and wondered what just happened. One minute she had the upper hand, so to speak, and the next she was on her back and he was buried to his eyebrows between her legs. Not that she was complaining. Hell no. But she was way out of practice with this sexual foreplay business. She'd barely had time to drive him wild with anticipation before he'd turned her into dinner.

She remembered Curt drawing her over to the bed. How she waited while he pulled back the spread and tossed it to the floor.

Oh yeah, that's when he moved on her with an animal rush and used his body to back her onto the mattress. Flush with excitement and surprise, she trembled as he stalked after her and caged her between his arms. It thrilled her when he coaxed her down on her back and began to kiss and lick a slow, meandering trail from her throat to her navel. He gave her belly button a playful tonguing before sinking between her legs and settling in with unmistakable relish. The man had skills and her control was slipping.

Her voice wasn't remotely steady when she asked, "How thin are these walls?"

He looked up, his eyebrows arched comically

over her mons. "Fairly thin." He reached out, caught the corner of a pillow, and tossed it to her.

Even stifled, Mia's ecstatic wail was impressive, growing like an old-fashioned siren. Curt was laughing so hard against her stomach when she climaxed that it was impossible to say who was shaking the bed more.

Gradually settling down again, she tapped him on the top of the head. He shifted to look up at her, sporting a wide grin.

"Are you finished laughing at me yet?" she asked impatiently.

"I don't know. Give me a minute."

She snickered. "Don't be a dick."

"I'll show you a dick."

"I wish you would. I don't have all night."

Curt crawled up and over her with a thrilling gleam in his eye.

"Wait!" she said in a sudden panic. "Protection?"

"I'm sterile."

Her palm landed with a slap on his forehead and held him at bay. "You're *sterile*?"

"I had a vasectomy last fall."

"You're kidding."

"I wouldn't kid about something like that. But if it makes you feel better, I still used a condom on the few occasions that called for one. I just figured you're a safe bet."

"Thanks for the reminder."

“But I love that about you,” he said in earnest. “My god, do you know how this feels to me right now? Knowing you’re about to give me something you’ve held back for so long?”

She didn’t want to cry. She really didn’t, but tears were prickling the corners of her eyes as she combed his hair back and admitted, “It finally feels right.” Stretching up, she gave him a soft kiss. “What are we waiting for?”

♡

The very first time he saw Mia he suspected getting entangled with her could complicate his life, yet he never wavered. He wanted her, deep in his marrow. Every cell in his body cried out for her.

With her extended run of celibacy in the back of his mind, Curt held himself in check, choosing instead to sink into Mia slowly so she could enjoy their glorious connection at time-lapse speed. No need to rush this or risk hurting her unintentionally. Already swollen, her body encased him like a snug glove. He shivered at how good she felt. It was harder, by far, to hold back his emotions because she was giving him a gift, the gift of herself, and it staggered him.

As he filled the hollow inside her, Mia’s fingers dug into his arms and she shivered. Worried, he looked to her for assurance she was okay. She nodded and broke into a tremulous smile as his pelvis locked against hers.

"This feel okay?"

Clearly amused, and perhaps a little touched, she stroked his face. "I'm not fine china. You won't break me." She gave him an encouraging bump with her hips.

"I can take a hint." Giving her what she asked for, Curt drove her back down to the mattress.

She lit up. "Mmm, very nice."

But he wasn't about to let her rush this. He took his time, angling himself inside her, pressing her down, drawing her up, rubbing, plunging, all the while slowly and steadily increasing the rhythm until they were both slick and shiny with perspiration.

He'd never experienced total intimacy with a woman like this. The feeling of skin on skin, skin *in* skin, was almost overwhelming. She'd surrounded him in a sensual embrace he had no desire to ever leave. Her arms hugged him close, chest to chest, beating heart to beating heart. Her legs crossed behind him and pulled him in. He'd thrust his tongue into her mouth, but she kept it there with tantalizing strokes and hungry suction.

Mia was visibly trembling now and he wasn't much better. She clasped him harder, pulling him in, thrusting up to meet him. They groaned as their lips sealed. Then Curt reared back and saw her eyes, her flushed cheeks and chest, and knew they were both on the edge. He reached between them to brush her clit. That was it.

She seized in his arms and cried out as if in free-fall while her pussy clenched around him. He let her drag him over the mental and physical ledge and into oblivion. Then, collapsing to his elbows, spent and panting, he nuzzled her cheek, feeling strangely giddy.

She reached up and combed her fingers through his hair as she fought to catch her breath. “Can I just say something?”

“Go for it.”

“Wow. I’m tingling from my scalp to my toes.”

Curt laughed and kissed her temple. “Tell me I don’t have to move just yet.” He burrowed deeper, hoping to convince her.

“Where’s your clock?”

“On your right.”

She craned her head around to check the time. “Sorry, big guy.”

“Damn. But we have to do this again.”

“Hell yes.” She sighed, a deep, luxuriant sigh that pressed her nipples into his chest. She broke the long pause that followed with a firm, “I said no.”

“I didn’t say anything,” he protested innocently while palming her breast.

“You didn’t have to. Like I’m not going to notice you’re swelling inside me as we speak. Oh god,” she groaned at the intimate nudge he gave her.

“I can’t help it. You feel fantastic.”

“Damn it. So do you.” Giving up, giving in, Mia hauled him down for a hungry kiss.

Curt let out a low growl and hooked her legs back with his arms then surged over her.

"Oh," she gasped. "What are you doing?"

He showed her.

"Ooo, don't stop."

He chuckled and thrust again. Her warm skin flushed with color before his eyes and Mia threw her head back and started to seize.

"Curt," she cried in a quivering voice. "You're going to have some pissed off neighbors in the morning."

He laughed and dropped down to swallow her ecstatic screams as his hips drove them out of her one staccato note at a time.

♡

Mia slowly opened her eyes and studied the sleepy man holding her. She'd been captivated by Curt's handsome face, his beautiful eyes when he climaxed. She'd never seen a man at such an unguarded moment. She'd always had her eyes closed with Greg, and honestly, it had been so long, she couldn't *remember* anyone else.

"Curt," she ventured hesitantly, hating to disturb him. "I have to go."

"In a minute," he murmured and hugged her closer.

She found herself nestling in, hooking her leg behind his bare hip even as she persisted in a whisper,

"I really do."

"Shhh."

Fifteen minutes later Mia woke up burrowed against him, sharing his heat.

"Oh my god. Now I've absolutely gotta go!" She rolled away from him and dropped right off the edge of the bed and onto the floor. Scrambling to her feet, she spun around to look for her clothes.

Curt sat up, naked and groggy. He rubbed the back of his head and muffled a deep yawn. "You could call."

"And say what?" She yanked her bra out of her twisted top.

When she reached for her panties, he spoke up. "Those are mine."

"Fine." She tossed them to him, amazed when he caught them, as drowsy as he was.

Curt let out a heavy sigh, got up, and snatched her jeans off the floor. He was ready when she held out her hand for them.

She tugged up her pants and finally looked at him. He was so rumpled and sexy. Was it any wonder her heart skipped a beat? He'd never looked more delicious, and that was saying something.

"My shoes?" she asked, trying to resist the pull she felt, even now, three orgasms later.

Curt found them under the bed and set them in front of her. He held out his arm so she'd have something to hold onto when she slid her feet home.

"Thanks."

He nodded and pulled on his bathrobe.

When Mia was ready for it, Curt helped her into her blazer and drew her purse up over her shoulder. They walked to the door together and paused for a last kiss, lingering over the sweep of tongue on tongue, lip moving over lip. Now that Mia was really leaving, she was awash in an impossible longing to stay. The aching regret seeped through her entire body and weighed her down.

She couldn't resist reaching inside his robe for one last, fond caress. Her hand closed around him and his lashes fell closed. His soft groan made her smile and she snuggled under the chin that was suddenly resting on top of her head. Finally, reluctantly, Mia withdrew her hand and squeaked in delight when his erection followed her out on its own. Curt was raring to go again. Unfortunately, so was she.

They both contemplated his erection for a second.

"Now look what you did," he reproached, the hopeful, melting look in his eyes hard to resist. "You're not going to leave me like this, are you? Stay, just a little longer."

She patted his cheek. "Sorry, babe, you're on your own this time." Stretching up on her toes, she gave him a quick peck then backed out of the door with a smile.

"That's cruel," Curt called softly as she fled down the hall with a muted chuckle.

♡

The movie credits were scrolling down the television screen when Mia got home. She walked into the living room and caught Greg and Liz snuggling on the sofa.

"Get a room," she teased.

"Perfect timing." Greg looked up with a smile and aimed the remote at the television. "Did you have a nice time?"

"It was great." Mia ejected the movie and snapped it into its case. Turning, she handed it to Greg and told them, "I couldn't believe it. Curt was playing guitar on stage when I got there. He's in a band." She felt like a dreamy school girl remembering the scene. "I can't thank you guys enough for tonight. I needed it *so* much."

"Our pleasure," Liz said coming to her feet.

They collected their things and Mia walked them out. They both got a grateful hug at the door.

♡

The pair was unusually quiet when they drove away, both privately mulling what they'd seen. It was Liz who finally broached the subject.

"Did you notice her shirt was—"

"Inside out?" he finished. "Yep."

"And what happened to the clip Mia was wearing in her hair when she left the house tonight?"

"I could hazard a guess."

"So you think they—" She made a circular hand gesture rather than say it out loud.

"Oh yeah. She was manhandled tonight."

Liz fell quiet, clearly bothered by something.

Greg glanced over at her. "What's on your mind?"

"Don't you think she's falling for this guy a little fast? I mean, she's so rusty and out of practice."

"Mia's a big girl. I'm sure she knows what she's doing."

"It's probably too late to slow it down now anyway. Kind of like the flu—you just have to let it run its course." Her eyes flicked over to him. "She's emotionally involved, you know. It makes me nervous. Whirlwinds always make me nervous."

Greg reached for her hand. "I met him, Liz, and he didn't strike me as the playboy type. I can't see him chasing someone like Mia, an older mom, just for the sexual kicks." He laughed at the absurdity of the idea. "He's a teacher. He seemed pretty stable to me. And I gotta be honest, being a teacher, I feel a little easier about him where Casey's concerned too." After a thoughtful pause he added, "Frankly, I'm relieved Mia's finally dating someone. I hated seeing her alone."

♡

Curt stretched across his bed on his stomach and

inhaled the faint, yet heady scent of their coupling on his sheets. He sighed and smoothed his hand over the surface and found something hard just under the edge of the pillow. He drew it out and smiled at Mia's hair clip. Rolling to his back, he toyed with it, lost in thought.

An unexpected knock pulled him out of his pleasant reverie. Glancing at the clock, he frowned. It was a quarter to eleven. Who the hell was here?

Curt climbed off the bed, adjusted his robe, and tidied himself before he looked through the peephole. Two more impatient raps hit the door.

"Fuck," he swore softly.

Drawing back from the peephole, he squeezed his eyes shut and took a deep breath. Only when he was ready did he turn the deadbolt and open the door.

"Come in, Holly."

Chapter 19

Holly's face fell when she saw the condition of Curt's bed. He silently groaned in his head at her predictable reaction. Closing the door, he waved her over to the chairs and took a second to toss the blankets back over the mattress in a messy heap before he followed.

"Give me a second," he said brusquely and walked into the bathroom and closed the door behind him.

He stared at the plain white tiles and all he could see were dancing spots as his eyes adjusted to the bright light.

"Ah, shit," he said in an angry undertone and went rummaging through his clothes hamper for something to put on. He wasn't about to sit in front of Holly with his dick swinging loose under his robe.

He turned up a pair of dark plaid pajama bottoms and yanked them on, nearly falling over the toilet in the process. Armored for battle, he reached for the doorknob.

When he walked out and saw Holly's face, he knew he'd screwed up. He should have handled this better. Their talk was long overdue and avoiding it solved nothing. Now, here they were, in his private space, at the worst possible time, having a discussion they should have had months ago.

Though he knew he should probably offer her something to drink, that was the polite thing to do, he refused. The minute she decided to drop by this late, and unannounced, she forfeited her right to the social courtesies. Besides, the last thing he wanted to do was drag this out longer than he had to.

He dropped into the empty chair—avoiding the bed and all the implications attached to it. "It's a little late, Holly," he said, leaning back with a frown. "This couldn't wait until tomorrow?"

She looked away, saw the disheveled bed and, obviously jolted by it, brought her eyes back to him. "No. You've been dodging me, Curt, and you know it. We rarely eat lunch together anymore and I never see you outside of school. So no, it couldn't wait."

Curt sighed. "You're right. I'm sorry."

"So now what, five years of friendship is down the tubes because we *fucked*?" Her eyes flashed in anger. "Get over it."

He flinched at the word. Holly didn't normally talk this way. "That's part of it," he admitted, but before he could explain further, she broke in with a vicious sneer.

"So what is it with you and this *Mia* anyway? You need a mommy to kiss you nighty-night and discipline you when you're bad? Hell, I'll bitch slap you. I've been dying to do it."

Curt stared at her, momentarily stunned. Calming himself before he said something he'd only regret afterwards, he modulated his voice. “Mia has nothing to do with this. Leave her out of it.”

“At least I didn’t catch her here,” Holly said sourly.

“Mia was here at my invitation. You’re not.”

Holly blanched.

Curt mentally logged that one into his regret column and tried again. “I’m sorry. I don’t want to discuss Mia with you. I wish I could, because you’re a good friend and I miss our talks, but things are different now. What happened in Madrid should have stayed in Madrid.”

“I thought it did.”

He slid his bare foot across the carpet and dug in with his toes. “I hoped it did. I’m not so sure.”

She laughed incredulously and shook her head. “Oh my god, you have one hell of an ego. If you think you’re the best I’ve ever had, you’re delusional.”

The corners of Curt’s mouth twitched. As tempting as it would be to argue the point, he understood her need to save face and preserve her dignity. Taking the high road, he let it go. “Do you mean that?”

“I said it, didn’t I?”

He blew out a breath of relief. “So we’re honestly good?”

“That’s what I’ve been trying to get through your thick scull. Yes, we’re good. Stop imagining I’m carrying a long suffering torch for you already and let's get back to being comfortable together. I *hate* this."

"Me too." He sat up, suddenly eager and excited. "You're going to like Mia. Give her a chance, okay? You two have a lot in common."

"She means that much to you?"

"It's getting to that point, yeah."

Holly shrugged. "Then I'll cut her some slack."

"Thanks."

Holly rose from her chair and Curt trailed her to the door and opened it for her.

She turned with a smirk. "Thank god we got this out of the way. I was starting to worry I'd be watching the World Cup all by myself this summer."

He laughed. "I'm still in."

"Good. So...lunch tomorrow?" she asked from the hall.

"From now on."

"See you tomorrow."

Curt closed the door, feeling as if the world had righted itself. He'd made love to the woman he wanted tonight and repaired his friendship with Holly. A sense of deep contentment filled him and he dropped backwards onto his bed with relief.

♡

Holly slid her key into the ignition and looked up at Curt's window as she started the engine. His light winked out the instant her headlights blazed on and she cursed under her breath and stomped on the brake pedal as she jammed the gear shift down.

"Son of a bitch," she muttered, snapping off the radio and pulling onto the street.

Well, if that's how she had to play it, she could still make this work. The best way to torpedo Mia was from the inside. They were bound to have fights eventually, and she was going to be in the perfect position to offer all kinds of advice from the middle.

Holly felt a pang of conscience at the thought, but it was easy enough to brush aside when she considered how long she'd been there for Curt. She'd paid her dues, damn it. She wasn't about to let some interloper sashay in and take him right out from under her like that. Whatever she decided to do to break this infatuation up was perfectly justified.

Chapter 20

For Mia, getting her head back into her normal routine the next day proved a bigger challenge than expected. It was impossible to focus on work. At best, she managed to float along on autopilot because something momentous had happened. She and Curt had sex last night!

It was still unbelievable, unreal. She tried the idea again. *We had sex last night, great sex last night.* She looked around her open cubicle, wondering if anyone was close enough to overhear the incomprehensible, yet exuberant bellow in her head. Nope. She smiled as she recalled every delicious detail, finally convinced she wasn't imagining the whole thing. It was time to face facts. She wasn't the same woman anymore, not even close.

When the lunch hour came, Mia and Jane changed into their walking shoes and hit the winding trails circling through the business park.

Though she considered Jane a friend, in reality they were primarily co-workers so she wasn't sure how much she should share when Jane started to press her for intimate details about last night.

Mia fed her a bone and hoped it would suffice. "Curt was playing in a band. Talk about surprised."

"You *know* that's not what I was asking." Jane said and greeted an oncoming jogger by name. "He's in a band? I thought he was a teacher."

"He *is* a teacher. The band is just a side thing. They're actually pretty good. Good enough to make money at it if they wanted to."

"Maybe they do during the summer."

Mia shrugged. "Possibly. All I know is Curt likes to travel during his summer vacations." She glanced at Jane. "Can you move over? You're crowding me off the path here."

"Sorry. So what does he play?"

"Guitar."

"Lead?"

"I have no idea." Remembering their configure-ation on stage, she added, "I don't think so. Oh, he sings too."

Jane smiled. "I see. You like the crooners, eh?"

"Just this one. He has an amazing voice." She sighed and her eyes defocused as she was transported back to him on stage, his intimate smile for her alone.

Jane noticed her dreamy side trip and laughed. "Mia, you are so *gone* on him."

"Don't even joke about that. I'm not," she protested in alarm.

"I hate to tell you this, but you're kidding yourself. Might as well accept it."

"No. No way. I *can't* fall for Curt. He's my trans-itional guy, my first adventure back into the scary world of dating. I just have to live in the moment because there is no future for us."

"Why not?"

"For one thing, we're not exactly age compatible. For another, Curt doesn't want kids. Need I remind you I have a son?"

Jane's eyes rolled skyward. "Not necessary. I'm just grateful you're finally talking about something else for a change."

Mia gave her a playful shove. "Ha ha. I'm not *that* bad."

Jane smiled. "Kidding. You're not bad at all."

"Anyway," Mia went on. "I like Curt—a lot. He's wonderful—interesting, intelligent, artistic, good company, and an incredible lover." It slipped out before she could stop herself. "But I'd be an idiot if I started to hope this—I don't even know what to call this. *Relationship?*—could last. I'm not deluded."

"Well, you just admitted you slept with him. Call it an affair."

"It's not an affair if neither of us is involved with anyone else. *Is* it?"

"I really don't care. Why waste time naming it anything? You're sleeping with a younger man. Fantastic. I'm proud of you." Jane grinned at Mia's deep blush. "What, you have a problem with that?"

She shook her head and laughed softly. "No woman with functioning ovaries would have a problem sleeping with him. I just need to remember Curt's not a long-term possibility in my life."

"Think you can handle it?" Jane didn't sound

confident.

"I have to." Mia slowed and she chose her words carefully. "I hear what you're *not* saying. I know this isn't like me at all. But I want it anyway." She glanced across the nearby pond and watched the ducks bobbing on the surface. It gave her time to organize her thoughts.

When she spoke again, her voice was as distant as her eyes. "It's kind of like the fall colors…when they're at peak. So beautiful, so intense it takes your breath away. But it's fleeting, which is why we get into our cars and drive up County Road eighty with our cameras every year. We need to appreciate those blazing colors before they flare out. Experiencing those highs makes coping with the lows a little easier." Mia's gaze dropped to the paved path before them and her words were hushed now. "I know my fling with Curt is going to end, but I still need to feel that rush, experience this golden moment while I can."

There was sympathy and understanding in Jane's expression when she nodded. "Come on, we're falling behind."

♡

By two o'clock, Mia was staring at her blinking cursor, the letters she was supposed to write shunted aside—their dry subject matter no match for the memories of Curt filling her head. She saw him again, every rumpled detail, down to the faint red mark her earring had left on his cheek while he spooned behind her in sleep. She recalled how his arm felt curled around her ribs, how the hair on his forearm brushed the undersides of her breasts. No man had ever made her feel so sexy, so...*delicious*. He'd made a meal out of her and loved it. Though blushing and embarrassed, she wasn't opposed to a lot more of the same.

Damn. She didn't want to miss him this much. It scared her. The office felt warm and oppressive all of a sudden. Mia plucked at her blouse and kicked off her shoes and sent them rolling under the desk. Hopefully that would help bring her temperature down.

But honestly, what was wrong with her? This was ridiculous. She wasn't an impressionable virgin. Why did making love to Curt last night short circuit her system? She'd always bounced right back after sex. She could pop out of bed without a backwards glance and get on with her day. She didn't dwell. So how come she couldn't master this one sexual encounter?

Her eyes ballooned. Did she just call what they did *making love*? Her warm glow flushed white and she went limp in her chair.

Oh shit. Is *that* what they did? Make *love*? She'd never fully appreciated the distinctions between having sex and making love until now.

There simply was no comparing her lackluster sex life with what happened last night. In less than two hours, Curt managed to blow the entire breadth of her sexual history out of the water and replaced what she thought she knew about sex with something far more emotionally potent. He'd left his imprint on her—oh god, *in* her—and changed everything.

Then Mia snorted at herself and turned her chair, and her back, on those uncomfortable reflections. She was being ridiculous. There was nothing out of the ordinary about their lovemaking. This was just her old reliable imagination screwing with her again. *Nice that it was back*, she thought dryly.

But then…why did she feel so different, so right today? What if she *was* falling for him?

That thought was too frightening to contemplate. No way. They were still learning about each other and she was far too practical to fall recklessly in love. Nope. Forget it. This was nothing more than lust. She was a woman hitting her sexual peak without a seat belt. She couldn't afford to let herself feel more, see it as more.

But Mia was suddenly afraid of becoming needy, even greedy for him. She recognized the symptoms. She wanted him here with her. Now. More precisely, she wanted to be with him away from here, anywhere else, doing anything else.

A flashback of Curt naked sent a rush of heat surging through her body, her veins practically humming with electricity. Fine, she could admit it. She craved more than just his company. Would she learn how to manage this sudden and insatiable appetite for him over time? Was that really something she should hope for? Never had Mia felt so animal in the most biological sense of the word.

It was time to have the dreaded relationship talk with Casey tonight. She'd avoided it long enough. Then she thought, why wait? Get it over with in the car, that way she could avoid eye contact. Was that cowardly? Probably, but it beat the heck out of a serious face-to-face chat.

Mia was a ball of nervous energy an hour later when Casey climbed into the truck outside the school. He tossed his book bag behind the seats and gave her a curious look as she drummed rapidly on the steering wheel.

"Want a little music to go with that?" he asked with a chuckle and reached to turn on the stereo.

Mia yanked her hands back with a guilty flush and turned the key. "Actually, I was hoping we could talk. Just leave the music off for a minute, okay?" She followed another car out of the parking lot and asked her standard question first. "Any homework?"

"A little math."

That out of the way, she took a deep breath and dove in. "You know Mr. Walden?"

Casey snorted. "Mom."

Her eyes cut sharply to her son. "This is serious."

"He's not moving in, is he?"

Mia's reaction to that question seemed to amuse the hell out of him.

"Why would you ask that?"

"Well, you're dating him, right? That's usually how it works in normal families."

"We're a normal family."

Casey snorted again. "No, we're not. I don't know one kid whose divorced parents are such good friends. And you like Liz too. That's not normal. And it's not normal that you never went out with other guys before Curt either. You obviously like him."

Mia was stunned. "I do," she admitted. "And here I thought this was going to be hard." Her eyes cut over to him. "So you're okay with me dating him?"

"Yeah. He's pretty cool and he makes you happy. You smile more now."

She was smiling more? Huh. Mia thought about that and realized he's right. She *was* happy, and surprisingly optimistic. She went to bed in a good mood and woke up energized and excited about the new day. She couldn't remember ever feeling quite like this. Had she used Casey as an excuse to avoid intimacy?

She reached over and affectionately tousled her son's hair as he turned the music back up.

It wasn't until they drove through the next stop sign that she noticed he'd started to fidget. His oversized shoes scraped together on the mat and his fingers were in nervous motion. Her heart dropped into her stomach when he dried his palms on his pant legs.

Dreading the answer, she still had to ask the

question. “What is it?”

Casey kept his eyes locked straight ahead, but his red cheeks betrayed him. “Safe sex, Mom. Okay?”

Mia’s jaw dropped. She tried to speak. Nothing came.

Chapter 21

Mia was starting the dishwasher when the doorbell rang a few hours later.

"I'll get it," Casey offered and put the leftover taco meat in the fridge on his way out.

She picked up the sponge and was wiping down the counters when Curt walked in, swinging his backpack off his shoulder. Mia lit up like a chandelier.

"Hey! You just missed dinner, but I can re-heat something if you're hungry."

"Thanks. I ate. I brought you something."

Aw. He'd been thinking about her too?

"You didn't have to do that."

"I know." He unzipped his bag and pulled out a sealed package.

She accepted it from him in confusion. "Light bulbs?"

He smiled. "It was cheaper than a new car."

"Ha. Here I was thinking flowers, candy."

"This is better—a gift that keeps on giving. I noticed you still use incandescent bulbs in your lamps. These cost a little more, but they use less energy. Hopefully you'll see a slight improvement in your rates after we switch them."

He was serious. This incredibly sexy guy was a nerd at heart. Who would have thought? Mia was still processing all this when Curt called Casey over and handed him a second package.

"Make yourself useful," he said with a grin. "How about changing the bulbs in all the lamps?"

Casey shrugged and took them into the living room.

Curt drew his hand lightly across Mia's waist on his way to the garage. She watched him go, immobilized by desire and *what* exactly? Then he reappeared with her step ladder and had to fight with her self-closing door to come back in. Amused, she raced over to hold it open for him.

"Thanks. That's one nasty spring."

"Try dealing with it when you're lugging groceries into the kitchen."

"Why don't you replace the mechanism?"

"I'm used to it."

Shaking his head, he opened the ladder directly under the kitchen fixture. "Would you hold this thing steady for me?"

She smiled wickedly. "I'll do it, *if* I can stand behind you."

He leaned forward and planted a slow, steamy kiss on her. "Hit the switch first, will you?"

He was already heading up the ladder when Mia scampered back. She grabbed the ladder with both hands—for almost thirty seconds. That's all the discipline she had before she began to follow the curve of his fabulous ass with her right hand.

"Hey." He looked down at her. "You're not

helping. Don't make me send you away."

"Sorry," she lied, not remotely sorry. Smiling to herself, she returned to holding the ladder.

Curt cautiously touched the glass fixture before supporting the cover from underneath while unwinding the retaining screws. He dropped the screws into the cover and handed it down to her.

"It's not hot, but I'll need a pot holder or a towel to handle the bulb."

Mia went into a drawer to get him one.

The kitchen done, they worked their way through the house, changing the entry light, the hall light, and finally both bedrooms.

"I wasn't sure what kind of bulbs you had in the bathroom. I guess I was a little distracted the last time I was in there," he said and winked at her.

Mia blushed. "Shh."

"Casey can't hear us." Curt helped Mia move her bed back into place. "Feel like testing that theory?" He eyed her bed with interest.

"No."

"Yoo-hoo! Is this a bad time?" Sally called from the front door.

"We're coming out," Mia shouted back and led the way.

Sally poked her head down the hall and her eyebrows shot up when they walked out of Mia's bedroom together.

"Hi, Sal. What's up?"

Sally's gaze shifted to the ladder. "I just dropped by to see if you wanted to run to Target with me. But I see you're busy."

Mia glanced at Curt. "*Am* I busy?"

"Actually, you're not going to believe this," he said with a laugh. "But I was going to suggest we go shopping. You still need a bike helmet."

"Are you kidding?"

"Nope." He looked back and forth between them. "Mind if I tag along?"

"Let's go," Sally answered for them both.

♡

Sally went right for a shopping cart as soon as they entered the store.

How much did the woman have to pick up? "Do you really need a cart?" Mia asked, dreading the answer.

"Have you ever gotten out of here without spending at least a hundred dollars? I'm taking a cart."

Curt chuckled at them then, craning his neck, spotted the sign for sporting goods. "Over there."

"Well I'm heading this way," Sally told them and cut to the right. "I'll be in toiletries."

The couple set off, hand in hand, jauntily swinging their arms as one.

"Remind me to pick up more double A batteries for Casey while I'm here," she said carelessly, then immediately turned bright crimson.

He grinned, missing nothing. "Is that what they take?"

"Some of them."

"Can I see your stash?"

"I don't think so. And I don't have a *stash*."

"How many?"

"I'm not saying."

"Does your favorite have a name?"

She gave Curt a long look. "Anonymous."

He laughed. "I think it's time Steely Dan took a vacation."

"I'm waiting for a postcard now."

He jostled her with his shoulder and chuckled. "Here we are. You know, we really should look into getting you a new bike. Yours is ancient."

"It's fifteen years old."

"You've made my point."

"I'm not getting a new bike."

"We'll see."

"I'm not."

Curt picked up a helmet. "What do you think of this one?"

"Barbie?"

"It would look cute on you."

"I don't think so." She sighed in disgust. "I hate every single one of these."

"Don't think of them as fashion, think of them as protection."

"Except I'm going to be tooling around town

wearing one of these. How am I supposed to ignore how I look in it?"

"You'll be cute no matter what."

"I'd rather be gorgeous."

"You're that too."

"That was convincing," she said dryly. "Except, you keep calling me cute. *Cute*."

"What's wrong with cute?"

"A puppy is cute. A kitten is cute. A baby is cute."

"You're cute too, but in a pretty way." He held the helmet out to her. "Try this one."

She plopped it onto her head and it immediately slid forward on her face.

"What size is that?" He grabbed it before it fell off.

That helmet went back to the shelf and Curt looked for a smaller size, coming up with a black number with a blue design. He put it on her head and tested the fit himself.

"How does it feel?" he asked, once he was satisfied.

"It's fine."

"Can you deal with this one?"

"It doesn't suck as bad as most of them."

"I'll take that as a yes." He tucked it under his arm. "Come on."

"Where to?"

"Bikes."

"I told you, I'm not buying another bike."

"I want you to try out a few seats. We'll compromise on a new seat—for now—and see how that goes."

He set her helmet aside and pushed on a few seats before rolling a bike out from the rack.

"That's a man's bike," she informed him.

"All I want to know is how the seat feels. Mount up."

"Bet you say that to all the girls."

"Only the cute ones," he said, teasing her.

"Cute." She shuddered and swung her leg over. "*Hey*, these shocks are awesome." She bounced up and down, impressed.

"But how does the seat feel?"

"Great."

"Try this one." He rolled another out for her and they swapped handlebars.

Mia hopped onto the second. "I think I liked the first one better. There's not as much bounce in these shocks."

He laughed. "You're thinking about a new bike now, aren't you?"

"With lots of cush." So she was weak.

"Okay. Let's find you something."

Curt carried Mia's helmet for her when she finally rolled her bike of choice to the front of the store. They found Sally looking at movies.

"What do you think?" she asked and turned the

DVD in her hand.

Mia shrugged. “Get it if you want it.”

Sally’s gaze fell on the bike. “And you teased me.”

“Buy enough toilet paper?”

“Hey. Those are paper towels. The toilet paper is underneath with all the soap and shampoo. What was I supposed to do? It’s on sale.” Sally dropped the movie into her basket and threw up her hand. “I think I’ve spent enough.”

“I know I have,” Mia agreed.

♡

They took Sally and all her paraphernalia home first then pulled into Mia’s driveway.

“Now what?” she asked as the garage door rolled closed.

Curt took the bike out of the back for her. Mia set her new helmet on the shelf above it.

He moved closer, an intriguing gleam in his eye. “I have a few ideas.”

“Oh really?” She smiled and crowded him back, willing to hear a few.

Their lips were a mere millimeter from touching when the door leading into the kitchen flew open and Casey stuck his head out. “Mom! Where are the flashlights?”

She froze; relieved he didn’t burst in on them a second later and catch her hands where they were about to go.

"Why do you need them?"

"Flashlight tag!"

Incredible as it seemed, Curt's face lit up and he broke into a huge grin.

"You want to play, don't you?"

"Hell yes!"

Little boys. Curt was so fricking cute right then she caved, ready to do anything to make him happy.

"Mind if we play too?" she asked Casey.

He was all for it. "The more the merrier."

"I guess I'm looking for flashlights."

♡

It had been decades since Mia ran around in the dark playing games. For reasons she couldn't begin to explain, she was never '*it,*' which suited her just fine.

There came a shriek and rapid footfalls off to her left as she crouched behind an overgrown viburnum bush in a neighbor's yard. She drew back deeper into the shadows as the sounds of a frantic foot race came closer than she liked. She expected the pair to appear at any second, but it was Curt she spotted first. He was hiding not twenty feet away when a light snapped on in the house directly behind her and illuminated a long stretch of lawn and him with it. He was going to be in trouble if he didn't move—now.

"Curt!" He didn't hear her. "Curt!" she tried again without success. He was backing away, but unfamiliar with the neighborhood, he was going to get burned.

She picked up an acorn and hurled it at him. He jerked and swore when it nailed him. He looked around, spotted her, and nodded when she urgently waved him over.

Making sure the coast was clear first, he made a beeline straight for her, keeping low and in the shadows.

"Sorry. I didn't know how else to get your attention," she whispered, crawling deeper into the bushes to make room for him.

"It's okay." His teeth gleamed in the dark. "This is a blast."

Mia let out a muted chuckle. "God, you're cute right now."

One look, one silly smile, was all it took for the two of them to attack each other. They rolled on the ground, limbs and tongues tangling. His left hand shot through her hair while the right went on expedition. She clung to the back of his head while frantically tugging his shirt out of his pants.

A light snapped directly on them and they froze in mid grope.

"You're—*Mom?*" Casey's initial triumph gave way to horror. "Oh geez. You guys are out."

"But who's it?" Mia giggled as Curt rolled off of her.

Casey turned his flashlight beam to the ground and walked away. "My mom and Mr. Walden aren't playing anymore," he called to the rest of the kids still hiding.

The adults were dismissed.

Taking their expulsion in stride, the couple wandered home arm in arm. Alone for the time being, they made out like teenagers on the couch, taunting and teasing each other, knowing full well there was no release at the end.

They jerked apart when Casey eventually came in and went right for the refrigerator. They could hear him pour something to drink while Mia stuffed her breasts back into her bra and Curt hastily zipped his pants.

They both looked guilty and disheveled when he walked past the living room. He shook his head and, with a snort of amusement, said, "Just keep it down out here, okay? I don't even want to know."

"Goodnight, Casey." Mia was blushing when he disappeared into his room and shut the door behind him.

"I should probably get going," Curt told her and got up.

"Yeah, I suppose so."

Parting was such sweet sorrow. A famous line, but Shakespeare knew what he was talking about.

Mia walked him out and they lingered on the dark driveway.

"Dream about me." He tweaked her under the chin.

Laughing softly, she pressed closer. "Considering the state you're leaving me in, count on it."

They shared one last, tender kiss then he threw his leg over his seat.

"Tomorrow," he promised. "We're breaking in your new bike."

"Okay." Smiling faintly, she watched him ride off then went back inside, locked up, and grabbed the new package of batteries off the counter on her way to bed.

She was going to hell.

♡

Casey came in with his new friend and asked, "Anything to eat?"

Mia turned from the stove, a wooden spoon in her hand. "Have some fruit. I don't need you spoiling your supper."

"Can Curt eat over?"

She examined this younger version of Curt and sexually stripped him with her eyes. Her mouth began to water. "Of course."

The boys went to sit at the table, talking away as she turned down the flame under her frying pan. She covertly watched young Curt from around the corner for a quiet, contemplative minute before wandering over and stopping beside his chair. He looked up in surprise with those heavenly eyes of his.

She gave him a slow once-over and licked her lips before casting a dismissive glance at her son. "Case, I need Curt to help me with something. Come back in a half hour."

The boys shared an uneasy look between them.

"Now, Casey," she said firmly.

He fled, and as the front door closed, Mia shoved the table back with her hip and spun around to straddle Curt's lap. The sizable bulge in his jeans thrilled her. She rocked against it, wet and ready.

"Don't look so scared," she cooed seductively, weaving her fingers through his hair. "You're going to love this. I promise." Holding his head immobile, she kissed the daylights out of him.

His shaky arms locked around her and she smiled, knowing she had him.

Mia woke with a horrified start as young Curt's spokes went *tick tick tick* in time with her racing heartbeat.

Chapter 22

Mia remained in an anxious ball on the sofa for the rest of the night. She zoned out with the remote in her hand, staring blankly at the channels flipping past, the rapid flashes illuminating the dark space around her like a slide show. She couldn't stop trembling, no matter how tight she wrapped the blanket around her. Hugging the pillow to her chest didn't help the shakes either.

The dream felt so real, so disturbing; young Curt vivid and adorable. But making a play for him was wrong. *Nasty.* He was Casey's age.

Then reality hit and she wanted to be sick. He actually *was* Casey's age when she'd conceived him. What was her subconscious trying to tell her?

She didn't want to go there or admit that she already knew what was wrong with this unwholesome picture. So she tried to desensitize herself with garbage. But poor quality reality shows, hard-sell infomercials, and old, grainy movies could not accomplish the impossible. There was something unsavory about taking a younger lover. She felt wretched and dirty, but even worse, emotionally vulnerable. She craved Curt in a way she shouldn't. Those luscious eyes of his were a narcotic to her system, and she was sinking into an addiction she didn't think she could survive.

Every flash of humor she saw in him thrilled her. Every lustful look intercepted made her heart soar. Even those quiet moments, when no words were necessary, seemed to seal their connection in a way she'd never experienced, certainly never expected with *him*.

It was obvious she was going to have to end things. The sooner the better. Call it self-preservation. It was going to be agonizing enough as it is. But just imagine even a month from now, when she wasn't just falling in love with him but was deeply and desperately in love and the axe about to fall. Mia shuddered at the thought. It made her ache inside, frightened and miserable. Tears rolled down her face and soaked the collar of her shirt as she watched the food processor dice perfect onions, make medallion carrots, and whip up a delicious fruit smoothie.

Like a Band-Aid, Mia. Right off.

♡

Except when Curt came over early Saturday, Casey was entertaining friends. After giving Mia a warm kiss good morning, he was lured outside to play basketball in the driveway with the boys.

The neighbors dropped by and Sally took a seat beside Mia on the grass as Larry stood at the edge of the driveway, watching with interest. Curt turned with a grin and fired the ball to him and Larry took off into the middle, cutting around one of the boys as he dribbled like an old pro. His shot bounced off the edge of the rim.

"Larry played in high school," Sally told her.

"Curt probably *still* plays in high school," Mia said soberly.

Sally laughed. "But they're having fun. I love to see Larry running around. The only exercise he gets these days is during sex. He gets so winded sometimes, I'm afraid I'm going to kill him."

Mia giggled. "Thanks for that update."

They looked up when Becky appeared and ambled over. As she crossed the driveway, her eyes were trained on the boys.

"Hi, Becky," Mia greeted the girl as she sank onto the grass next to her mom.

"Hi." The girl nodded toward Curt and said, "So it's true. You're dating Mr. Walden?"

Mia colored. "Looks that way."

"I know a lot of girls who are going to be bummed about that. A couple teachers too."

"I've met one."

"Ms. Fields?"

Who the hell is Ms. Fields? "No, Ms...shoot, I forgot her last name. She teaches Spanish. Holly something or other."

"Oh, Miss Patton."

"That's it." All three females watched Curt as he attempted a shot. Larry blocked it with his long arms. "So who's this Ms. Fields?" Mia asked casually.

"She teaches algebra."

"Is she pretty?"

"Not as pretty as you."

Mia gave her a grateful smile. "Thanks. I needed that."

Becky grinned. "I don't think you have to worry about him. He keeps coming back here, right?"

Mia smiled, her eyes following the man of her heart without hesitation. "He does."

"I think everyone should head over to our house after this," Sally suggested. "We'll fire up Larry's new grill and put him to work. He's been dying to show it off."

"You sure you want all of us?"

"What's a few extra burgers and dogs? I'll throw together a pasta salad and who knows what else. Open a jar of pickles. Maybe olives."

"I'll scrounge through my cabinets for something. I might have beans."

"We need chips, Mom," Becky spoke up.

"Why don't I run to the store?" Mia offered. "Let me know what we'll need and I'll go get it."

"Good idea. I'll take inventory and write up a list."

"Don't forget pop," Becky called to Sally as she walked back to their house.

"Got it." Sally waved a hand in the air.

"Does Casey like cream soda?" Becky asked Mia.

"He'll drink anything. Lately, he's been asking

for ginger ale. I don't know why."

Becky smiled as he ran shoulder first, right into another boy and bounced off of him. Casey landed on his ass.

"That had to hurt." Mia laughed as Larry yanked her son back to his feet.

"He's getting so tall, but he doesn't have the weight yet," Becky observed.

"True. Sometimes I don't even recognize his voice. He's starting to sound just like his dad."

Becky giggled. "The way they all talk right now is so funny. Like a graph. Their voices are up here, then suddenly down low in the basement." She tried to imitate what she meant as she spoke.

Mia laughed and watched her son clomp around in his seriously large clown shoes, amazed they actually fit him. "He needs a razor."

"Oh no," said Becky then stopped herself with a blush. "I'm just…I like his mustache."

Mia gave the girl a playful nudge. "You find the peach fuzz sexy, eh?" All kidding aside, the long suspected crush was now confirmed.

"Well—" Becky shrugged, embarrassed.

"I won't tell. Come on." Mia pushed up to her feet. "Let's see if your mom has a list ready yet and we'll go shopping together, okay?"

"Okay." Becky got up and brushed off the back of her shorts.

Curt looked over at Mia. "What's going on?"

"We're throwing together a barbeque. Don't stop."

He nodded and turned back to the action and the girls continued on to the house next door.

"It's on the counter," Sally called out when they walked into the kitchen. She set a pan on the stove for boiling water.

Mia picked up the list and read the items. "Vanilla ice cream?"

"For root beer floats." Sally salted the water and turned on the burner. "Unless you think sundaes would be better."

"I'm good with floats." Mia looked at Becky. "Come on. Let's go interrupt their game."

Sally popped up from behind the open fridge door, a jar of mayonnaise in her hand. "Don't do that. Take my Jetta."

"You sure?"

"Just watch Larry's car when you back out of the garage." Sally tossed her the keys.

"Will do."

♡

The two friends were patting out hamburgers when the guys ambled in. Curt drifted over to Mia and kissed her on the temple.

"So you *do* sweat." She laughed and drew back from him. "Go use my shower. Take Casey with you, while you're at it. We'll be here when you're done."

"I would, but I don't have a change of clothes." Curt popped a grape into his mouth.

"No problem." Sally looked at her husband leaning against the counter mopping his brow with a damp paper towel. "Larry, go find something Curt can borrow while his clothes are in the washer."

He gave a tired nod. "Give me a sec."

"Thank you," Curt called after him.

Mia laid another patty on the waxed paper and said, "Washer and dryer are downstairs. Could you have Casey throw his dirty stuff in there too?"

"Sure. Anything you need or want washed while I'm at it?"

"Not at the moment."

Larry returned with a clean t-shirt and shorts. "I figured you'd rather go commando than borrow someone else's underwear."

Curt laughed. "Good call. Thanks again for the loan." He winked to Mia. "I'll be back."

While the guys cleaned up, they shifted the party outdoors.

♡

The Larson's backyard was large, sunny, and bordered by flowers. Relaxing under the pergola out of direct sunlight, and with appetizing smells wafting out of the nearby grill made it very pleasant. Larry was in his element with his long handled spatula. And Curt…well, Curt sauntered out looking indescribably yummy in his borrowed shorts, loose tee, and damp hair. A cold beer hung from his relaxed hand.

Mia sidled over to intercept him and took a nice long drag of his fresh, clean scent. “Mmm, much better.”

He smiled, crooked his arm behind her head, and pulled her in for an arousing kiss. As their breath mingled she discovered that, though she wasn’t a fan of beer, she didn’t mind the taste on him. Not even a little.

She eased back to whisper, “So, you’re swinging free and unfettered?”

He laughed. “Yep. You could join me in the fun.”

“I don’t think I could handle it.”

“Coward.”

“Soup’s on!” Larry called from the loaded picnic table.

The kids started a game of ladder golf afterwards, while Mia and Sally put away the leftovers.

“I’ve made a decision,” Sally announced. “The guys are doing the dishes. There isn’t much.”

Mia agreed.

Curt got up from the table. “I should throw the clothes into the dryer first.” Mia glanced at him and a hungry look passed between them. She shot up too.

“I’ll go with you. My dryer has a few quirks.” She turned to Sally and added softly, “We’ll be back in a little bit. Don’t make Larry do everything on his own.”

She snorted. “I’m sure he’ll wait.” Leaning in

with a sly grin, she said, “We’ll keep Casey busy.”

“Thank you.” Grateful, the pair took off.

The second they were through the front door, Curt backed her against the wall and attacked her neck.

“How much time do you think we have?”

“Tough to say.” She grabbed him by the hair and kissed whatever she could reach. “I want you so bad. But not here.”

“Bedroom.” He grabbed her hand and towed her down the hall. They spun through the door and he gave it a graceful kick closed behind them.

“No lock?” he asked, noticing the knob.

“I’ve never needed one.”

“I want to undress you but…” he began.

“I know,” she finished. “Just strip.”

They tackled their own clothing and dove to the bed, bare skin on bare skin, slipping and sliding over each other and relishing the full body contact.

“Damn,” he groaned as their chests brushed together.

His tongue plundered her mouth. His fingers penetrated her body. Mia trembled and strained, but this wasn’t what she wanted. He was wasting time.

“No!” She tore her mouth from his. “You! I want *you.*”

More than happy to oblige, he shifted and entered her. She flexed her hips to take him deliciously deep. There they held a moment and gloried in the rightness of their bodies intimately coupled. She couldn’t get enough of him. There'd never be enough.

Curt kneaded Mia's breast and plucked her nipple while her heels scrabbled for purchase on the blankets. She could feel the rough scrape of his cheek along her jaw when he dipped to kiss her ear, flick her earring with his tongue, and suck her lobe.

"Mmm. This feels way too good," she said with a delirious quiver.

"No," he whispered and softly bit her shoulder.

"Yes."

"Never *too* good."

Then he gave her more, feeding her by inches, and she blossomed, the heat building inside her radiating out through her pores.

Mia's climax struck like a crack of lightening and she threw her head back and cried out. Curt covered her mouth with his and shared her passionate gasp while wringing another and another out of her until she finally returned the favor.

Spent, he collapsed beside her with a breathless confession. "I love making love with you." He gave her a sated little smile.

"Me too." She snuggled in his arms as the magnitude of her immediate happiness obliterated her earlier misgivings—for now.

♡

When the lovers rejoined the party next door, Larry dragged Curt inside to tackle the kitchen while

Casey and Becky chose to add to the mess by making root beer floats.

Left on their own, the two friends soaked up the peace and quiet. Blissfully loose and relaxed, Mia dropped her head back on the chaise lounge while Sally rocked lazily in the chair beside her.

"You know, Mia, I've never seen you more beautiful."

She turned her head languidly to the left and saw Sally's soft smile of amusement. "Seriously?" *What did that mean?*

"Curt's so nice—so good for you," her friend went on.

"He is nice, isn't he?" she agreed, carefully sidestepping the second half of that statement.

"Casey approves of him, you know. And you weren't fooling anyone today."

"He knew we were—"

"Of course. But I wouldn't sweat it. He's taking it in stride. Kids these days are a lot more aware than we were."

Mia cringed. "Am I a bad mother?"

Sally snorted. "Hardly."

"I feel like I'm neglecting him lately."

"You're not. You're just loosening the apron strings. I think he appreciates it."

Mia thought about it and her brief smile flickered out. "I guess I did sort of stifle him for a while there." She was uneasy when she looked at Sally. "Still got that dustpan?"

"Dustpan?"

"You know, to sweep up the pieces of my heart, remember?"

"Oh yeah." Sally waved her off. "I don't think you'll need it."

"Just in case."

"That bad?"

She nodded. "I've fallen for him, Sal. *Bad.* What the hell am I supposed to do now?"

Sally leaned across and put an arm around her. Mia buried her face against her shoulder and trembled at the repercussions.

"Who knows, Mia? You might be the one who kicks *his* ass to the curb. Maybe he's got these faults you aren't even aware of yet. Something you won't be able to stand."

Brushing away a couple of tears, Mia sat back and asked weakly, hopefully, "Like what?"

"He's king of karaoke?"

They shared a lethargic laugh.

"Not bad, if I didn't already know he has a beautiful voice. Remember, I've heard him sing. He could turn me to mush just by humming in the car."

"Hmm." Sally snapped her fingers. "I know! How about his alter ego as a rodeo clown?"

Mia considered it. "That might work. I'd get some serious ice cubes in my panties with that one."

Sally smiled. "Good. There's got to be a bunch of

stuff we can make up about him if we need it. Does he have any kinky or disturbing fetishes?"

"Not that I've noticed."

"Check his dresser drawers. Maybe he's a cross-dresser."

Mia laughed. "Thanks. I needed this."

"Anytime."

She was just pulling herself together when Curt appeared with root beer floats for both of them. He presented them with an exaggerated flair.

"Enjoy, ladies." he said with a playful wink and returned to the house.

Sally eyed Mia closely as she poked her straw up and down in the foam. "Are you going to tell Curt you love him?"

"Are you insane?"

Chapter 23

Their little party broke up at dusk. Casey went inside with Becky to play video games and Mia and Curt said goodnight to their hosts. He'd hinted earlier in the day that he wanted to take her on a late bike ride but he was mum about the details so she didn't know where they were going or why they were waiting for nightfall.

He led her to the school. They rode across the empty parking lot and cut behind the sprawling brick building.

"Are we allowed to be here after hours?" she asked when they propped their bikes against the wall.

"I have a key."

He let her in through a back door and they followed the dark corridor to the even darker science wing.

She giggled, though softly. "I feel like a cat burglar sneaking in. I'm afraid to make noise."

"We're the only ones here."

"I know. *Still*."

"You probably never misbehaved." He chuckled, amused. "Here we are." Curt unlocked his classroom and reached in to flip on a couple of switches. It was enough light to see by, but not enough to blind them.

She followed him in and looked around. "This takes me back." She walked between the raised lab tables, their stools overturned on top. "It even smells the same—the odors are so strong."

"Are they?" Surprised, he took a testing sniff. "We only use a fraction of the formaldehyde we used to. Honestly, I barely notice the smell anymore."

She spotted the row of sealed jars lined up on the back counter and the variety of creatures preserved inside each. Her head turned slowly to follow them before she visibly shuddered and spun away.

Which disturbed her more, he wondered, *the pale squid or the phallic looking sea cucumber?*

Mia walked around one of the tables, drawing her hand along the smooth black edge. "I actually got sick in biology once. Did I ever mention that?"

He laughed softly. "No."

"Oh yeah. I admit I was always queasy during dissections. Just doing the worm grossed me out. I could barely look at the frogs. When the teacher cut open the pregnant cat and the piglet, I hid in the back so I wouldn't have to watch. I swear the worst was the small shark. The smell was so bad it made me gag. I got cold and clammy. My friend told me I was as white as a ghost. You wouldn't believe how fast I ran out of there to get some fresh air."

"At least you didn't faint." He sympathized. He'd seen it before.

"I was this close." She flashed a small gap between her index finger and thumb. "Just walking through the science wing the rest of the week brought me out in a cold sweat. I barely passed the class."

"I wish I'd been there." He imagined them taking the same class. Knowing he would have had a major crush on her, he would have done everything he could to help her get a better grade.

But Mia mistook him and imagined it differently. "I probably would have tried harder to stick it out, paid a little more attention if *you* were my teacher."

Letting it go, Curt smiled and made a considerate suggestion instead. "Why don't I grab what we need and we can head outside, okay?"

"Good plan." Her eyes swept the classroom. "At least now I have a visual so I can picture you when you're working. I've tried to do it in my head a few times." She laughed softly. "Okay, more than a few times. Do you walk around or hover in certain spots around the room?"

"During classes, I pace. During tests, I circulate. I guess it all depends on what's going on."

"Interesting." Her eyes tracked him to the built-in cupboard in the far corner. "What are you after?"

He grabbed a pair of binoculars and a green Army blanket from inside. "These."

Rejoining her at the door, he flipped off the lights and closed it behind them. The corridor was entirely dark except for the glowing exit sign at the very end. They went out that way. Since there was no way to open it again from the outside, he wedged it open with a large rock.

"Now what? Where are you taking me?" Mia asked.

"Out there, across the field."

Holding hands, they left the sidewalk, crossed a utility driveway, and stepped onto the damp grass on the other side, every step taking them farther away from the lights. Without the moon in the clear night sky, he wasn't surprised when Mia stumbled.

He was ready and kept her on her feet. "Watch your step."

"I would if I could see anything."

"Need to slow down?"

"I'll be fine."

He led her across the wide expanse of mown grass to the far edge of the football field and the un-developed acreage beyond.

"How much farther?" she asked a half second before he let go of her hand.

"We're here." Curt spread the blanket out on the ground. The sounds of crickets and frogs came at them from out of the darkness. "Sit." He sank onto the blanket and drew her down with him.

"Now what?" The playful innuendo in her voice implied she already knew the answer.

She didn't.

Chuckling softly, he set her straight. "We're going to stargaze. This is the perfect night—no moon and we're as far as we can get from the lights. Hopefully, we should be able to see something." Even though he knew she could barely make him out, she was staring at him anyway. It amused him. Curt stretched out on his back and gazed up into the inverted bowl of sky over them. "Mia, lie down. I won't molest you."

"Now you tell me," she grumbled and dropped to her back.

He was smiling when he said, "Pick out a spot in the sky and really look at it. Try to notice how many points of light there are in it."

♡

Mia could hear the teacher coming out in Curt's voice, the gentle direction. She liked it. She never noticed how soothing and persuasive his voice was because his heavenly eyes and his sinful body were such a distraction. It was a very stupid oversight. Now she knew she didn't have to see him to respond.

Following his lead, she chose a cluster of stars just over her head. "Okay, I've got one."

He gave her the binoculars. "You might need to adjust the focus. There's a knob on top."

She brought them to her eyes and fiddled for a second. "All clear."

"Good. Do you remember your spot? Find it again with your naked eye. Then, when you're ready, look at the same area through the binoculars."

"Wow." She was amazed. "There's so many. A lot more than I realized."

"Imagine what you could see through a telescope. I'll have to set one up for you when the moon is out sometime. You'll love it." He was relaxed and silent at her side for a few minutes while she continued to investigate the night sky.

"Hey! Check out Mars," he said.

"Where?"

"Right under Leo."

"Leo being?"

"Shit. You don't know your constellations, do you?"

Mia nibbled her lip, embarrassed. "I know the Big Dipper."

He laughed and sat up. "Come here." Spreading his knees, he created a back rest for her with his body. "Lean against me."

She scooted between his legs and dropped her head back on his shoulder.

He swept her hair aside, out of his way. "Okay, I'm going to direct you."

"What am I looking for?"

"About one o'clock." He positioned her head back a little more. "I want you to find Leo with your naked eye first, because if you use the binoculars you're going to have a harder time picking out the constellation."

"Let's give it a shot."

"Now picture a crane or a flamingo. Can you see my finger?"

"Sort of."

"Follow it. Imagine the corner of the body on the left, the arch of the back. Here's the head right here looking to the right. Have you got it?"

"I think so."

"Damn. I wish I had a book with me."

"Sorry."

"No worries. We'll get you there." He gave her leg a reassuring pat. "Follow my finger again. We're going back to Denebola—our original star. Still with me?"

"Yes."

"Now let's shoot straight down. See that planet?"

"Can I actually see the red?"

"Yes. Keep your eye on it so you can find it with the binoculars."

Mia located Mars and laughed with excitement. "This is so cool."

"Welcome to my world." He hugged her.

"I've never done this before." She panned away, then back and wondered if she'd be able to find it again without his help.

"I couldn't tell," he teased and was rewarded with an elbow to the solar plexus. After a beat, he pointed out the faint arc spanning horizon to horizon.

"See the dusty curve across there?" His arm followed it.

"Yes."

"Focus on it."

"Whoa," she said with a breath of wonder.

"That's the Milky Way, our galaxy. Just imagine, we're only one of those specks within that mess of specks—from any other point of light, indistinguishable from the rest."

"Incredible." She raised the binoculars again and exclaimed, "Hey, there's a plane *way* up there!"

Curt laughed, shaking her gently. "You've just had your virgin satellite sighting."

"Really? Cool."

She passed the binoculars back so he could focus on his own points of interest. Just when she was starting to understand the appeal of stargazing, a dark shadow swooped over their heads. She shrieked and ducked, cowering against him.

"Was that a bat? I think it was a bat."

"You're okay. Calm down. They're not interested in us." His soothing teacher voice was back. "I put bat boxes all around this field to attract them. They're extremely beneficial. You wouldn't believe how many insects a single bat can eat in one night."

She shrank again as another flew a few feet in front of them. While she continued to scan for more bats, he went back on topic.

"It's too bad we aren't outside the glow of the city. That's when you'd really get a shock at how much it interferes with night sky viewing. Sure, I could set up a telescope," he went on. "But even with a nebula filter, visibility isn't great and the stars themselves will look dimmer."

He eased down on his back and took Mia with him. "Fortunately, there's a movement now to reduce light pollution and shade or direct city lights downward where they belong. Without government involvement though, astronomers face real challenges with their big telescopes."

Mia turned over and kissed him, effectively cutting off his lecture.

He ruffled her hair and laughed. "Enough?"

"For now."

"Okay." His smile was barely visible when he asked, "Wanna fool around?"

"You read my mind."

Mia curled over him, molding her body to his as they kissed. Curt's hand came up behind her head and locked her mouth to his and the kiss deepened, leaving her breathless. She could feel him thicken and grow under her pubis. Inspired, she rubbed against him, more than ready to take things to the next level.

"This time, I'm on top," she informed him in a sexy purr and sat up to straddle him.

He gave her an encouraging bump from underneath. "Whatever makes you happy." He fished his hands up the front of her shirt and gave her breasts a rousing squeeze.

"Mmm. You do that so right." She leaned into his palms with a throaty moan.

"Um, Mia? You're crushing me."

"What? Sorry!" Horrified she'd hurt him, she slid back enough to take her weight off of his restricted erection and allow her access. "This should make you feel better," she promised and drew the tab down to give him a little relief.

She was just running her thumb teasingly over the bulge swelling out of his fly when a black shadow dive-bombed her head. Mia screamed and dove for the blanket. She flattened out on her stomach next to him. "Fucking bats!"

The sexy mood now completely blown, Curt sighed, tucked himself back, and zipped up. "Well, it was a nice thought. But I guess this isn't happening tonight. Come on." He climbed to his feet and waved her off the blanket.

She rolled to the side, but kept her head down. "Don't fold it. I'm going to hide under it."

Laughing, he dropped it over her. "It's yours. Maybe I'll take you to visit the planetarium instead."

Mia got pretty warm under the heavy blanket. But as she warily scoped the sky for more flying rodents—and yes, she knew bats weren't technically rodents—she still preferred it to going back to the school without it.

She waited just inside the door while Curt returned the binoculars and blanket to his classroom then locked it again. He tested the outer doors to be sure they locked automatically behind them.

"I'll follow you on our way back. You should

wear something reflective next time we do this. I don't want you to get hit. I'm easier to see."

Mia couldn't help but think *my hero* as she threw her leg over her bicycle.

Was it any wonder she'd fallen for him?

♡

There was a light glowing in Casey's room when they rode up the driveway. The rest of the house was dark. Mia walked her bike into the garage and set her helmet on the shelf behind it.

"I wish..." she said softly and turned to him.

"Yeah, me too."

Curt tipped her chin up and kissed her. Mia slid her arms around his waist, then down to cup his muscular derrière.

"When can we work something out?" he asked. "I want to spend a full night with you and not have to flee in the morning like a criminal."

She smiled and rolled her forehead against his chin. "I'd love that."

He drew back and kissed her again while swaying her gently in his arms. "This weekend."

"This weekend?"

"Can you arrange it? I'll make reservations."

"I'll pick you up from school."

He smiled, clearly excited at the idea. "Can we really do this?"

"I hope so. I'll call Greg tomorrow and see if I

can arrange something. He might even offer to take Casey Saturday night too."

"He'd have my undying gratitude."

Mia laughed. "Mine too. I can't wait."

Sinking into another heady kiss, neither seemed eager to part.

She drew back with disappointment and concern. "Are you sure you'll be safe riding home? It's pretty dark out."

"I'll be fine." His perfect smile glowed.

She walked him to his bike and her heart fell as he slipped on his helmet. He was going. He had to, of course, but she didn't have to like it.

He straddled the bar then reached for her hand and squeezed it. "I had a great day with you."

"Me too." Her hand felt cold, heavy when he let go.

As Curt rolled down the driveway, she called softly after him, "Be safe."

"I will. Goodnight, Mia."

She turned away, the ache in her chest already unbearable. How could she miss him this much? He just left! He was just leaving *now* and she felt devastated? This was awful. She was in way over her head. *Her head?* No. Way over her heart.

Worried at the prospect of more unsettling dreams to come, she went back into the house, afraid of facing her empty bed alone.

Chapter 24

With the end of the school year right around the corner, Mia only got to see Curt once that following week, and that was for a hasty meal Monday night before he ran back to the school to set up for his classes the next day. He was simply too busy to give her anything else at the moment, what with a flurry of late assignments coming in, reviewing the last quarter with his classes, setting pop quizzes, and planning his final test. She had to cope without him.

It wasn't easy. Now she understood the full and unpleasant meaning of the expression pining. She was pining for her lover—big time.

Every evening she took her phone into her bedroom when she turned in, knowing Curt would call to say goodnight. It was his Tuesday call that transformed every one afterwards into a sexy little secret between them. There was an understanding now that they'd both be in bed by then.

"What color is it?" he asked softly.

Mia pressed the phone against her ear with her shoulder and pulled her bedside drawer open. Her hand closed around the vibrator hidden inside. "Baby blue."

"Is it loud?"

"Not under the covers."

"Put it under the covers and turn it on. I want to

see if I can hear it."

She did and held her breath, waiting for the verdict before finally asking, "Well?"

"Pretty quiet. Make a little noise for me."

"I always do."

"I know. I love it." God, that seductive tone of his always got her going.

Mia laughed. "What are *you* doing?"

"Wishing this was your hand and that was me between your legs. Pretend it's me, okay?"

"That would take a stretch of the imagination."

"What can I do to help?"

"Talk me through this?"

"Squeeze your breast and tell me what you feel like under the covers."

"Soft, wet, swollen, yet empty at the same time."

"We can't have that. Turn it back on."

She gave the vibrator a twist and it hummed to life.

"Good girl. Let's make you moan. Moan for me, Mia."

♡

With her romantic weekend coming up, Mia dragged Sally to the spa with her Thursday right after work. They were separated for their body treatments, but afterwards sat together for facials and pedicures.

"I could get used to this," said Sally, blissing out over their foot massages, a white wine spritzer in her hand.

"It's decadent, but what the hell? I'm worth it," Mia agreed with a lazy laugh.

"Curt better appreciate all the work you're going through for him here."

Mia smiled. "No doubt. We suffer for beauty."

"That's right." Sally took another sip.

Mia held up the bottle of polish in her hand and nodded slowly. "You know, I'm going to like this on my nails. You're right about the darker shade for my toes too. It's gonna look great." She handed the second bottle back to the woman exfoliating her feet.

"I like the reds better myself, but those work on you."

Mia slowly sobered. "This is weird. My life has changed so much since I met Curt."

"He's so *hot*."

Mia laughed. "He is. He really is."

Sally looked at the woman working the scrubbing cream up and down her calf and explained. "Mia's got herself a boy toy."

The woman grinned. "Lucky you."

Mia didn't appreciate Sally's characterization of her relationship. "Curt's not a boy toy. He's almost thirty." *In two years.* Sally gave her a long look and Mia buckled. "Well, thirty*ish*."

"I don't know why that bothers you. He...is...prime."

There was no denying that assessment.

♡

It was Curt's last period before the big weekend. He leaned back against his desk with his legs outstretched and watched the students file in. When the kids noticed all the stools were moved across the room away from their lab tables, the noise level rose by two decibels.

Curt stood up and all eyes turned to him, their chatter dying out.

"You'll notice there are four stations set up at each table and on the counter behind you. Every station is numbered to coincide with the questions on your test sheets. When you get to the specimens, you'll see there are numbered flags on every pin stuck in them. Name the organs and explain the function. No cheating and no copying. I'll be watching closely." He circled one of the tables, making eye contact here and there as he walked between the kids. "You have three minutes to answer your questions before I hit the buzzer and move you to the next station. Everyone should move in numeric order. There will be no skipping around. If you begin at station eighteen, you will move on to nineteen and so on until you've hit every station in order. Time is short, people. Leave your books and bags on the stools. Mindy, Brian, the tests are stacked on the counter behind you. Please take one and pass them around."

Once everyone was in position, Curt nodded.

"Begin." He hit the buzzer and clicked the stopwatch in his hand.

Then he sat down on the edge of his desk and gave the kids half his attention. Okay, so he fibbed a little, but monitoring a test wasn't exactly the most demanding part of his job so he could afford to let his mind drift off and on to Mia.

What was she was doing right now? He conjured a picture of her typing away on her computer or answering her phone. He smiled when he imagined her abandoned shoes tipped on edge under her desk. She wanted to curl her legs up underneath her, but with a skirt on, she had to settle for flexing her nylon-encased toes instead. Maybe she was staring off into space, absently tapping a pen on a stack of papers, as lost in thought as he was.

Curt glanced at the time. There was less than a minute to go so he waited it out and hit the buzzer.

"Next station." He reset the stopwatch once the kids were ready then slid back into his own reveries.

Was Mia thinking about him too? He saw this weekend as a significant step in their deepening relationship, a major indication of their feelings for each other. They were on the same page, right? It wasn't just about the sex. No question, he was looking forward to the sex, but being naked with her was also a euphemism for opening himself emotionally too. Did she understand that? He was ready to connect with her on every level, without barriers. It was a big step, maybe even a premature step, but it felt right.

He stopped the watch and hit the buzzer. "Time."

Curt wasn't the type to pursue women casually, nor did he engage in promiscuous sex, though he could have. Easily. The opportunities were certainly there. But he was too smart, too cautious to gamble with his health. And, like it or not, he never could view sex as a simple bodily function. He didn't understand how some people could divorce their emotions from something so intimate, so he'd cared, to some degree, for every woman he'd slept with.

As a teacher, he couldn't afford to be cavalier about his conduct in that regard either, even if he wanted to. No, he was his mother's son, a romantic at heart. He wanted to fall in love like his parents had and be loved for who he was, *what* he was. He never realized how hard it could be to find that. Now at twenty-eight he knew better. His face drew women, but his convictions, his feelings weren't as acceptable to them. Every woman in his past had wanted to catch him then gradually change him.

"Time."

The teenage shuffle around the tables continued, as did the stopwatch in his hand.

Curt wondered if Mia could fall for him. Could she truly care about *him* with no maternal agenda driving her interest? Would he finally be enough for a woman as a man, a lover, a friend, a partner? Was she the woman who would see him as more than a warm body to throw into an adjustable tuxedo all for the inevitable purposes of contributing half his DNA to the future generation? He hoped so. He was already nursing a serious crush and he wanted to be open, share everything up front with her so there weren't any surprises between them. He was ready to blow his caution all to hell for this woman. It was—

"Time."

♡

The buses were long gone when Mia pulled into the school parking lot to meet Curt. The sun hit him full-on as he walked out of the building and her heart skittered erratically. Anticipation of their intimate weekend ahead made her wriggle in her seat, her body suddenly warmer than moments ago. With his pack slung over one shoulder and that sexy smile, he dazzled her.

"Hi, gorgeous." He climbed into the passenger side and reached across to cup her cheek and plant a delicious kiss on her. The warmth inside her spread to every extremity. Her panties clung.

"Mmm." She drew back slowly so she could focus on his wonderful face. "Are you ready?"

He buckled his seatbelt. "Ready? I'm stoked," he said with a devilish laugh.

Amused, she grinned and pulled out of the parking lot. "I guess we go to your apartment first?"

"Yes. My bag is packed and waiting right inside

the door."

"Good. I don't want to sit outside getting weird looks from your neighbors."

"What? They're harmless."

"I'm sure. But it's embarrassing."

"Ah." Now he understood what she meant. "You're remembering your teakettle impression."

"It might have crossed my mind."

He rubbed her leg and made a suggestion. "We could give them an encore—just for kicks."

"I don't think so."

She pulled up along the curb in front of his apartment building a few minutes later and Curt hopped out. He was back in a flash with his bag and they continued on to her house.

"Just wait 'til you see what I've got planned," he told her with a promising smile.

Chapter 25

When they got to the house, Curt hopped into the shower while Mia refreshed her makeup. It was a pretty flimsy and transparent excuse to watch his naked reflection enticingly displayed behind the rippled glass without being completely obvious about it. Still, he wasn't fooled.

"You know, you could join me," he suggested.

"If I get in there with you, we're going to miss our reservation," she said touching up her lipstick.

"But it would be worth it."

She turned to enjoy the show. "True. But I didn't starve myself all day just so you could beg off on dinner at the last minute, no matter how tempting the reason. Now hurry up."

"She wants her dinner." He turned off the water and slid the door open.

Mia tossed him a towel. "And cover yourself, quick before I lose what little backbone I have."

He laughed and wrapped the towel around his hips as she hustled out.

Ten minutes later she looked up from the magazine she was skimming and just about swooned when Curt emerged, dressed and ready to go. The only thing better than looking at him was getting close enough to touch him. She tossed the magazine back onto the coffee table and sauntered seductively over to meet him.

Mia's hands rode up his chest and she nuzzled close. Then her eyes widened in surprise and she felt the fabric more carefully. "What are you wearing? It's so soft."

"Bamboo."

"I've heard of it." She touched him some more. "Nice."

He laughed and offered his arm. "Shall we?"

"So where are you taking me?" she asked as they strolled out.

"The Coral Reef." He pulled up short, his eyes wide. "Oh shit. I never asked if you can eat, or even *like,* seafood. You're not allergic, are you?"

Amused, she reassured him. "No. I love it."

He playfully mopped his brow with the back of his hand. "Whew."

♡

Though Mia knew the Coral Reef by reputation, she'd never been there. The interior was tastefully designed using built-in tropical fish tanks to break up the space into smaller sections. The color of the walls reminded her of warm sand. The woodwork was even warmer browns. The setting managed to bring her first ever Curt fantasy back in a sexy rush. She'd imagined him on a beach, then emerging from the surf, a wet and wonderful piece of eye candy.

He noticed her mysterious smile and returned it

without a hint of suspicion at what prompted it.

They were seated at the long, gracefully curved bar. Right away, Curt ordered two plum and white wine infusions then sat back with an air of contentment and grazed the top of her hand with his fingers.

"What do you think so far?" he asked.

"It's beautiful." Mia looked up from the menu. "I need a translator."

"I'll help you order."

He told her he'd asked to be seated at the bar when he phoned in their reservation, though she didn't understand why until they were front and center for the culinary show. Two men, wielding utensils and wickedly sharp knives, chopped and sautéed until the delectable aromas had Mia's mouth watering.

"Are you interested in an appetizer?" Curt asked.

"That's a big *yes*. But I don't know what I'm even looking at here," she answered helplessly.

Smiling, he drew the menu out of her hands and gently closed it. "Will you trust me?"

How could she resist an appealing appeal like that? She nodded.

When their drinks arrived, Curt ordered something that sounded ominously like Harumaki. Mia wanted to have an open mind about everything, but watching some of the strange things thrown together in front of her was bringing her out in a sweat. Science lab all over again.

Her handsome date raised his glass and prompted her to do the same. They tapped them together and he made a toast. "To a beautiful weekend and a beautiful woman." The look in his luscious eyes underlined his words in bold. "Go on. Try it."

Blushing now, she took a sip and was pleasantly surprised. "Hmm. It reminds me of a wine cooler."

"Would I steer you wrong?"

"I guess not." She laughed.

Their server stopped back and Curt went into action, scrolling down the menu with his finger and selecting for them both. A few minutes later a plate of spring rolls was set between them along with two side plates and dipping sauce.

"Egg rolls?" she asked with relief. "You ordered egg rolls?"

"Their version anyway." He chuckled. "You'll enjoy these."

She took a careful bite and nodded with approval. "Good call."

They ate with their fingers, gingerly, because it was incredibly hot and there wasn't any silverware, only chopsticks on the counter in tall decorative jars.

Then their appetizer plates were cleared away and their entrées placed in front of them. Curt plucked two sets of chopsticks out of the jar and handed her one.

"Um, I don't *do* chopsticks," she informed him.

"Have you ever tried them?"

"Once. It was a disaster."

"When was that?"

"I was a teenager."

"You might be better at it now. Come on, give it a try."

Grimacing with trepidation, she took the set he held out to her and carefully copied his finger placement.

"No. Hold the bottom stick stationary. Bring the top stick to it. Like this." He adjusted her hold and guided the motion. Three hands didn't seem to be enough to help her.

When she felt marginally ready she attempted to pick up a crunchy looking battered thing on her plate and nearly sent it across the counter. Only Curt's quick grab saved it from landing on the floor. They were both laughing when he dropped it onto his plate and picked it up the right way so he could feed it to her.

"Fried shrimp!" she exclaimed with a big smile.

"Tempura," he corrected with a wink. "Like it?"

"Love it. Can I eat with my fingers now?"

"What about the rice?"

Her heart sank. Yeah, what? "I don't know."

"Hang on." Chuckling, he raised his arm and motioned an employee over. "Can we get a fork for the lady, please?"

"Sure. No problem." The young man went to get her one.

With fork in hand, Mia was able to enjoy her

tamari and ginger seared asparagus and her julienne carrots without sending them flying. Every new taste brought an ecstatic moan and a big smile.

"What's that?" she asked, pointing to his vegetable with her fork. "Some type of broccoli?"

"Broccolini."

"Good?"

"Awesome."

"I'll trade you one of my asparagus spears for one of those."

"Deal."

"Everything is so good," she said between fervent bites. "I'm *really* enjoying this."

He chuckled. "I can see that."

"So what's that you're eating?"

"Sashimi. Do you want a taste?"

She looked at it suspiciously and he gave her a little nudge. "Come on. It's good. One bite."

Though she hesitated, a little prodding finally convinced her to try. He picked up a thin slice, dipped it, and then brought it to her mouth, his hand underneath to catch any drips.

Mia took a cautious bite. He smiled patiently while she chewed, his grin growing as her eyes transitioned from reluctance to unabashed wonder.

"Wow. That *is* good," she whispered, shocked and afraid to be overheard and look like an idiot in front of the already initiated.

"See. I'm glad you tried it."

From that point on they shared almost everything on both plates. He ordered her another glass of plum wine while he switched to sake. She was willing to try a taste of that as well, though she found she preferred the wine.

They flirted outrageously through the rest of the meal and finally left the restaurant satisfied, but not uncomfortable.

Curt was doing the driving tonight so Mia had to wait while he personally opened her door and tucked her into the passenger seat. Evidently, he wanted to give her the complete date experience. She felt pampered.

When he got behind the wheel, she turned with a contented smile. "Dinner was amazing. Thank you."

He started the engine and smiled back. "My pleasure. You've fed me a lot lately. I wanted to do something special in return."

"Well, it was new to me."

"No!" He feigned surprise.

She laughed and swatted him on the arm. "Cut it out."

He chuckled. "If you're good, this won't be the only pleasant surprise you get tonight."

"Ooo. Mr. Mysterious."

"Just you wait."

It was strange to see someone else in her driver's seat. Giving up the keys back at the house wasn't easy for her. She didn't know what kind of driver he was.

However, it didn't take him long to reassure her. Now, merely a passenger on his magic carpet evening, she was finally able to relax and enjoy how it felt to let someone else take charge for a change. Her discovery that she actually liked Curt in this role was an even bigger revelation. But she trusted him implicitly now—with her vehicle, her safety, her son, and her body. Her heart, she held in reserve.

Oh, it was his. No doubt about it. He'd seduced it away from her some time ago. But that didn't mean she felt safe telling him. That admission would give him too much power over her. Feeling every chink he took out of her protective armor, Mia simply wasn't ready to remove it and hand it to him. He'd already disarmed her. Why make it easier for him to wound her?

They pulled into the garage and Curt cut the engine. As the door rolled closed behind them, he released his seatbelt and turned. Without a word, they moved together for a heated kiss.

Eventually easing back, he gave her an intriguing smile. "Come on. Your surprise is in the house."

"What are you up to?" she asked and hopped out of the truck.

Smiling, he kept his secret as he ushered her in.

"Wait right here." He left her standing between the kitchen and the dining area.

Okay, she was more than a little curious now. He returned with a small gift wrapped package and held it out to her.

"Oh." Melting, she touched her chest. "You bought me a present?"

"To make up for the light bulbs."

She laughed. "You didn't have to do that."

"I know. But I wanted to. Open it."

He seemed even more excited to see her open the present than she was. It must be good.

The paper came away in her hand and she stared into the little box. "Is this what I think it is?"

"I thought we could add to your collection. I understand these are pretty popular. Besides, I'm not looking to be replaced." At her blush, he explained, "I just thought it might be fun to incorporate it this weekend. I figured after our nightly phone calls recently, we've basically answered the electronics question."

Hard to argue with that. Mia wandered over to the table and set her purse and gift down. He followed and wrapped his arms around her, pressing tight against her back.

"You don't have one of these already, do you?" He nuzzled the side of her neck and Mia sagged into him.

"Not one of those."

"Then this really is a night of firsts for you."

"You could say that." She succumbed to the seductive pull of his mouth on her ear.

He was already hard. Aware and aroused by it,

she rubbed and ground against him. Humming low and deep, Curt slid his hands up the front of her shirt and unclasped her bra. Her breasts dropped free, but he was there to catch them. Gripping her firmly, he pulled her against him with deep, mind-numbing squeezes. Mia felt her limbs go slack, her back arch. She suddenly needed his support.

"I can't think when you do that," she said with a low groan.

"Is that a complaint?" he asked, a knowing chuckle behind the question.

"An observation."

His hand flowed down to her hip and the side zipper that ran along the seam. She let out a helpless gasp when he popped the button and took hold of the tab.

Licking behind her ear, he murmured, "Should I continue?"

"I think you'd better."

He laughed softly and squeezed her nipple, drawing it out as he pulled the zipper down.

"You feel incredibly soft," he whispered, his warm breath tickling her ear.

She shivered. "I had a body treatment yesterday."

"Nice."

Sally would be thrilled to hear he appreciated the effort. *Later*.

Using both hands, he eased her skirt down her hips. When it dropped to the floor, he stepped back in surprise. “I like the hosiery.” He ran his finger over the wide lace tops of her thigh highs.

“I thought you might,” she said, pleased.

“Keep them on.” He ran his hands up and down her thighs with approval. “Oh yeah, I definitely like these.”

As he relieved her of her lacy panties, she shed her blouse and bra and dropped them with the rest of her discarded clothing.

“This is an image I’ll never forget.” He stroked his hands down her arms and took a long, flattering look at her. “Thigh highs and a smile—gorgeous.”

The look in his eyes was intense, smoldering. She knew she was running out of time. Pulling him in by the front of his shirt, she went to work on the buttons. Equally motivated, Curt popped his fly and slid his trousers off while she peeled his shirt away, freeing one arm at a time. He kicked his pants aside and sent his loafers flying at the same time.

Naked, they both stood back and took a moment to drink each other in. Mia’s nipples tightened under his bold stare. He grew visibly harder under hers.

Tension seemed to stretch and pulse between them until whatever force held them back suddenly snapped and they sprang together. The hard slap of their naked bodies drove Mia back against the tabletop. His right hand locked behind her head as their mouths sealed. His left snaked around her waist and held her flush against him.

Even with a week of fantasizing about being in his arms again, Mia wasn't prepared for the violent yearning she felt as their tongues and loins fought for the finite space between them. She was going to give way. There was nothing she wanted more urgently than to yield to him because, even in surrender, there was triumph.

The hand behind her head eased off and his heavy lidded eyes drew back. Without warning, Curt lifted her off her feet and set her on the table. He used his body to coax her down on her back, squeezing and kissing her breasts and nipples the entire way.

Slowly working south, he spread her knees farther apart then dipped to taste her. With lips and tongue, he pleasured her; though it was clear he relished it as much as she did.

Already familiar with how much she liked it, he brushed his rough cheek along her sensitive inner thigh and watched with unmistakable enjoyment as she broke out in goose bumps. Their eyes connected and the hungry look that passed between them spoke volumes. Curt stroked down her silky stockings, caught hold of her ankles, and raised her legs to his chest. She watched all this with rapt anticipation, her breathing shallow, and her sexy pumps in the air. Then, with gentle pressure, he tugged her to the very edge of the table and penetrated her.

"Yes!" Mia arched back with a groan of relief.

Smiling, he closed his eyes for a quiet beat to

savor their connection. "I love how you feel around me. Warm and snug. Mmm."

"I want to touch you, but I can't like this," she whispered, hating to interrupt his moment.

His dark lashes swept open and he shook his head. "It's okay."

Resigned for now, she focused instead on the exquisite sensations of him moving in and out of her. She was being invaded, stretched, and deliciously filled. The pleasure was so intense, she quivered.

He noticed and gave her thigh a squeeze. Pressing forward again, deeper this time, he said, "I can't get enough of you. I'm blown away by it. Do you know what I mean?"

All she could manage was a whispered, "Yes."

The pure bliss on his face expressed exactly what she felt as he thrust and rolled his hips in deep, lazy circles. Reaching out, he caressed her breast. She covered his hand and they laced their fingers together.

Mia flexed toward him, her bottom rising off the tabletop. She turned her head and smiled at where she was. "I'll never be able to eat here again without thinking of this."

He chuckled. "I was thinking the same thing."

Every time he withdrew, her body seemed to sink with disappointment. But then he'd reverse and press into her again and suddenly everything was right with the world.

Curt was in no mood to rush. She could tell he

savored every sensation as he fed himself to her one easy glide at a time. Mia couldn't say the same. She was ready to fly, with or without him. He'd brought her up, now it was time to let go of her damn parachute and allow her to jump. Hoping to spur him on, she began to reward his faster, harder drives with an encouraging clench.

He took the hint. The tempo of his thrusts increased, as did the force behind them. Her excitement off the charts, she strained to take every glorious inch of him and felt the quickening in her chest, the flutter in her belly.

"Mia." Hearing the anticipation in his voice, she focused on him. "Pick up your toy." He spread her legs like a fan and gave her an encouraging nod.

The thought of using a vibrator in front of him made her cheeks flame with heat. No. It would be too embarrassing. She couldn't. Could she?

He gave her a quick jab and she gasped with pleasure.

"Try it, Mia. Come for me. There's no reason to be afraid or ashamed. It's just us." He locked eyes with her and kissed the inside of her calf.

Still uneasy, she reached back and picked it up. She held her breath, twisted it on, and then slid it slowly down her body. She could see the tension in Curt's face. The muscles in his neck and shoulders stood out tight and defined. His biceps bulged. No question he was having a hard time holding back.

“Go on. Touch yourself.” He plunged deep and drove a gust of air right out of her lungs.

Bashful and tentative, she touched the buzzing vibrator to her clit—and screamed.

Her body exploded in a shattering orgasm that set her bucking and convulsing so violently on the table she actually kicked Curt back. Out of control, her head slammed against the wood surface and she yelped again as pain and pleasure rode her thrashing central nervous system without a saddle.

The speed, the power of her climax, shocked the hell out of them both.

Equally amused and amazed, Curt helped her sit up then rubbed the back of her smarting scalp.

“Well, that was interesting. I guess we learned we should confine toys to the bedroom.” He started to chuckle. “Are you okay?”

Okay? She was delirious.

“I never expected—” Her voice trailed off in wonder.

“I know.” He kissed her on the forehead. “That wasn’t so bad, was it?”

“Not bad?” She laughed and slapped him on the bare ass. “Can we take this into my room?”

There was triumph in his eyes when he stepped back and tugged her to her feet. “Lead the way.”

Chapter 26

They made love differently this time. Mia insisted. Unable to forget their aborted starlit encounter on the blanket a week ago, she was determined to reclaim the seat of power tonight. She brought him back by hand and mouth first then rose over him and sank slowly, taking him into her body. The deep plunge was so exquisite they both groaned.

He gave her an encouraging nod and urged her on as he kneaded her breasts and she proceeded to move on top of him.

It felt good, so good, but the position began to exhaust her. He could feel her, hot and swollen around him, but her breathing was labored. Her head hung lank, her pretty face obscured by her hair. The nails that had lightly teased his chest hair now scored his skin.

"You've got this, honey. You're almost there. I can feel it."

She shook her head from side to side and denied it. "I don't think I'm going to come this way."

He could feel his own climax gaining on him and didn't want to finish without her.

"Let's see." He reached for her toy and slipped it under her.

Mia's orgasm was instantaneous and just as spectacular as the first. It brought her crashing down on him, her sex contracting around him.

Unable to hold off any longer, he threw the toy aside, planted his hands and heels on the mattress, and drove straight up into her and gave Mia's hungry body something to swallow.

Then, their energy spent, they collapsed to the bed and held each other, their chests rising and falling as they panted for air.

He was shaking as much as she was. Amused by it, he laughed at himself and wrapped her even closer. They settled in for the night, their breathing gradually slowing as they drifted off to sleep.

♡

Curt woke up alone the next morning. Yawning and stretching, he spun and found the floor with his bare feet. Only now did he notice the extra blanket on the bed. Mia must have put it over him when she got up because it wasn't there when they...when they...hot damn, they were something last night!

Chuckling softly, he smiled and scrubbed his face with both hands and basked in the wonder of it all over again. He could still smell her on him. *Mmm.*

His bag was on the floor in the corner and he went over to it and pulled on the pair of plaid pajama bottoms he'd brought, sans underwear, and his gray t-shirt before padding into the bathroom.

He could smell the bacon all the way down the hall when he came out. Making his way to the kitchen, he found her. She looked gloriously mussed. *I did that*, he thought proudly. There was a light in her eyes, a glow to her cheeks, and her smile was off the charts.

He gave her an intimate smile of his own. "Is that coffee?"

"I'll get you a cup."

"I can get it." He didn't want her waiting on him. He opened the cupboard and chose a mug. "I'd rather be gardening?" He turned it to her and grinned.

She laughed. "Sally found that one for me. Irony, don't you know."

"Ah." He filled the mug and set the pot back down. Bringing it to his nose, he inhaled the rich aroma. "How long have you been up?"

She was in the middle of turning the bacon with a fork so it took her a second to answer him.

"Thirty minutes maybe?"

She put the fork down. He set his mug aside and opened his arms. She walked right into them without hesitation and melted against him. They held each other for a full minute, simply needing to get their first touch of the day out of the way.

Finally, Mia stepped back and kissed him lightly on the lips. "How do you like your eggs?"

"Over easy."

"Perfect."

"Should I make the toast?"

"That'd be great. Bread's in the drawer there." She pointed.

He pulled the toaster out and stuffed all four slots. Since he had time, he retrieved his coffee and took a heady swallow. "Ahh. That's better."

"You need your morning coffee, do you?"

"I need my *everything* coffee. Let me remind you that the first time we undressed each other with our eyes was in a coffee shop."

"You didn't undress me." She brushed off the very notion with a roll of her eyes.

"I had you in panties, garter belt, and a smile, sweetheart."

Poised to light the burner under the second frying pan, she turned, her hand frozen on the knob. "Seriously?"

He raised his eyebrows. "Would it bother you?"

"No."

To his delight, she blushed and turned away, adjusting the flame under the egg pan as a flimsy excuse to avoid eye contact.

"You're better than the fantasy, Mia."

"So are you," she said softly, her head still down.

Curt walked over and moved her hair aside so he could kiss the nape of her neck.

"Are you sure you want to start that again?" she asked, shivering against him.

He didn't get a chance to respond because the toaster buzzed and tossed the four slices into the air.

"Damn thing jumps like you did last night." He laughed and went to pick up the toast.

"And you," she reminded him.

"And me," he agreed.

They lingered over breakfast, simply talking for another hour.

"Didn't you say you had a sister?" she asked him.

"I do." He traced the top of his mug with his index finger. "Heidi's one year younger and three years older—give or take."

"Huh?"

"Well, at least through our teens. Girls tend to mature faster than boys. Believe me, I've seen it firsthand."

Mia laughed. "Okay. I get it now. What's Heidi's story?"

"She's currently a stay at home mom. Jeffrey's going on three," he added with an affectionate smile. "And wife to Jason. That's a strong marriage."

"They're lucky."

"We had a good example, so I guess we both have high expectations."

"Do you see your family much?"

"Not as often as I'd like, or should." He tipped his cup to see how much cold coffee was left in the bottom then set it back down and slid it away with a sigh.

"I can make another pot," she offered.

"Nah. I've probably had enough caffeine." He kicked back in his chair and relaxed. "What about you? Any siblings?"

"I wish." Her shoulders sank. "My mom had several miscarriages after I was born. The doctors eventually recommended a hysterectomy."

"Are your parents in the area?"

"They moved to Portland nine years ago. They hardly know Casey, though they try to keep in touch with him by phone. He's a lot closer to Greg's parents. We both are."

"You still talk to his parents?" He was surprised.

"All the time. I love them." Smiling, she changed the subject. "What should we do today?"

"Would it bother you if I said absolutely nothing? I just want to be with you." *Bond with you.* "That's it. We can fill in the details as we go."

"That sounds wonderful. I'm all yours, income-municado to everyone else for the weekend."

"That's exactly what I wanted to hear."

Their eyes met and held for several beats before she looked away and announced, "Well, the kitchen won't clean itself."

"You cooked so I'll take care of the dishes."

"Really? Thanks. I guess I'll go run a comb through my hair and brush my teeth." She picked up the jam and honey on her way out.

Curt collected the plates and followed. "Tell you what." He set the stack in the sink and opened the dishwasher. "I'll make lunch and we'll have dinner delivered."

"The only thing we can get delivered around here

is pizza or Chinese and I'm not really interested in either."

"Hmm," he said thoughtfully. "Maybe we can make a quick run to the store and bring something back."

"I like how your mind works."

He gave her a wicked smile. "I noticed."

Mia laughed. "I'll see you in a few."

♡

They went outside so Mia could water her window boxes and her newer plantings. Curt pitched in and filled the various bird feeders around the yard for her. Afterwards, they relaxed with a few games of backgammon before retiring to the sofa.

Mia sprawled on top of him and finally began the romance they'd bought together. It was soothing to hear his steady heartbeat under her ear while he rubbed lazy circles on her back.

She found it amusing he'd brought his fantasy along too. With his arms around her, he read his book behind her head. When necessary, he'd lift his warm hand to turn a page then resume rubbing her back again. It was heaven.

"Hey. Tell me when you reach a juicy part, okay?" he said out of the blue.

She shifted to look at him. "Why?"

"So you can read it to me." He grinned, not remotely apologetic.

"I'd rather not. I don't like to read aloud."

"Then I'll read it to you."

"Seriously? You'd do that?"

"If it gets you hot? Damn right I will."

She laughed. "But you already get me *hot*."

"What's your temperature right now?" He placed his hand on her forehead and feigned concern.

"I think I'm running a fever," she said in a breathy, sexy voice.

"You're burning up," he agreed. "Smoking."

"Maybe I'm catching something."

He chuckled and corrected her. "No. You've *caught* something. Me." Then, tossing his book aside, he dragged her up his body so he could kiss her properly. She loved it when his legs came around her and completed the embrace.

"Something on your mind, Mr. Walden?"

"I'm getting hungry."

"Anything I can do?"

"I was hoping you'd ask."

Thirty minutes later, they returned the upset coffee table to its usual place then Curt collapsed onto the couch, taking Mia with him.

"This is going to be one hell of a weekend." Her limbs were like jelly, her head still spinning as she sank on top of him.

It took him a second to catch his breath before he agreed. "I can't fault how it's going so far."

A happy little laugh escaped her as they snuggled.

Contentment, on a scale she'd never experienced, permeated her body. She could almost imagine it modifying her DNA.

No. It was dangerous to experience this level of bliss. She mentally pushed back at it, afraid to acknowledge the feeling for what it was. It was easier to accept that these were live-in-the-moment experiences with Curt, nothing more. She couldn't afford to build castles in the air. Taking that reminder to heart, she did allow herself to admit, "I'm glad you're staying over."

His arms tightened around her and he kissed the top of her head. "Me too."

Hearing that was enough for her. It had to be.

♡

Curt didn't mean to doze off later in the day, but when he woke, all he wanted to do was hold Mia while she slept. Her cheek looked so soft. It would be nice to touch it, but worse to disturb her. There was a little smudge of mascara under her eyes, a hint of shadow. He liked it. Resting here in her bed together was a simple pleasure, but a seductive one. He could imagine making it a habit. Unfortunately, he had to move. The call of nature was an indifferent task master. He eased out of bed and quietly left the room.

She was just coming around when he lifted the sheet and slipped back in beside her.

"I must have dropped off." She covered a yawn.

"I wore you out," he said, pleased about it.

"You did." She wore a lazy smile and nothing else. "But that was the idea this weekend, right?"

"Screw until we can't walk anymore?"

She wriggled against him and flicked her tongue across his collarbone. "Mmm-hmm."

He smiled, rolled on top of her, and burrowed between her legs. His erection probed for entry and she flexed up to welcome him home. "We're gluttons for punishment."

♡

The early evening sun was angling through the leafy canopy above the deck when Mia wandered outside. She tossed the deck of cards onto the table and indulged in a luxuriant stretch. She suddenly realized with a smile that the world was a beautiful, wonderful, glorious place. Had she ever felt so loose and relaxed in her life?

Of course they'd completely missed their lunch—by a few hours. Now they were starving. With this appetite, she decided even pizza was doable. At least clean up would be a snap afterwards.

She dropped lazily into one of the deck chairs and winced. Note to self: ease down next time. She glanced up when Curt walked out carrying two glasses of red wine. He handed her one and bent to kiss the top of her head before taking the opposite chair.

She brought the glass to her nose and inhaled the

complex bouquet. “Good choice. Would you care to shuffle?”

“Sure.” He took a sip of wine first, then picked up the cards and tapped them out of the box. She watched him cut the deck in two.

It was nutty, more than a little ridiculous, but Mia loved the way he shuffled. Why stop there? She loved pretty much everything he did. A fresh lick of lust flared deep inside of her and she tried to tamp it back down.

Not now, for god’s sake!

She’d just finished thoroughly using and abusing the poor guy. Give him a little time to recover his strength. She was sick. That’s all there was to it. She was a sick little momma.

“Who won last time?” he asked, dealing the cards as smoothly as he did so many other delightful things.

I want him again.

“Do you remember?” he asked, startling her.

“Hmm?”

There was comprehension in his little smile. “Who won our last game?”

“I did.” Ignoring her cards for a second, she reached for her wine, hoping she wasn’t throwing accelerant on the flames.

“That’s right.” He set the remainder of the deck face down and flipped the top card. “Are you ready?”

Silly question. She’d always be ready for him.

Curt turned his chair toward her and Mia placed

her bare foot between his knees.

He smiled down at her toes. “Nice polish.”

She flashed her fingernails too. “I went for it.”

“At least four times now,” he said with a chuckle.

“Yeah, but that’s the thing about oral. You eat and twenty minutes later you’re hungry again.”

“Like Chinese food.”

“Exactly!” She raised her glass in agreement.

He laughed and shook his head. “You are the most surprising woman.”

She was enjoying Curt’s attention, enjoying simply watching him wander through her space. She felt his presence in almost every room now. It was comforting, comfortable.

She looked at those long and oh-so-talented fingers holding his cards and her eyes went all soft and dreamy.

God, I love him.

Four simple words that made Mia jolt in alarm because she’d heard them, clear as a bell.

Shit! Did I think *that I love him or did I actually* say *it out loud?*

Chapter 27

"Mia?"

She jumped. "What!"

"It's your turn."

Mentally slapping herself back to her senses, she apologized. "Sorry. I must be hungrier than I thought."

"Food's coming."

But she couldn't lie to herself. When this affair ended she was going to be devastated. This was a beautiful, yet fragile interlude in her life. She had no idea what it would inevitably mean to him. She hoped he would look back on it fondly someday.

But getting involved with Curt was reckless, falling for him, predictable. He was too young for her, or she was too old for him. Either way, she knew it. He had to know it. And the woman who was waiting not very patiently to replace her obviously knew it. Was she making a fool of herself? If she was, the joke was on her, and it was cruel and painful.

Forcing herself to focus on their game, she studied the cards in her hand. She passed on the card face up and drew from the deck. Discard.

He picked it up and dropped an eight of clubs. He was going to win this thing if she didn't pay attention. Her old competitive spirit rallied and she sat forward and casually picked up his ten of hearts. She discarded a two of diamonds.

"So you want tens, eh?" he said, eyeing her speculatively. "Or hearts?"

Giving him a nonchalant shrug, she kept her secrets. She was getting good at it.

He considered his next move as he toyed absently with her foot, the pressure just hard enough not to tickle her. How did he always know exactly how to touch her?

Inspired, she reached out with her foot and did a little toying herself.

"Careful," he warned and gently moved her foot off his groin. "These things are spring loaded."

Mia wiggled her eyebrows suggestively and he laughed. God, she loved that smile of his.

If she got any wetter she was going to slide right off this chair. Just looking at his arms coming out of his rolled up sleeves was foreplay. Her eyes traveled to his open collar and she hungered for another tactile tour of his chest. Mia longed to see his eyes, see the expression in them, but he was looking down so they were hidden by his thick fringe of lashes. Now she knew how his lids tasted, how the soft, delicate skin felt against her lips. Now she knew how his lashes gave way under the gentle brush of her tongue.

Curt placed a card and she admired his hands. They were good hands, strong yet gentle, his long fingers capped by perfectly shaped nails. She remembered, all too vividly, the pleasure those fingers could deliver.

It was too late to fight her way back to sanity. She wanted him again.

He looked up from rearranging his cards and set down two runs. Leaning back with a challenging smile, his eyebrows shot up at the frank expression in her eyes. It was carnal, hungry.

He gave her a wicked grin. "Something tells me you want to take me inside and have your way with me again."

"Is it that obvious?" Her voice was a sexy purr.

He shifted in his chair. "Glaringly. And I'm glad." He set his cards down as he stood.

That's when the doorbell rang.

His eyes fell closed and he sighed. "And here's the pizza."

♡

They ended up cuddling on the sofa after dinner. There, they polished off the first bottle of wine and uncorked a second, though half of that one remained when Mia stood and turned, an unspoken invitation in her eyes. Curt smiled, clicked off the television, and tossed the remote aside.

"It's our last night," she said with a disappointed sigh of as they went to check the lock on the front door.

"I know." He didn't need reminding. The end of this beautiful weekend together hung over him like a heavy cloud. Sadly, life made demands they couldn't ignore. Casey would be back tomorrow and *he* had to go home. Feeling melancholy himself, he wanted to savor what little time they had left.

Curt caught Mia's hand and spun her into his arms and proceeded to sway with her on the hard foyer floor.

She laughed in delight. "I *knew* you could dance."

He brushed her hair back and kissed her lightly. "I'm okay."

"You're better than okay."

He kissed her again for that then turned them into a quick and thrilling spin.

"Mercy." She was captivating, her face glowing. Everything about her touched him.

He went still. "Kiss me."

Mia rose up on her toes and met him halfway. It was sweet. It wasn't what he wanted this time.

"*Kiss* me," he repeated.

His command made her bold and she grabbed him by the head and took him to school for the challenge.

When Mia slowly eased back, she started at the look in his eyes. Did his intensity frighten her? He felt a heady rush of relief at her next words.

"I want you too."

Overpowering lust lashed like lightning between them. No matter how often they fed the desperate hunger, it was never appeased. Desire crackled in the air, sharpened his senses, and made every inch of his body aware of hers.

"Here," he said firmly.

"Here?"

"Right here." He tugged Mia to him by the hem of her shirt and whipped it up over her head. Then, with a burst of laughter, he smoothed her hair back down and tried to tidy her again. "Sorry about that."

Chuckling along, she said, "No problem."

She went for his shirt, her fingers racing down the buttons. He loved the brush of her fingers on his bare skin. She spread his shirt apart and pressed her hands, her lips to his chest. "You feel as good as you look."

Could he get any harder? "How do I taste?"

She ran her tongue across his nipple and said, "Delicious."

Curt took her against the wall, the disarray of their abandoned clothing all around them on the floor.

With every slow, deliberate thrust Mia slid up the wall behind her. He held her pinned between his body and the hard surface as he fed himself to her over and over again. Clinging to him, she held on, her feet hooked behind him as he supported her weight, using it at crucial times to drive even deeper inside her.

He gave her another good, solid bump and licked the side of her neck before locking onto it with a light suction.

"No marks!" she gasped as he drove her up by several inches with his next thrust.

"Don't worry. If I was going to mark you, it would be somewhere no one else would see."

Clearly titillated, she asked, “Like where?” then gasped with his next drive.

“Your inner thigh,” he said on the downslide. “Your luscious breasts.” He locked hips and lips with her again. “Your beautiful ass.” He squeezed both cheeks.

Mia groaned and clenched tight around him. He knew the signs. She was one thrust away from total nuclear meltdown.

“Yes,” he whispered. “Come for me.”

Wanting it, he pulled her down on him as he thrust forcefully up at the same time. Mia’s eyes shot wide and she exploded in his arms with a loud scream of pleasure.

Her powerful climax staggered him and he sank to his knees as her body held him in a grip that threatened to wring him dry. He turned from the wall and lowered her to the floor then, taking full advantage of her rhythmic contractions, quickly joined her in release.

They lay connected, absolutely exhausted and panting for air. Her rapid heartbeat banged against his ribs, an echo of his.

“Don’t expect me to move for a few minutes,” he warned her. “I can’t. You drained me.”

“I wouldn’t dream of it.” She nestled beneath him with a blissful smile, her arms around him.

Curt eventually turned his head and kissed her on the brow before withdrawing. He rolled to his side and welcomed her against him and they lay silent for several contemplative minutes.

Sober, spent, and raw in every possible way, Curt came to accept that he'd fallen in love.

The evidence was indisputable. He wanted this woman—all the time. He craved her company, her laughter, her softness, her passion. The sound of her voice was music to his ears. Her soft breath had the power to intoxicate him.

What if she didn't feel the same way? Could he risk his heart? Dumb question. There was no avoiding it at this point. It was already hers.

♡

The rest of the evening was filled with sweet tenderness. They fit together so well, and not just sexually, though that was undeniable. It was more than that—deeper. Mia fought the idea, but it persisted. Had she finally found true compatibility with another person? There was an unmistakable softness in Curt's eyes when he watched her. No question she looked at him the same way. They seemed to have stepped beyond the normal courtesies and into something far richer and more meaningful. Unsure of how to process the change, and frankly more than a little frightened by it, she chose to push it to the back of her mind.

It wouldn't do to try and interpret their affectionate gestures and warm caresses. This was enough. Just this. No promises, no declarations. It was better to be content with what was freely offered without reading too much into it on either side.

Curt woke Mia with playful kisses on Sunday morning and they made love leisurely, stepping into the shower together afterwards. It was like old times. She silently wished this weekend could stretch on indefinitely, but that was impossible.

Their morning was filled with significant glances and tender touches. That Curt seemed just as incapable of walking by without reaching out to brush hands, make some kind of contact, was a comfort to her.

It was closing in on noon and they were sprawled lazily on the sofa with the many sections of the Sunday paper scattered around them when Curt told her he should leave soon.

"With Casey coming home, it's only right. You two deserve some time on your own."

Mia's disappointment was crushing, but he was right. His suggestion was kind and thoughtful. *Damn!* There was no objection she could make without looking like a selfish ass herself.

They snuggled together for a little longer before he got up to pack his things. Mia followed just to be near him. She was silent while he stuffed his clothes into his bag, her heart a dull, aching weight in her chest. He looked just as miserable when he turned. They shared a weak smile, devoid of light and sincerity. Her heart crumbled a little more and Curt came to her and pulled her into a one armed hug. She turned her face into his shoulder and held him for strength.

Why was this so hard?

They walked out together, hanging on each other the entire way, and she took him home.

She didn't bother to shift the truck into park when they pulled up outside his building. It would only make driving away more difficult. He must have understood because he gave her a reassuring smile.

"Thank you for the beautiful weekend."

"You're welcome," she said softly, fighting to hold it together. "I'm sorry it's over."

"Me too."

They sat there another minute simply looking at each other before Mia remembered to mention the wedding.

"Damn, I forgot. Greg and Liz are getting married a week from Saturday. I was going to ask if you'd be my date, but I dropped the ball. Is it too late?"

The backs of his fingers grazed the edge of her face before Curt flipped his hand over to cup her cheek. Her eyes drooped closed as he traced her lips with his thumb. "A wedding, huh?"

"Yes." She wished his touches could continue.

He smiled when she opened her eyes. "I'd like that."

"Think outdoor tea party dress," she said with a catch in her voice then kissed the back of the finger brushing her open lips.

"I should be able to find something."

"Good." She was grateful, relieved.

"Will I see you at the Stylus on Thursday?" The hope in his eyes, his voice, spoke volumes.

She'd been expecting the question, and as much as she wanted to commit to it, she hesitated. "I'm not sure yet."

Her problem was guilt. She'd been spending a lot of time with Curt lately and now this very selfish weekend alone with him. It shamed her to admit that poor Casey hadn't drifted through her mind even once. A little atonement was in order.

He slid his hand behind her neck and into her hair, giving it a gentle tug. "If you don't come to see me, I suppose I'll have to come to you."

Her heart melted. "You'd better."

They shared a tender kiss then Curt got out. He grabbed his bag off the backseat, closed the door, and gave the window a final slap as he stepped clear. Firming up her emotional backbone, Mia nodded and pulled back onto the road, not strong enough to watch him walk away.

♡

Curt entered his apartment and gave his bag an underhanded swing onto his bed. He fell back against the door clutching his head with one hand and rubbing his pounding chest with the other. Only now did he speak the words out loud for the very first time.

“I’m in love with Mia.” He shook his head at the crazy, exhilarating truth of it and tried again. “I love Mia.”

Cool—now what?

Chapter 28

Casey got home a half hour after Mia returned from dropping Curt off, but he wasn't interested in hanging around. He put his bag in his room, hit the kitchen for a snack, and announced that he was on his way out to meet up with his friends.

She chased him to the front door and asked, "What do you mean you're taking off? You just got home. You can't spare fifteen minutes for me?"

She was a little hurt, and even more put out, because Curt went home so he wouldn't be in their way. Evidently, that consideration was unnecessary.

"We can talk at dinner, okay?" Impatient, Casey tossed an apple from hand to hand.

"I know, but we haven't seen each other all weekend."

He gave her a pained look. "You're gonna tell me about something that happened this weekend, aren't you?"

Hell no!

"No. I just missed you, honey." She walked over and hugged him.

"I missed you too, Mom. But the guys are waiting for me." He gave her a pleading look. "Please? Can I go? I'll see you later. Promise."

"I suppose."

He gave her a grateful hug and hit the door

running, nearly plowing into Sally on her way up the front steps.

"Sorry," he said, darting around her. Then he was gone, sprinting across the grass.

"I thought my number was up for a second there." Sally laughed and patted her chest.

"Just wait 'til he's driving." Mia held the screen door open for her friend.

"Scary thought."

"Tell me about it." Mia waved her into the kitchen and pulled a bottle of wine out of the fridge. Holding it up in front of Sally, she asked, "Interested?"

"What are we drinking to?"

"Being fucked—in every conceivable way."

Sally's eyebrows shot up. "Pour."

Mia took down two goblets and gave them both a generous portion. "Where should we do this?" she asked, turning and handing Sally her glass.

"Wherever you want, sweetie."

"Let's go out on the deck."

They sat at the glass table and Mia tipped her head back and took a hard swallow. She came up coughing, her eyes watering.

"Holy shit, Mia. Slow down," Sally said in alarm. "What the hell happened here this weekend? Was Curt rough with you? Should I send Larry over to kick his ass?"

"No," Mia said bleakly, her sad eyes welling. "He was wonderful."

"Then I'm not following this."

Mia dropped her forehead onto her hand and shook her head, laughing at herself. "How could you? I'm totally screwing *everything* up."

"Because you had your first romantic weekend in how many years?"

"That's part of it. The rest is being stupid enough to think I could handle an affair without complications."

"Complications being...emotional involvement?"

"Yes." Mia ventured a sip of wine this time.

Sally sat forward, her goblet hanging from her cupped fingers. "You might not believe this, but I *never* thought you were getting involved with Curt for the sex."

"You didn't?"

"No. *God no*. I saw how you two looked at each other that first time. I've watched you together since then, and there's no easy way to tell you this, honey, but you're in a serious relationship."

Mia laughed, resigned. "At least on my end."

"Don't sell Curt short. That's not like you."

"I don't mean to. But I'm afraid to hope."

"Then open your eyes."

"I can't see through the hearts dancing in them."

Sally gave her a bolstering smile. "If you don't tell him you love him—soon—then you really are as stupid as you think."

"Easy for you to say. You're not the one who'd be

laying it all on the line."

"I think you'll be pleasantly surprised by his reaction."

"Then what? He's eight years younger than me. How can something like that work?"

"Oh, I don't know, maybe with mutual love, respect, simply enjoying the same things and each other's company—not to mention a shocking amount of passion. Isn't that all it ever boils down to for every couple?"

Mia dropped her head back and stared up at the leaves fluttering against the deep blue sky.

"I've never felt closer to anyone in my life," she confided. "He's reached inside me on so many levels that it's sort of frightening. How do you find the courage to hand someone the last piece of yourself, the final bit that you've held protectively in reserve?"

"You realize he's doing the same thing."

The corner of Mia's mouth trembled. "I'm not sure I'm ready."

"You'll know when you are."

♡

If Curt thought he was busy the week before, it was nothing compared to this final week of school. He had very little time to devote to his pursuit of the woman he loved.

The woman he loved. He still couldn't get over it.

Their private bedtime calls continued, only now

they both strayed into more familiar territory, using everything in their very personal arsenal to arouse each other. It wasn't ideal, but it was the best they could do under the circumstances.

He tossed the damp washcloth aside and pulled the sheet back up, one arm going behind his head as he sighed into the dark room.

"We're getting better at this," he said into the phone.

Mia's laugh made him smile. "I never thought I'd look forward to phone sex."

"In a pinch…" The tone of his voice sank an octave.

"Don't start me up again. You know how turned on I get when you talk that way."

Now it was his turn to laugh. "I'll stop. Can I see you tomorrow?"

"I have yoga. Wednesday?"

"I wish I could. How about Thursday? Come by the Stylus and watch me play."

"Okay."

He gripped the phone, excited and surprised she agreed. "You will?"

"I think I have to. I'll never make it to Friday."

"Me neither." He paused, unsure about pressing his luck then threw it out there anyway. "Come over afterwards."

"It's a school night."

"I'll allow myself a later bedtime."

"I can't. You know that. And Casey's going to be home—alone."

"He's a big boy."

"So are you."

"Touché."

"It isn't that I don't want to. I do. You know how much I do."

"You don't have to explain, Mia."

"Thank you."

"Sleep tight."

"You too."

♡

Mia was late getting to the Stylus on Thursday because of her exhaustive emergency preparedness lecture. When she actually pulled the fire extinguisher out from under the sink, her very impatient teen marched her to the door and thrust her through it.

"Have a nice time," he said and shut the door.

"You little shit," she said with a startled laugh. "I *will* too!"

Curt's group was on their last song when she walked into the pub. She was sorry she'd missed their set.

Wending her way back to their table, it was impossible to miss the look of relief that crossed his face at the sight of her. He must have been climbing the walls with worry. She mouthed a silent *I'm sorry* as she walked over. He sent her a subtle kiss in return and Mia blushed on the outside and melted within.

Only now did she notice Holly and another young woman seated at the table. Mia's footsteps faltered.

"Hi." The unfamiliar young woman greeted her.

"Hello." Mia pulled out the chair across from them.

"I'm Desiree. Brad's wife." Her smile was warm and friendly. It beat the hell out of the catty one Holly gave her.

"Nice to meet you, Desiree. *Holly*," she acknowledged the competition. "I'm Mia. Curt's newest groupie."

Desiree laughed. "I love it. He told me to look out for you."

"Did he? *Aww*." Mia swung around to the stage. He must have been watching her because he winked.

She was a mooning, sappy mess when she turned back and found Holly's sharp glare fixed on her like a burning laser. "Are you feeling all right, Holly?" she asked pointedly.

Though still hostile, Holly hid it from Desiree. "I'm fine. Why?"

"You look like you have indigestion." Mia feigned concern. "I might have antacids in my purse. Let me look."

"I'm fine," Holly repeated firmly.

"Curt said you're a sweetheart," Desiree told Mia. "Probably because you're a mom, right? Is it true your son actually gave him your phone number?"

Holly looked positively green at that. Mia laughed lightly and explained. "Yes. But Curt asked him for it." The dig was purely unintentional, and *delicious*.

Desiree beamed at her. "That's awesome! He's such a great guy."

All three glanced over at him. Mia quivered at the warm look that passed between them. "I couldn't agree more." Turning back to her new friend, she asked, "Where's the baby tonight?"

"My parents are watching her. Brad and I are getting a rare night alone. I can't remember the last one. Of course, we'll probably fall asleep as soon as we get home. We're both tired all the time."

"Do yourself a favor. Stay awake," Mia advised.

Desiree blushed prettily. "That's my plan."

The guys finished their song and cleared the stage, stowing their instruments away before joining them.

Rollie cut over to the bar for a fresh pitcher of beer. Curt came straight over and dipped to kiss Mia before claiming the seat next to her. His arm slipped comfortably, even possessively, behind her. Oh yeah, Mia was enjoying this.

"Hey there," he whispered, his eyes sparkling.

"Hey." Mia returned his smile.

"I'm glad you made it."

"Me too."

Then he noticed the table in front of her and frowned. "Where's your drink?"

Mia shrugged. “I don’t have one yet.”

He stood. “What do you want?”

“You don’t have to fetch me anything.”

He gave her a look. “Are you going to share in the pitcher of beer or would you rather have wine?”

He was handling her and she didn’t even care. “I’d prefer the wine,” she admitted with an apologetic shrug.

“Thought so. I’ll be back.” He squeezed her shoulder and walked away.

“What did I tell you?” Desiree asked with a smile.

Nothing Mia didn’t already know. “He’s sweet and attentive.”

“Enjoy it while it lasts,” Desiree pouted at her husband.

“Hey,” Brad spoke up in protest. “I’m always doing things for you.”

She touched her husband’s cheek and laughed. “I know. I was teasing. You’ve been great since the baby was born.”

Seeing Curt waiting at the bar, Mia finally noticed something and asked, “Isn’t there a server on tonight?”

Eric spoke up. “Crystal ran for limes. I guess they didn’t make the delivery.”

“Ah. How’s the job hunting going?” she asked.

“I’ve got a couple of potentials. Nothing confirmed yet. Don’t want to jinx ‘em.”

“Gotcha. I won’t pry.”

Mia saw Brad lean in to nuzzle his wife’s ear. He

whispered something and she giggled and whispered back. Romance was in the air. Good for them.

"Here you go." Curt set a glass of red wine in front of Mia and reclaimed his chair. He leaned in and told her, "I noticed the three of you getting friendly down here. Good." He gave her knee a happy squeeze.

Mia smiled, but kept her comments to herself.

He didn't notice Holly's insincere smile because Brad broke in with a question.

"Say, Curt. Are we going to keep playing over the summer or are you doing another dash on us?"

Mia's ears weren't the only ones to perk up at the question. Holly practically came out of her chair to hear his answer.

Curt turned his speculative gaze on Mia before saying, "I don't plan on going anywhere this summer." Then in an undertone, he added to her specifically, "At least not alone."

Her heart skipped a beat at the news. He leaned in and kissed her, lingering afterwards to nuzzle noses. The unexpected intimacy was icing on the cake.

Holly shot up from her chair, startling everyone. She yanked her purse off the back and slipped it over her arm. "Sorry guys, I've got boatloads to do. I just wanted to drop by my old haunt and see everyone again. It's been real."

Curt was surprised and disappointed. "What? You're leaving already?"

"Gotta. You know how it is. Finals tomorrow.

But this was fun. We'll have to do it again."

"I hope so."

"Good seeing you again, Holly," someone called as she headed out without looking back. Only Mia understood what had happened. What she didn't know was if Holly was admitting defeat or regrouping.

Did it matter? Curt had innocently made his choice clear in front of everyone. No one said Holly had to like it. Her open animosity killed whatever sympathy Mia was capable of feeling for her.

By the time everyone parted an hour later it was just assumed Mia would give Curt a lift home. They went straight to her truck without unnecessary explanations.

She pulled into his parking space at his apartment building and they turned to each other. His gaze was sexually potent, even in the most innocuous situations, but when it picked up the glow of the streetlamp behind her, his eyes were downright mesmerizing. She caught the flash of the silver post in his ear and felt weak and breathless as he moved in to kiss her. The brush of his lips was the most necessary thing in her life at that moment. She couldn't resist, didn't want to as he took the kiss deeper, showing her all the paths yet to be explored, all the pleasures to discover with only their mouths engaged. Overwhelmed by heat and need, it took every ounce of strength she had to resist the pull of his lips, his body, and his bed.

He pushed her shirt up, her bra down and latched

onto a puckered nipple and took her to the moon and back as she combed her fingers through his soft hair.

"What if someone sees us?" she asked, too aroused to be all that concerned, but obliged to mention it anyway.

"We could go inside," he reminded her, circling her areola with his tongue before sucking it into his mouth again.

"You know I can't."

"You can."

"I shouldn't."

"I need your taste on my tongue."

She held her breath as his hand slid under her skirt and followed her inner thigh to her panties. Her hips slid forward of their own volition and he kissed her as he slipped his fingers under the elastic to toy with her slippery sex. She rocked against his hand, painfully aroused.

"Please," she whispered, beyond reason or caring.

Chuckling softly, he slipped her his tongue while feeding her one digit, then two. She let out a hungry groan and devoured his mouth, her pelvis rising off the seat with every thrust of his hand.

Curt was rock hard and getting harder as she stroked him through his fly. They were both groaning now. If he didn't end this, he was going to be sporting a wet stain on the front of his pants when he climbed out of her truck.

Shifting his hand slightly, he strummed her clit with his thumb. That did it. Mia cried out and her hips bucked involuntarily up from the driver's seat. He was glad his arm wasn't between her and the steering wheel or it would have been crushed.

As her eyes slowly refocused, she gave him a faint smile and asked, "Does this mean you're not going to call me now?"

He laughed, eased his fingers out of her, and drew her skirt back down. "Do you want me to call?"

"I wouldn't mind it," she admitted casually while tucking her breasts back into her bra.

He grinned. "I'll call. Be ready."

Chapter 29

It was just after noon when Mia pulled up in front of Curt's building the Saturday of the wedding.

He greeted Casey in the back as he climbed into the passenger seat. "Hey, Case. No cast?"

"Hi, Curt." The kid held up his arm. "Nope. Dad took me to get it off yesterday. I have a small brace now. It's a lot lighter."

"Nice." Curt's eyes lit on Mia in her summer dress and he clutched his chest and smiled. "Wow. You look beautiful." He reached over and stroked her bare arm.

His warm approval made her cheeks burn. "You look pretty amazing yourself."

She snuck another peek at him and felt the heat spread all through her. It was an understatement to say the man was gorgeous. He always looked good. But this was the first time she'd seen him in a blazer, and though it was a neutral, almost oatmeal color, it went great with his chinos and white shirt. He'd skipped a tie, but that didn't hurt him at all. This look suited him better.

"Are you excited, Casey?" Curt asked him.

"I don't know. I guess."

Chuckling, Curt turned to Mia. "Thanks for letting me go in on the gift with you. Let me know what I owe."

"Don't worry about it. You're my guest. I don't think you're obligated."

"Mia, I *want* to contribute."

"Fine. I'll figure it out."

She reached for his hand and gave it a squeeze. They ended up holding hands most of the trip.

Even though it was a beautiful, warm day, they drove with the windows up and the air conditioning on to preserve Mia's carefully styled hair.

It took twenty minutes to reach the arboretum. They were stopped at the gate house where Mia showed their invitation to the attendant and received a map of the grounds in return before they were allowed to continue down the graceful hedge-lined drive.

The arboretum was originally a private estate. The main house resembled an old Tudor manor, all stone and enormous beams. It was striking. Inside there was a small café, a gift shop, and a bookstore, along with immaculate restrooms. The second floor housed offices. There was an exquisite ballroom on the third floor that was rented out for functions. However, the building was not their destination.

The grounds around the estate stretched over one hundred and twenty breathtaking acres, the more formal gardens situated closest to the house. There was a winding circuit around the estate that offered panoramic views and larger specialized gardens and plantings interspersed with natural woodlands and water features. Most people chose to drive, though there were walking paths for the more hearty visitors as well.

Mia parked in the lot closest to the building while Curt opened the map.

"Where are we going again?" He glanced up to take in the layout.

Mia read the invitation. "The Lilac Sanctuary."

He took their bearings and pointed southwest, away from the house. "It's over in that direction."

They locked the vehicle and followed the inter-connected series of paths. Casey led them past a variety of very different garden settings.

Mia looked longingly at the picturesque rose gardens as they walked by. "Have you ever been here?" she asked Curt.

He smiled at her. "A couple of times. I liked it. I suppose you must come here a lot. It's right up your alley."

"I wish. Not since Casey was a baby."

"How come?"

She shrugged. "Nobody to go with me."

He caught her hand and gave it a squeeze. "I'll take you. Anytime."

Her heart swelled with tenderness. "I'd love that."

"Me too."

Mia noticed the many visitors wandering through the topiary garden when they passed. "I feel over-dressed."

"You look wonderful, perfect for an outdoor

wedding."

"Thank you."

They smelled the sweet fragrance of lilacs and heard the melodic sounds of a violin and cello duet before they actually saw the border of the Lilac Sanctuary. Passing beneath a picturesque archway, they joined the mingling guests who were, for the moment, ignoring the chairs set up on the lawn.

Mia spotted Greg's parents and brightened when they waved her over.

"Casey, there's Grandma and Grandpa."

They went to join the older couple.

Greg's mother's hand went to her throat when she saw her grandson. "Who's this nice looking young man?" she asked her husband.

"Hi, Grandma." Casey went forward for a hug.

"Don't you look sharp?" Grandpa agreed.

"And Mia." Gloria Page extended both hands to her former daughter-in-law. "You look lovely." They hugged with affection.

"Don't forget me." Greg's dad gave her a warm kiss then leaned back just enough to get a good look at her. "Why, Mia, you're positively glowing. Gloria, doesn't she look radiant?" He winked at Mia, the twinkle in his eye bringing her out in another blush.

"Let her go, Earl," said his wife. Her gaze moved to Curt. "I take it this is your young man?"

Full of blushes today, evidently, Mia reached back for his hand and drew him forward. "Curt

Walden, I'd like you to meet Earl and Gloria Page."

They shook hands, and as they made small talk, Mia took a mental step back to ponder why Gloria had called *both* Casey and Curt young men. She found it more than a little unsettling. What was Gloria implying? One guess? Greg. That bastard probably warned them she was dating a younger man. It would certainly account for his dad's insinuation about her glow.

Damn it! Greg's parents obviously thought she'd found herself a scrumptious boy toy. Oh, there was going to be hell to pay for that.

Lost in a swirl of suspicion, Mia had to quell her anger when Greg found them. It wasn't the best time to ream him out.

He gave their son a hearty pat on the shoulder and his parents a quick embrace. Then he smiled at Mia and pressed her hand before turning to enthusiastically pump Curt's entire arm.

"I'm glad you made it," Greg told him. "It's nice to see you again."

Curt grinned. "Big day."

"I'll say. I'm nervous as hell." He shot an apologetic look at his mom. She waved off the slip with an understanding laugh—considering the pressure he was under.

"Where's Liz?" Mia asked him.

"I haven't seen her yet. She spent last night with her folks. She didn't want me to see her ahead of time.

Who knew she'd want to observe that old custom?" He shook his head in amazement. "Well, I have to steal Casey now. We need to go over his part in all this."

They walked off, leaving the others to mingle. Mia introduced Curt to old friends and former relatives, gauging their reactions even closer now that she knew the innuendo was alive and well. In the end it was a relief to be called to their seats.

The wedding itself was beautiful. When Liz finally appeared, looking elegant in an antique, ivory tea length gown, it was transparently obvious to all how deeply the couple loved each other. Mia's eyes weren't the only ones tearing when Greg's face transformed at the sight of his bride walking toward him. Mia loved them both so much at that moment, and with Casey right beside his father, looking all grown up and dignified, her heart swelled with pride.

Curt glanced at her, pulled a tissue out of his pocket, and slipped it to her. Mia laughed and dabbed her eyes as he put his arm around her in support. She rested her head on his shoulder for a tender moment. How did he know she'd forget tissues?

Greg and Liz spoke their own touching and heartfelt vows. Then Casey came through with the ring on cue. Greg slid it onto Liz's finger and there was a collective sigh when he lifted her hand to his lips and kissed it right in front of everyone.

The judge smiled. "Congratulations."

That was all the prompting Greg needed. The newlyweds shared an eyebrow raising kiss while their guests erupted in exuberant applause.

The day felt golden as everyone went back to their cars to caravan to the restaurant and the lunch already waiting.

♡

Mia was distant on their way to the reception. Curt assumed it had something to do with seeing her ex-husband remarry. After all, they'd had a ceremony of their own once. But from what she'd told him, he didn't think they'd ever looked at one other like that. Still, it must be strange to watch your former husband take a new wife. Did it hurt her, even a little? Did seeing Greg speak his vows take Mia back to their ceremony?

Out of concern for her, Curt was especially considerate at the reception, though as time wore on he wasn't sure she noticed. He found himself tending her like a nurse, placing a glass of champagne in her hand, putting a plate down in front of her and urging her to eat a little, just a little. Later, he really began to worry when she brooded over the wedding cake he shared with her.

When Earl and Gloria Page stopped by to ask if their grandson could stay with them during summer break, Curt had to jostle Mia to get her attention. She seemed startled to find someone speaking to her but agreed to arrange a visit soon.

That was it. He needed to get her out of there. Even though he questioned the advisability of saying goodbye to the newlyweds, protocol demanded it. Curt brought her over to offer their congratulations and wish the couple well. Liz surprised him with a welcome-to-the-family kiss and Greg pulled him in after their handshake for a one-armed bear hug and pat on the back. Unfortunately, Curt was too worried about Mia to fully appreciate it. With a nod to Casey, they took her out.

She didn't question him when he put her in the passenger side of the Explorer. She was simply too preoccupied to manage the drive.

They drove with the windows down, their hair flying. It took the pressure off the need to talk. It was a relief to finally pull into the driveway and shift the SUV into park. Curt pressed the button on his visor and opened the garage door for Casey so he could get inside.

He glanced back at the kid in the rearview mirror. "Hey, Case? We need a few minutes out here. Okay?"

Good kid, he didn't question or argue. He just got out of the truck and disappeared into the house.

Now, alone with her, Curt reached over and took Mia's hand. "Are you going to be okay?"

She looked puzzled. "Yes. Why?"

"I'm worried about you. That's all." He massaged soothing little circles on the back of her hand with his thumb. “You seem a little thrown. It must have been hard for you.”

“*Hard*?” His meaning dawned on her and she shook her head. “No, it isn’t that. I’m truly happy for them.”

Curt’s tense stomach muscles relaxed. “Then can you tell me what it is? I’m here if you need to talk.”

She looked at him in a surprisingly seriously way. “I don’t know if I should.”

Maybe he’d relaxed too soon. He didn’t say anything, just looked at her, waiting, feeling a tad uneasy all of a sudden.

“Fine,” she muttered. “I did *not* appreciate being the butt of everyone’s jokes out there today.”

He couldn’t even begin to process what she meant. “Say again?”

“Asking me ‘is this your *young man*’? Saying I have a healthy glow—nudge, nudge, wink, wink. I could have screamed at their innuendo and insulting assumptions. Totally offensive!”

Curt was stunned. “You’re kidding right? Please tell me you’re kidding. Were we even *at* the same wedding?”

“You can’t tell me you missed all those significant looks going back and forth right in front of us?” She glared at him in disbelief.

“I don’t know what you’re talking about.”

“You’re not *that* naïve. Give me a break. Everyone was snickering at us. At me! There’s Mia with her boy toy, her bump and grind. I've become a laughingstock and I'm pissed about it."

Her words, her characterization of their relationship left him chilled. "Are you completely insane?"

Mia crossed her arms over her chest and scowled straight ahead, fuming.

"Wow." *Breathe. Just breathe.* "It didn't take much for you to let your true feelings out, did it? For your information, 'young man' is an old expression. I didn't take offense, nor was I expected to. My god, Mia! The people I met, we talked with, were nice, courteous people. *Nothing* they did or said even came close to suggesting they thought I was some *kid*, let alone your 'bump and grind' and it hurts me that you just threw that in my face. I was accepted as your date and your equal—at least by everyone I met today. I didn't realize *you* haven't accepted me yet." he added solemnly.

"You're twisting what I said. Everyone was looking at me, judging me," she insisted.

"We were at a wedding." He tried again, as patiently as he could. "Believe me, you were *not* the starring attraction. That you even imagine they were fixated on you is ludicrous." He shook his head, thrown by what he was hearing. "I never would have thought you could be so egocentric."

"You don't understand. I *know* those people."

"I'm beginning to seriously doubt that. They were great. Ready to celebrate a wedding between people they care about. Any delusions you're suffering from are beside the point."

Mia glared at him, obviously furious he was arguing with her about it.

He sat back in resignation. "I give up. Clearly you have unresolved issues with our age difference. I thought we'd dealt with it. Evidently not." He was heartbroken and extremely disappointed in her. "I can't believe how cheap you've made me feel. You cheapened what I thought we had together."

Nothing. She sat there, angry and unmoved. He couldn't reach her.

Fine. He focused on breathing in, breathing out, but it didn't make him feel any better. He was reeling and there was no way to stop the motion sickness.

"I've gotta say this. You might be comfortable with me in the gigolo role, but I'm not. Take all the time you need to decide what you want from me, if anything. Just don't bother calling until you know the answer. Now, I think it's best if I go home."

With that, he fired up the engine and backed out of the driveway. Mia silently simmered the entire way. Curt was equally upset, but he kept it hidden behind a grave mask. He wasn't mad, just deeply wounded. This was a sucker punch to the kidneys. Here he thought they were happy. *More than happy*. Last weekend was a turning point in their relationship. He'd reached a level of intimacy with Mia that he'd never even flirted with before, and he'd welcomed it, relished it. All he could think about since was how much he looked forward to seeing how their future together would unfold.

Not this. No, definitely not this.

He didn't bother to pull into his parking lot. Instead, Curt stopped along the curb and left the engine idling when he got out. He crossed the lawn without a backwards glance.

Chapter 30

Mia walked around the vehicle and got behind the wheel. She was shaken, fuming at Curt. How could he miss so much? The innuendo was glaringly obvious. Men! Was he really that blind? She was absolutely certain she was right. When Curt had time to re-examine the day for himself, he'd ccme around.

However, being confident did not remove the chill their argument left behind. Why did their first fight have to feel so final?

It was only later she realized if she was right, and people *were* indulgently amused by her relationship, she had a difficult decision to make. Was she uncomfortable enough to end it with Curt? That thought really gave her something to sweat over.

All Sunday, Mia's certainty remained. She *knew* she hadn't misread any of the reactions she saw at the wedding—and there were more than just Greg's parents involved, thank you, very much. She replayed the dialogue, as she heard it, over and over again in her mind and was convinced, more than confident, that there was a measure of mockery and amusement in it, as if she were the gay divorcée, personified.

She could just imagine what they were thinking when she dragged Curt around, introducing him to everyone. She seethed at their understanding, tolerant smiles. *Oh yes. Let Mia enjoy her fling. Let her have some fun. Why shouldn't she bring her gigolo to her ex-husband's wedding? Poor neglected thing.*

Gigolo?

Mia's eyes bulged at the word. Where did that come from? Oh right. Curt tossed the word around so casually yesterday. *She* never used it—until now. She cringed at how quickly her mind seized on it.

By Monday, however, it was slowly dawning on her that perhaps all of the ugly images and terms that could possibly be applied to their relationship may have been generated in her own mind. Had *she* planted and extracted all the looks and thoughts herself?

With growing horror, she came to the inescapable conclusion she'd been wrong. Curt was right and she owed him a big apology. If that weren't serious enough, it was time she admitted that, not only was she deeply in love with him—throw-caution-to-the-wind kind of love—but her very happiness rested in his hands.

Oh god! What had she done? She felt sick. Her chest ached at the pain she'd caused him, at the damage she'd inflicted on their relationship. Every recollection was pure torture, coming at her with a clarity she hadn't exhibited in days. Remembering the look on his face, the disappointment in his eyes, nearly suffocated her. She'd wounded him. Mia turned the blame gun on herself now, where it should have been pointed in the first place.

She sank into a funk of self-loathing and mental

abuse. How could she even risk throwing someone so precious from her? She had to make amends right now.

Mia picked up the phone and dialed his apartment. There was no answer. Could she blame him? If he'd treated *her* like that she might be reluctant to hear from him again too.

His cellphone sent her calls directly to voicemail, yet she continued to try to reach him throughout the day anyway, ignoring the work piling up on her desk. Every time she dialed, the words *I'm sorry, please pick up* repeated in her head, yet it didn't change the inescapable fact that he wasn't answering.

On the way home from work, she drove past his apartment. His bike was locked up outside. She stopped and went in, only to hesitate outside his door. She stood there, afraid to knock, so she put her ear to the wood and listened instead. Silence. Desperation took over and made her knock several times. There was no movement, no answer, nothing. She left with a heavy heart and heavier feet.

On Tuesday, Mia's depression infected the entire office and made everyone gloomy. Jane tried to get her to open up and talk about it, but she just waved her off.

"I can't," Mia said miserably. "I've been a complete idiot. Let's just leave it at that."

She knew if Jane looked at her with any more sympathy, she was going to fall apart right in front of her. She'd never been an overly emotional person, at least not at work, so there was a good chance she would freak everyone out and create a new impression of herself she really didn't want. It was easier—well, maybe just better—to keep her chin up and pretend nothing was wrong.

Already exhausted, Mia didn't even want to cope with making dinner. She stopped off and bought a frozen pizza. The house was empty when she got home. Casey called shortly afterwards and asked if he could stay longer at Tony's. Under the circumstances, she didn't object. She threw the pizza into the freezer, rather than the oven, and poured herself some wine instead. Her appetite was totally shot.

Unable to shake the despair, Mia called in sick on Wednesday. That's when she hit her lowest point—lower than she thought she could sink. She'd cried so much she had a sore throat and a runny nose on top of everything else. She wasted hours on the sofa, a weepy lump in her fuzzy robe with the remote in her hand, zoning out in front of daytime television.

Her head hurt, her heart ached. She was a mess and she blamed herself, sometimes out loud. Spiraling into self-loathing, she wondered if maybe she belonged in a psychiatric ward.

Casey wasn't faring much better. Having always been on the receiving end of care giving, he seemed lost in his new role and unsure of how to help her. He could see she was suffering, could hardly look into her bleary, bloodshot eyes without wincing in pain himself. The mass of tissues littering the floor around her made him pace and fret. Her litter visibly upset him. Understandable, she supposed, considering she was usually tidy, whereas now she wasn't even trying to hit the waste basket she'd brought out from the bathroom. When Casey pressed, Mia insisted she was just under the weather. Clearly, he didn't buy it. Why would he? Curt was over so often he'd become part of their household. It had to feel weird not to see him around all of a sudden.

"Did he dump you?" Casey asked when he took her empty mug off the end table.

Mia glanced up, dabbing her tender nose with a fresh tissue. "What?"

"Well, you're not even talking to him on the phone anymore."

"We just had an argument, that's all. Everything will be okay."

She wished she could believe her own bullshit.

Casey shook his head on his way to the kitchen, obviously not convinced either.

♡

Wednesday, and nearly six o'clock already. Curt tried to ignore the time, but everywhere he turned it was right there in front of him—on the stove, the microwave, even that stupid teapot clock his sister had hanging next to the door. Brad knew he wasn't coming to the Stylus to play tomorrow and in true Brad fashion, hadn't asked why. Curt appreciated it.

He turned back to Heidi and watched while she finished matching up the socks in her basket. His three-year-old nephew charged into the room.

"Unca Curt!"

"What is it, Jeffrey?" He gave the boy a listless smile.

"Spin!" Jeffrey tried to tug his uncle off the kitchen chair.

"No," he said wearily. "I told you. I'm all spun out. Maybe later, okay?"

"Up!"

It was easier to give in than to fight. Curt stood and picked up the boy.

"Jeffrey, stop bothering your uncle," Heidi scolded.

"It's okay." He looked at the boy in his arms. "You ready?"

"GO!"

They spun in a tight circle in the middle of the kitchen as Jeffrey broke the sound barrier. When they ground to a stop, Curt was afraid his ears might be bleeding.

"More!"

"Once more." He relented.

They spun again and the boy's laughter brought the first genuine smile to Curt's face in days.

"Okay, time to get down," Heidi told him as she

picked up the stacks of clothing from the table.

Jeffrey suddenly threw himself backwards off his perch on Curt's arm, his hands reaching for the floor. Curt flipped him over and set him safely on his feet. The little boy stomped with glee.

Heidi pointed him out of the kitchen. "Now go play until I call you for supper."

Jeffrey threw his arms around Curt's legs and gave him an unexpected hug. Touched, he ruffled the boy's hair. A heartbeat later, the moment was over, gone with the laughing child as he ran from the room. Heidi followed him out with her basket and Curt sat back down at the table and picked up his beer.

When Heidi returned, she paused in the doorway, clearly shaken to have caught him in a dismal funk.

"Would you talk to me, damn it?" she snapped and, storming over, dropped onto a second chair so she could look him in the eye. "Your sadness is like a knife in my chest. It's killing me to see you like this."

"I'm fine."

"You're not fine. Lean on *me* for a change. I know you're not the most forthcoming guy, but I want to help. Confide in me. Who else have you got?"

"There's nothing you can do."

"Sometimes just talking helps." She threw up her hands when he remained silent, and bent to scoop one of Jeffrey's little trucks off the floor instead. She set it on the table with an exasperated sigh. "Fine. Keep your damn secrets. Get an ulcer. I've got enough to worry about just picking up after Jeffrey. He's going to break someone's neck if we're not careful."

Curt rolled the little truck along the tabletop. "I don't know how you do it."

"What, parenting?"

"Yes."

"I know Jeffrey can be a little bugger sometimes, but then, when you least expect it, he charms the living hell out of you." She laughed softly, her gaze unfocused. "It makes up for everything else." Then she shook herself and watched him play quietly with his nephew's truck. "Are you ever going to have a kid?"

He laughed. "No. At least, not the biological kind. But I was really starting to consider something else recently," he admitted cryptically.

Though confused, she didn't ask him to elaborate. "Well, you'd be great. Jeffrey loves you."

"I think maybe I'm better uncle material."

At the sound of the garage door opening, Heidi popped out of her chair with a big smile. "There's Jason. Good. The chicken is about ready."

She opened the door for her husband and he caught her around the waist as soon as he walked in. They shared a tender kiss and Curt found himself smiling because they had the kind of relationship he wanted, what their parents had. Watching this couple together made him happy.

Jason looked over at their visitor. "Hey, Curt."

"How's it going, Jason? Don't worry. I'll be out of your hair in the morning."

"You don't have to leave."

Hugging her husband, Heidi agreed. "Jason's right. Stay as long as you want. We're here for you."

Curt smiled. "I don't want to cramp your style. Besides, you two look like you want to be alone."

"Trust me. You're not interrupting anything. We have a three year old who isn't exactly crazy about sleeping in his own bed." Jason chuckled. "You aren't planning on climbing in with us too, are you?"

Curt laughed. "I don't think so."

"Then you're welcome to stay," Heidi told him.

"You know I can't. I have a flight in the morning. Are you sure it's not asking too much for a ride to the airport?"

"It's on my way to work." Jason helped himself to his wife's glass of beer. "I can easily drop you off, if that's really what you want."

♡

Casey tidied up around his mom and forced a cup of hot tea on her before heading out the door.

Five minutes later, Sally barged into the house without knocking. She stared at Mia in dismay.

"Casey came to get me. What happened here?"

Mia sniffled. "I blew it."

"With Curt? What'd you do?"

"Picked a fight. Hurt him. Sally, I really offended

him."

"Then fix it."

"I can't. He's not home and he won't answer my calls."

"So you're just going to throw in the towel? Lay there in your rumpled jammies and nasty hair?"

"I don't have the energy to do anything else."

"Have you eaten?"

Mia gave a listless shrug. "I ate a little something on Monday."

"That's what I thought." Sally tugged the throw pillow off Mia's lap and threw it to the other side of the couch. "Get into the shower and I'll make you something to eat. Whether you can fix this mess with Curt or not, life goes on. You can't mope around here looking and smelling the way you do."

"I don't smell."

"You're used to yourself." Sally put her hand on her hip and shook her head. "You're freaking out poor Casey."

That was the reality check Mia needed to pull herself together. She nodded and dragged herself to her feet.

"Give me fifteen, twenty minutes," she said and shuffled into the bathroom.

The television was off, the lap blanket was folded and draped over the back of the sofa, and the mound of tissues were sitting in the waste basket by the garage door when Mia came back, rubbing her head dry with a towel.

"You can put your own snot rags in the trash outside." Sally turned and handed Mia a grilled cheese sandwich on a plate. "Want a baby dill with that?"

"Yes, please." Mia ate it at the counter, her eyes filled with gratitude. "You're a good friend, Sal."

"I know."

♡

Mia went to work on Thursday, though she was still drained and listless. Jane made sure she ate the lunch Sally packed for her, whether she wanted it or not. They must have talked to one another. She appreciated it.

Since Casey planned to stay over at Tony's that night, Mia took great pains with her appearance before driving by Curt's apartment again. His bike was in the exact same spot and the windows in his apartment were dark. Clearly, he hadn't been home in days.

She needed to do something constructive, like staking out the Stylus. There was a good possibility she'd find him there. He'd have to talk to her then. No way was she going to let him avoid her this time.

Mia didn't want her surveillance to be obvious so she parked down the block and slid low in her seat. Time passed and she grew restless, wondering if he was even in there. Rocking in her seat, kicking her feet, she finally began tapping out tunes on her steering wheel after she'd chewed her thumbnails down to ragged nubs.

Eric and Rollie were the first to leave. They lingered on the sidewalk, their voices rising occasionally, but still indecipherable. Brad walked out and the friends said goodnight and split up to go to their cars. Minutes later, the glow of their taillights a distant memory, Mia found herself alone again, abandoned and forlorn on the empty street. She held her breath and waited for Curt. She *had* to wait. There was nothing else to do. She held onto the infinitesimal, though flagging hope he might still be inside.

And if he was? Her ever helpful mind began to torture her with worrisome thoughts. Eventually it nudged her outside and over to the windows. She peeked in, hoping she wouldn't catch Curt pouring his heart out to a falsely sympathetic Holly. That would actually be worse than seeing him flirt with Crystal or anyone else. Flirting was nothing. Holly had an agenda.

Mia's fears proved groundless. There were only a few people in the pub now. Curt wasn't one of them. This had all been a complete waste of time.

She wondered how weird it would look if she went inside and asked if they knew where he was. As his girlfriend, shouldn't she know? In the end she chickened out and went back to her truck and drove home with a sinking heart.

Chapter 31

Curt didn't plan to drink on the plane, but when the flight attendant asked, he found himself ordering a screwdriver, then another.

Halfway into the first is when the flush of cold reality hit him. Boarding the plane was a big mistake. The second drink was meant to chase away the clammy dread once he could admit he'd screwed up.

He had to go back. He wanted off this damn plane. Now. Good luck with that. They were miles above the Atlantic and would be for some time yet.

Shit.

He'd messed up when he walked away from Mia. He should have gone head-to-head with her. They should have fought it out then and there. Instead, he retreated to lick his wounds. Why, because he loved her? He picked a hell of a way to prove it. Now he itched for a fight. He wanted the confrontation, the raised voices, the fury and unfettered passion twining around and between them.

He remembered how angry she'd looked in the car and he smiled. Oh no, he could do better than that. She wasn't nearly pissed off enough. He'd never seen her screaming mad, shouting mad, and he was looking forward to it. Her sexual animal wasn't the only one he could arouse in her. She needed a real temper explosion too, and he was the right man for the job.

Curt checked his watch and tapped his foot with impatience. He was turning right around and grabbing the first available seat back as soon as they landed at Heathrow.

He glanced at the passenger next to him and snorted softly. The man was tuning him out, trying hard to ignore Curt's simmering mood by burying his nose in a magazine. Well, that was just fine. He didn't want to spend this anger on the wrong person anyway. Hell no! He was taking this battle to Mia's door. There was no way he was going to let her fucked-up notions drive a wedge between them. He loved her, damn it, and what they had wasn't an illusion. It was real. He'd bet the farm it scared the shit out of her too.

Love hurt. He knew that going in and still felt it was worth it. Now it was time for Mia to stop holding back and acknowledge she loved him as desperately as he loved her. She needed to stop fearing him, fearing her feelings, but most of all she had to stop using their ages to create an arbitrary distance between them.

Sometimes it took rage to unlock the softer emotions hidden behind it, especially love, but it would take a delicate touch to get her juices boiling without them spilling out in the wrong direction. Raw, naked emotion was a volatile thing. Trust a science teacher to know about the dangers of mixing chemicals.

♡

By Friday morning Mia was determined to pull herself together. She had finally accepted that it was all in Curt's hands now. If he wanted to see her, or reach her, he knew how to find her, which was more than she could say. Clearly, he didn't want to deal with her right now. Well, she was done making a fool of herself. She wasn't going to chase him anymore. If this was how he wanted it, fine. She had other concerns—a son to consider.

Just shake him off, Mia. You can survive this.

She'd always expected things to end with him eventually. At least now she wasn't left waiting for the swing of the blade. There was a perverse comfort in that…sort of.

Honestly, what was one man anyway? Really, all he did was reintroduce her to the unpredictable world of dating. Sure, she had a few scuff marks on her ass and elbows, but she could get back up and dust herself off again, right?

She blocked out the irritating voice that kept reminding her she wouldn't be in this predicament if she hadn't behaved like a total shit.

♡

It was just after two in the afternoon when the taxi pulled up in front of Mia's office building. Curt leaped out with his bags swinging from his hands and bolted into the cool interior. Mentally stoking his anger to keep it pumped, he stormed across the large lobby to the elevators and punched the up arrow. His roiling tension was so strong, simply waiting for the elevator was damn near impossible. The door slid open and he lunged inside and jabbed the button for the fifth floor.

The dark look on his face startled the receptionist when he strode out of the elevator. Guarded now, she didn't offer him a friendly welcome.

Curt didn't exactly care. "Can you direct me to Mia Page's desk?"

Her eyes narrowed with distrust. "Is she expecting you?"

"No."

"Then take a seat over there and I'll put a call through to her." She pointed to one of the sleek leather sofas.

His whole demeanor changed, startling her for the second time in as many minutes. "Please don't do that. This is a surprise. I just raced over here from the airport to see her."

The receptionist considered him carefully, stretching her neck over the top of the desk to take a look at his luggage.

"That's not our policy." She hesitated, clearly uncomfortable with the decision he was asking her to make.

Curt didn't bother with words again, which was better because his eyes were locked and loaded and he knew how to use them. When he gave her the full blast, she didn't stand a chance. Honey versus vinegar, who knew?

She expelled a heavy sigh and Curt knew he was in.

“Take that hallway to the left. When you reach the coffee room, take another left then a right. She’ll be in the cubicle at the end.”

It might be pushing it, but he had to ask. “Would you mind if I left my suitcase here for a few minutes?”

“I think that would be best.” She gave him an accommodating smile. “Put it by the potted palm.”

Curt bestowed his most charming smile on her yet then took off in the right direction.

Several people stopped what they were doing to gape at him as he walked briskly through the office, a stranger in their closed environment. He ignored them.

The last cubicle was ahead and he slowed. His heart was pounding more violently than it had on his race over here. He could feel the last of his anger drain out of him. Their battle would have to wait. He took a deep breath and ventured forward. Mia’s back was to him as she worked at her computer, but that didn’t stop the rush of tenderness that swept through him at the sight of her.

He inched forward, his voice barely a whisper. “Mia?”

She spun in her chair, her reaction too complicated to decipher. “Curt?” She took in his disheveled appearance, his conflicted expression. “Where have you been?”

"At my sister's."

Her anxious gaze went to his shoulder bag. "Are you coming or going?"

"Both."

"I don't understand." Her voice broke.

"I was on my way to Rome—" he began.

"Rome? As in *Italy*?"

"Yes. But just minutes into the flight, I knew I'd made a mistake. It should have been you sitting next to me, not some stocky guy with a bad comb-over. Every minute in the air was agony because all I wanted to do was turn right around and get my ass back here—to you. Mia, I want you to come with me. We have so much ground to cover together."

He wore his feelings openly now. It wasn't what he'd intended to say, but he had a change of heart the second he saw her. Screw it, they could fight later.

Curt dropped to his knees in front of her. Ignoring the group of people gathering behind him, he grabbed both armrests and trapped her in her chair. "*Voglio sposarti*," he said softly.

"Is that Italian? It's beautiful," she said, visibly softening. "What does it mean?"

"I'll tell you later." He smiled, knowing he'd just said, *'I want to marry you,'* in front of at least twenty strangers. "Mia, I don't know how else to convince you our age difference doesn't matter except to say that I love you. We belong together. I knew it the first time I smiled at you and you blushed. There's nothing

I want more than to spend every possible minute I can with you. We've wasted enough time already. Don't rob me of a second more. Please?"

♡

Mia glanced over his head at the collection of faces smiling at them, and blinked. "You *love* me?" she asked softly, hopefully.

Curt nodded, his eyes trained on her alone.

She tried to blink back her tears. She failed. "I was hoping it was mutual. I love you too."

She couldn't tell if he rose to hug her or she collapsed onto him, but all of a sudden they were holding each other and there was nowhere else in the world she wanted to be. Home was wherever he was.

Curt eased back, his hands framing her face, and kissed her softly. "Come with me. Let's work this all out."

Mia melted into his eyes. It was a warm and wonderful place to be.

Looking up at her co-workers, she spotted Jane nodding enthusiastically while blatantly checking out Curt's ass. She gave Mia a big thumbs-up. A woman from the next department over was smiling and nodding as well, her hands clasped in front of her. Mia sought her boss in the mix of faces and the corners of her mouth twitched when she found him beaming back at her.

She swiped under her eyes and sniffled. "Um,

Bill? Can I have a little time off? I have vacation coming."

"Two weeks enough?"

She laughed. "Plenty."

Curt turned, finally acknowledging their audience. Then the meaning of Mia's request sank in and he spun around and stood, drawing her out of her chair and into his arms again.

She was lost in the moment, sinking into his kiss. A loud and enthusiastic round of applause broke out behind her, accompanied by a few whistles, and she tucked her blushing cheek against his chest, suddenly embarrassed by all the familiar, and not so familiar, people gawking at them. Curt must have dragged everyone with him because she thought the office was practically empty when she got back from lunch. One thing was certain; everyone here would be talking about this for a week—at least.

Moving out of his arms, she said, "Just give me a minute to turn off all my stuff, okay?"

"Don't even think about it," Jane said sternly, and stepped into Mia's cubicle. "I'll do it. Just grab your gear and go." She smiled at Curt. "Nice to finally meet you."

He gave her a cockeyed smile. "Jane, right?"

"Yep." She nodded and hugged Mia.

Curt walked over to Bill and clasped his hand. "Thanks. Thanks a lot."

"Just make her happy."

He laughed, undeniably happy himself. “That’s my plan.”

Her purse over her shoulder, Mia reached for Curt’s extended hand when, suddenly remembering she had one loose end to tie up first, she pulled back and swung around to grab her phone instead.

“What are you doing?” he asked, leaning over her shoulder.

“Hang on.” She’d already pressed one of the speed dial numbers so she held up a finger for silence and smiled at the voice on the other end of the line. “Hi, Mom? It’s Mia. About your offer last weekend… how soon can I bring Casey over?”

The End

Books by Tara Mills

Accidents Make the Heart Grow Fonder
Caution: Filling is Hot
Forest Fires
Friends and Lovers
Going Solo
Grading on Curves
In Love and War

Novellas, Short Stories & Teasers

If You Want Me
Sexcapades: Britt and the Butler
Sexual Politics
Falling
Stolen Moments
Holiday Kisses
It's in His Kiss

The Pelican Cay Series

Intimate Strangers – Book One
Tarnished Hero – Book Two
Dark Storms – Book Three
Sweetest Taboo — Book Four

About the Author

I write the kinds of stories I love to read, contemporary romance with authentic characters and realistic themes. From suspense to comedy, I've got you covered. Escape with me into books.

Please visit my website
www.taramillsromance.com
or *Like* me on Facebook. I'm also on Google +
Pinterest and *occasionally* on Twitter

Made in the USA
Charleston, SC
23 January 2016